THE LAST THING I SAW

ALEX SINCLAIR

bookouture

Published by Bookouture in 2018

An imprint of StoryFire Ltd.

Carmelite House
50 Victoria Embankment
London EC4Y 0DZ

www.bookouture.com

ISBN: 978-1-78681-435-7
eBook ISBN: 978-1-78681-434-0

This book is a work of fiction. Names, characters, businesses,
organizations, places and events other than those clearly in the
public domain, are either the product of the author's imagination
or are used fictitiously. Any resemblance to actual persons, living or
dead, events or locales is entirely coincidental.

Previously published as DON'T LET ME DIE. This edition
contains significant editorial revisions.

THE LAST
THING
I SAW

To my wife and daughter
Thank you for your support and inspiration

PROLOGUE

I stared down at the gun trembling in my hands, knowing in my heart that I could never go through with what needed to be done. Once I did, my life would be over. This one act would shatter my world into a million splintered pieces and destroy me forever. But despite the consequences, I aimed the gun at his head.

A scatter of noises competed in the dark void of the freezing night for my attention as he continued to beg and plead with me. But I couldn't hear him. He sounded like he was underwater, drowning beneath the surge of a raging tide there was no point fighting. I couldn't comprehend anything but the static of fear below me, creeping out into the night sky. All I heard was a desperate utterance escaping his lips, starving to live.

"You don't have to do this," my husband Darren said as I aimed the pistol. My finger wrapped around the trigger as a decision entered my brain.

I'd run out of time and options. I'd run out of excuses. There was no other choice, and my refusal would have a far worse outcome. He had gone to great lengths to bring us all to this moment. How had I not seen this coming?

The signs had all been there. The warnings had been clear. His past threats floated into the forefront of my mind on a loop, preventing me from thinking of an alternative.

"I have to," I whispered, eyes closed. My words were weak and crippled, but they could all hear me.

"Please," Darren said. "There has to be another way. There's still time to undo this."

I opened my eyes and felt my aim tighten. The trigger began to squeeze. I saw the scene again, like a nightmare I couldn't wake from. My eyes wouldn't shy away from the misery before me. I wasn't given that dignity, not while he remained alive.

I sensed the pressure all around me and understood that this was the end. There was no coming back once a decision had been made. If I survived this moment, I would never be free.

All I could wonder in those dying seconds was why was I here? And how did everything come down to this moment?

CHAPTER 1

Before

Our house was only three years old when we first moved in. Now, after nine years of family meals at our oak dining table, of scuff marks and dents left on the walls, of growing feet dragging stains over the carpet, it felt like it had been around for half a century. It wasn't the physical state of our home that gave it this age, but the inescapable drama my family seemed to fall victim to.

The four-bedroom, three-bathroom modern colonial had originally been built by my husband, Darren, and the construction company he once worked for in our quiet town of Clearwater Hills, Illinois. When news got around that the owners had lost the house after failing to make timely repayments on the loan, Darren practically begged for us to buy the dream home he'd built for someone else. Seeing as the house was only across town and up for auction, starting at a once-in-a-lifetime price, I had no choice but to agree. What a mistake that would turn out to be.

"God, this was a steal," Darren said the day we moved in. He kept muttering about how lucky we were and how satisfied he was to finally live in a house he'd put together with his own two hands. He was proud to put our names down on the contract, Darren and Emma Turner. The global financial crisis made the house affordable at the time, but the same event caused my husband to lose his job six months later.

So the cycle of fools buying property they couldn't afford continued on a steady yet predictable path. For the next four years, we struggled. Darren went from one job to the next, doing what he could to help make ends meet. I maintained a full-time admin position at the University of Chicago, while also running our household and getting our son, Jayden, off to school each day.

Life remained hectic, to say the least. I managed a strict weekly routine that the flap from a butterfly's wing could disrupt. I'd run between Jayden's responsibilities, work, and home, on top of keeping Darren's spirits afloat. I felt like I had four different jobs and got paid for one. When my father died in a car crash, the system came to a grinding halt.

My dad lived in town, on his own. My mother had passed away a few years prior, succumbing to breast cancer. Once the pain of her loss began to fade, he put all his energy into being a lecturer at the university. His death was a gut blow, not only to me but also to the faculty, especially considering his age: sixty-three. He was in those prime years to unload his knowledge onto the world. Instead, he died pointlessly when a truck plowed into his car at an intersection he'd been through countless times before.

My dad had been at the school for most of his career and secured me the admin job I currently held after failing to show the same effortless talent for academia he had at the same age. Despite my inabilities, he never once made me feel less important or like a failure for not rising to his level.

With Darren between paying jobs during a time when the country possessed too many houses and not enough employed people to live in them, we were struggling more than usual when my father's life was cut short. His death, however, came with a silver lining in the form of a substantial inheritance, the size of which would change our lives and allow us to keep our dream home during the rough seas ahead.

The timing was insane given how close we came to losing it all. Every time I've looked at our house since that day, I have thought about my father and the hard work he put in over the years. I didn't want a single cent of his money to go to waste. But, of course, the purest of intentions inevitably fail.

A few months after we got back on track, Darren came to me with a proposal of sorts. He wanted to take the plunge and start up his own construction business.

"I know all the talent around town," he said to me. "I know all the best suppliers and can lock down some solid connections. I just need the start-up money to get this going."

Everything he said sounded safe on paper. The financial crisis was in the past, and the construction industry had started to pull itself out of the ashes. People were building houses again. Darren argued that it would be the ultimate time to take advantage of the rare situation. How could I say no? He was the person I loved more than anyone else in the world, short of our son. I not only believed him, I believed *in* him.

That was five years ago. Now, after nine years of living in our home, I was thirty-seven. Darren's business was thriving, and our fourteen-year-old son, Jayden, spent his days at Clearwater Hills Middle School. Everything was on track for our perfect life in our quiet American town.

So why did the well-maintained house my husband had constructed seem so old to me now? Because our seemingly perfect life was far from the pure and enviable domestication it appeared to be. Our world was about to come apart, and we had no idea.

CHAPTER 2

"Have you seen my phone?" Darren asked me as he scurried around the kitchen, tossing and turning old newspapers and dishes to find his smartphone. I handed the device to him from the pocket of my dressing gown, unsuccessfully hiding a smirk.

"You left it in the bathroom again, honey," I said as he yanked it out of my hand. I wished he wouldn't snatch things like that.

"Stupid." He gave himself a mock slap on the head, not thanking me for finding his cell. I could see the wrinkles around his eyes creasing harder than usual. His misplaced phone wasn't the only reason he was pretending to hit himself.

"Is everything okay? You seem a bit frazzled."

He stared at me for half a second with his mouth partially agape. "Nothing. Just trying to organize a world full of idiots on this never-ending project."

"The contract? How's it all going?"

"Crazy, of course. We've still got thirty houses to build, and not enough time to do it in. Typical corporate developers never think of how these things are supposed to go. They slap down some concept art with a 'Coming Soon' sign and expect the rest to fall into place. Whenever things slow down, their answer is to just throw money at you."

"But money is good, right?"

He shook his head. "Not if time's against you."

I could see his shoulders tensing up with every word. I inched closer to him and put my hands on his biceps. Even they felt stiff and full of stress. "You've got this, okay? If any company can pull this contract off, it's the team from D. Turner Construction. Believe in yourself." I played the role of supportive wife on autopilot.

His eyes didn't project back the confidence I tried to beam into him. He scratched at his scruffy hair and let his hand fall to the two-week-old beard he had been growing.

"Thanks for the pep talk, honey, but I've got to go." He moved away from my grip and seized his oversize travel mug, which was filled to the brim with double-strength coffee. I might as well have said nothing.

"Are we still on for tonight?" I asked him as he made his way to the front door.

"Uh, yeah. Of course," he said without looking back. "I'll be home by six. Love you."

I never got to say the words back to him as the door slammed shut. I found myself edging up to the small glass window by the entry to pull aside its curtain. Darren was already climbing into his work truck, on the phone, blasting out the next person in the chain that needed a kick in the pants to move the project forward. I didn't envy him, but at the same time, I wished he'd pay me some more attention. This contract had been going on for far too long.

I thought back to some of the potentially questionable activities Darren had had to do in order to keep this contract afloat. The timeline simply didn't seem possible, given my knowledge of how long it took to build a house. All I hoped was that Darren wasn't cutting any corners.

The sound of blaring headphones interrupted me as Jayden came into the kitchen with his usual sour seven-in-the-morning face he'd decided to wear of late. The kid was fourteen going on forty as teenage angst began to set in. Not that long ago he was still happy playing with toys and enjoying life. Now, every day was a struggle.

Jayden sat down by the kitchen counter and poured himself some cereal, splashing milk half into the bowl and half onto the counter a moment later. He slurped down his food without taking his eyes off his smartphone for more than a second.

"Jayden, honey?"

He glanced up at the interruption with a scowl and waited for me to speak.

"What was our rule about music and phones during meals?"

His face twisted up. I prepared myself for the daily morning argument.

"This isn't a meal," he said as he removed one earbud. The white cord dangled around his black zip-up hoodie, swaying for a moment, letting out the many decibels of noise that had been destroying his eardrum. I didn't want to get into this fight again.

"Yes, it is. Now turn that music off and put your phone face down on the counter."

"This is such bullshit," he muttered as he slapped the device down and pulled out the second headphone.

"Language, Jayden."

"Whatever," he said before continuing to eat. He didn't bother to turn the song off. I could now hear with clarity some heavy metal racket laced with cuss words. I decided not to start on him about his choice in music. One battle at a time was about all I could face.

"Did you finish your homework last night?" I asked. My simple question was about to commence another thread in our ongoing war. When he didn't answer, I moved farther into his field of view with both arms crossed. "Well?"

Jayden's phone buzzed and moved slightly on the kitchen counter. He snatched it up to read the notification. "That's Ben. I gotta go." He leaped from the stool, leaving behind his half-finished meal and mess.

"Jayden." I used what little command my voice carried. "Show me your homework."

He span back to me as he grabbed his backpack. "I gotta go, Mom. Ben's dad is waiting for me."

There was a time when he had been happy for me to drop him off at school, right to the front door. Now, I couldn't take Jayden there without embarrassing him, even if I let him off half a mile away. There's nothing that could make a mom feel any lower than her own child rejecting her.

A honk of a car horn confirmed Jayden's ride had arrived. I couldn't stop him from leaving without upsetting Ben's dad. Knowing what that man was like gave me my answer.

"We'll talk about this when you get home."

"I won't be home tonight, remember?"

The door slammed before I got to say anything else. Another victory for me, if winning involved giving up at the drop of a hat. Darren and I were heading out for dinner while Jayden was going to stay at a friend's house for the evening. By the time we were all home together, I would have forgotten about his homework, and he knew it.

I let out a long-winded sigh and moved back to the kitchen with a huff. I wasn't due to start work until nine, so I spent the next hour cleaning up the mess my family left behind for me on a daily basis. I swore Jayden and Darren did it on purpose just to see if I'd continue to serve them.

Most days it didn't bother me too much, but Darren's distraction and Jayden's teenage moods were starting to make the task of supportive wife and mother a cumbersome effort. Of course, that was the perfect moment for our chocolate-brown Labrador to begin barking her butt off at the back door. I yelled out to our dog, shouting her name, Bessie, while a wineglass caught my eye. I resisted the temptation to pour myself a drink while the sun was still rising. Things hadn't reached that point just yet. I tightened my dressing gown and headed for the still yapping dog.

"What the hell is your problem today?" I yelled, unloading all the crap of the morning on Bessie. She was the final member of my family deciding to push me over the edge.

Despite my gruffness, she continued to bark at the back door. "Do you want to go out?" I asked with both hands out wide, searching for an answer to the dog's sudden irrational behavior.

"Jesus Christ," I said as I unlocked the thick door and let her scurry through the slightest of gaps. I decided to peek outside to see what all the fuss was about. As I predicted, nothing but our oversize backyard met my view. Darren had promised to do some landscaping when we first moved in. Now, he was far too busy with his construction company.

Bessie ran straight toward the side fence that bordered the street of our corner block. She honed in on a single location, not letting up with her loud noise. The neighbors would be thrilled.

"Bessie!" I shouted, possibly louder than the dog. She didn't respond, forcing me to venture outside. It was another freezing, snowy morning. Usually, I didn't brave the weather without a decent coat on, but today I had no choice. I felt every bark out of her mouth edging me ahead.

I stomped up to Bessie and saw her scratching at the fence like a wild beast. "Stop it!" I yelled.

As if noticing me for the first time, she cowered down, tail between her legs. She backed away for a moment and whimpered toward the fence. Something was really getting to her.

"There's nothing there, Bessie. Now come inside and stop embarrassing me." I grabbed her by the collar and led her back toward the house. She continued to stare at the fence and whined.

"Leave it. It's just a fence," I said, utterly confident that the animal had lost her mind.

How truly wrong I was.

CHAPTER 3

The rest of my day went by as it always did: I cleaned the house in a rush, commuted to the university in easing gridlock, and settled into work with some gossip before getting on with the numerous tasks that needed completing. My job was simple on paper, but in reality, we were pulled in every possible direction the university could legally force us. Still, I enjoyed the work.

When I left not long after five, I noticed one of my colleagues crying in the parking lot. A young girl who'd only started two weeks ago one department over from me, also named Emma, was leaning against her car. Seeing the poor girl reminded me that I would occasionally have to work with another Emma. I groaned at the thought, not needing the extra confusion.

I thought about leaving, not wanting to become involved, but my parenting instinct kicked in, not allowing me to escape.

"Emma?" I said quietly as I approached, making sure not to startle her.

The twenty-something blonde tried to turn away briefly to cover up her tears. She spun back to me with a forced smile. "Yes?"

"Is everything okay?"

She sniffed. "Everything is fine, sorry. Don't worry about me."

"But you're crying. Has something happened?"

Emma shook her head at me. "Nothing. It's fine. I'll be okay. I just…"

I took a quick look at my watch as subtly as I could. I needed to move on if I was going to make it home in time for dinner with Darren. We had reservations for a five-star Italian restaurant.

Jayden was going to visit a friend and we'd pick him up later. I couldn't miss this meal. We hadn't spent a night alone together in months, maybe longer. We needed this time together.

Emma continued. "It's nothing. Just boyfriend troubles."

I stared past the words coming out of her mouth and could tell she was lying. Having a teenager gave me the uncanny ability, even though I barely knew Emma. Still, I didn't have time to delve deeper, so I used her lie as my out.

"Right, well, you tell him not to mess you around. I'm really sorry, but I need to go." I thumbed toward my car.

Emma's eyes went wide. "Oh, of course. Don't worry about me. I just need a few seconds to work this out, and I'll be fine. Please go."

"Thank you," I muttered as a lump of guilt sat in my throat. After my unceremonious morning with my family, I had almost run out of care and needed something to go my way for a change. "I'll see you tomorrow," I added as I backed away without grace. I'm sure karma would see me pay for that.

Emma's sniffing continued for a moment as I left. I put her problems out of my head and hurried toward my car before I changed my mind. Any other day I would be willing to hear it, but not tonight. I had finally managed to lock Darren down for a meal in town. I tried to remember how long it had been since we'd done such a thing. Our marriage needed it. Things hadn't been great.

After I reached my car, the usual blurry trip home flashed by as I drove on autopilot, listening to some drive-home station. The general mix of songs I used to enjoy blended seamlessly with depressing news and traffic reports. I almost turned the noise off before making it home. For some reason, I couldn't stand it anymore. It had all become too much of a routine.

When I arrived home a touch after six, I saw the driveway was devoid of Darren's work truck. "Of course," I said out loud. I resisted the urge to curse. Instead, I gave him the benefit of the doubt. It was only ten past the hour, so I couldn't lose my cool just yet.

Another twenty minutes disappeared as I adjusted my makeup and changed outfits inside, desperate for my husband to hurry the hell up and come home. Our seven o'clock reservation loomed. The grandfather clock in the hallway outside our bedroom ticked loudly, reminding me that soon I would have no choice but to reach for my phone and blast Darren the second he answered my call—if he answered my call.

Seven o'clock came and went, and I found myself sitting at the end of our bed with only the light from our attached bathroom illuminating the room. I was too angry to make the call. The phone sat in my tightening grip, the background photo of our family staring back at me. There I was, snuggled in close with Darren, while Jayden stood in the middle of our hug. The photo was more than four years old. It was the last time I remembered such a happy moment. Between now and then, things hadn't been smooth sailing. Darren's business had managed to grow every year, but at a cost to the family. The more his business expanded, the less time he reserved for us.

This wasn't the first dinner Darren had missed. My previous attempt to force him to spend time with his wife after hours had failed even quicker than this one. He had supposedly had an emergency to handle concerning the contract his business so sorely depended on. I still remembered hearing his secretary Jessica's voice in the background, urging Darren to hang up the phone. She wanted him to get back to work. Or was it so he could get back to her? I tried not to let my mind come to such conclusions.

The rumble of Darren's truck filled the driveway, prompting me up from my position at the end of the bed. I put my game face on and readied myself for another argument I didn't want to have. Anger, however, pushed me forward. Instead of eating a beautiful meal made by anyone other than myself, I would be wasting my night with shouting and silent fuming.

As I prepared to leave the bedroom and face Darren head-on, I shook my head at the lingerie I had foolishly left out in preparation for our return home from the restaurant. I grabbed the silky, black garment and shoved it into the drawer, slamming the dresser shut a moment later. A picture frame of our wedding day fell over and made a loud snap. I picked it up to see the glass had shattered across both of our faces.

With no energy to deal with the broken frame, I hurried down the stairs and caught Darren the second he walked into the kitchen. We both maintained our silence as I strolled toward him with crossed arms. He dumped his bag on the clean counter I had scrubbed that morning, sending construction dust in all directions. He kept his eyes on the surface, never once glancing up. His beard seemed thicker than before, his eyes bloodshot.

"I realize that you're pissed," he started, "but I had a good reason for—"

"I don't want to hear your excuses. I really don't."

"Emma. Please, I—"

"No, screw you. You didn't call or even send me a text. What was so important that you couldn't spare a single second for me, huh?" My arms crossed tighter over my chest. He kept his eyes glued to the counter as he scratched the back of his head.

With a raised palm and closed eyes, Darren tried to give me whatever bullshit line his male brain could generate, but his words never came out.

"Can't think up an excuse, can you? Why am I not surprised? Do you even care about me anymore?"

"Of course I do!" he yelled. His eyes flicked to mine. Now the argument was about to start. Some days I fought with him like this so I could spark a reaction. It was better than being ignored.

"You know I care," he continued. "I'm out there busting my ass, seven days a week."

"And what am I doing? I not only work full-time, but I also keep this household going."

Darren waved me off. "That's not the same as running a business. I'm responsible for ten guys. Their livelihoods depend on the decisions I make every damn day. You want to compare that to your job and this house?"

I was expecting that. Darren's go-to excuse for all matters was the stupid business. I'd set his precious company on fire if so much of our lives weren't tied up in it financially. I wished I'd never funded the idea.

I turned away, both arms still crossed, and went to leave. I couldn't be bothered arguing for the rest of the night. The passion it once evoked wasn't burning in his eyes anymore, so what was the point? He didn't respect me enough to see things from my perspective. If he couldn't understand how unimportant he made me feel compared to his business, then maybe this marriage had run its course.

"Emma, wait," he said as I cleared the kitchen and headed for the stairs. He chased after me, and I found myself wondering why. Darren had never been the sort of man to pursue me when I was angry. His typical, lazy response involved letting me cool off for a day or two. Sometimes I thought he pissed me off on purpose to secure some time to himself. Something was up.

"I'm sorry I didn't call, but..." He let his voice trail off.

I turned around with one foot on the steps. "What?" I asked with a furrowed brow. I could see agony in his eyes that made me slow down for a moment. He wanted to say what was in his head, so I gave him one last chance to make things right.

"We lost the contract today. It happened at lunchtime. I couldn't stand the thought of telling you, so I didn't call or text.

I even sent Jessica home. I've just been staring at the walls of the office, not knowing what to do next."

My heart sank. It had taken six months and hundreds of hours of preparation just to secure the deal in the first place. I'd lost count of the number of sacrifices I'd had to make so Darren could work on the damn thing. The real work had only been underway for the past two months. It would be a tremendous blow to the company and to Darren's reputation.

"I'm sorry," I said. I walked back toward him and placed both hands on his forearms. "Are you okay?" I was still pissed at him for not calling, but I accepted why he hadn't.

"No. This was a huge deal. I've fronted a lot of money to get things going. I wasn't going to break even until at least half of the houses were complete."

My mouth fell open. We generally never discussed anything to do with the finances of Darren's company. He never wanted me to take on that stress, he would say. I didn't even have access to the business accounts to get a picture of where it all stood. Most people would have thought I was crazy to hand over such a large chunk of my inheritance for something I had no real clue about, but that was how much faith I had in my husband. Until now. How much had he kept from me?

"What happened? Why did we lose the contract?" They were the only two questions my brain could handle asking.

Darren shook his head and let out his breath. "I didn't tell you, but a week ago we had an accident on site."

"An accident?"

"Yeah, one of my guys fell from a frame and broke his spine. He's in the hospital right now."

"Oh my God. Why didn't you tell me? Who was it?" I knew Darren's team well. We had company dinners every three months. Most of them lived in the area.

"Victor," Darren said as he scratched his beard.

"Jesus." Victor was the most experienced guy he had. The man never made mistakes. He'd never taken so much as a sick day. It would be a significant blow to the team.

"I know. It's messed up. I don't understand how this happened, but he fell off the second level of one of the houses and landed right on top of a stack of lumber."

I groaned with the pain I imagined that kind of impact would involve. Victor was in his fifties, with no experience in any other profession. I lowered my head as the gravity of the situation pulled me down.

"But that's not all." Darren's voice sounded shaky—something I'd never experienced with him. My brows rose again as I stared him in the eyes. What else was in that head of his? How could this get any worse?

"He's suing me."

"What? Why?"

Darren gulped in a deep breath. "He reckons the site wasn't up to code. Says he fell because of that."

"That can't be right," I said, doing my best to support him.

"Tell me about it. I make sure everything is done by the book. Not one thing out of place. It costs me a lot, but I make the job a safe one."

I wondered how true his words really were as I moved in closer, sensing his stress levels bordering on the edge. "So how can he be suing you then?"

A nervous laugh crept its way out of his mouth. "His lawyer got the site independently evaluated a few days after. According to them, there were several violations, meaning my insurance won't cover any of this: Victor's time off, his medical expenses, the lawsuit. None of it. Oh, and to top everything off, we lost the contract because of the accident. So, yeah, everything is basically fucked. How was your day?"

My heart sank as my head began to spin. How could there be violations if Darren thought the site was safe? Was he lying to me?

I stared around at our house, knowing without a doubt in my mind that if we went to court and lost, the home Darren built, the home that we paid off with Dad's money, would be liquidated in the legal mess.

"We should have never started this business," I said.

Darren forced a laugh. "Don't put that on me again. Don't give me that shit right now."

"What?" I asked. "It's true. This business has been nothing but a sinkhole for the money my father left me."

"Left *you?*" Darren yelled.

"Yes, me," I replied. I took a few seconds to realize I was letting myself lose control. I closed my eyes for a moment and remembered to breathe. "I didn't mean it like that, sorry."

"Whatever," Darren said as he ran a hand through his hair, the other gripping his side. He paced on the spot as the wrinkles across his brow thickened.

I stopped his movement and held on tight to his sides as I stared into his eyes. "What are we going to do?"

CHAPTER 4

After

Where am I? I stare up at a blurring ceiling as it rolls by me, confusing my sense of time. I can't be at home. We don't have this much space in our house. Sharp fluorescent lighting dots the way, temporarily blinding me with each pass, forcing me to turn my head to the side as much as I can.

I try to sit up, but my body seems to be held down by an external force. I swear a dozen hands are pinning me in place, but no one is hovering above. The only person I can half see is the man who is guiding me around in this bed. His hairy knuckles grip the barrier that surrounds me as I am wheeled along.

It hits me after too long a delay that I must be in a hospital bed. Have I been in an accident? Am I dying? My heart thuds hard against my chest and a wave of panic floods down to my core. All I can do is breathe. In and out. Slow and steady.

I begin to calm a little and decide to check the rest of my body. I'm not wearing my usual clothing, only a thin hospital gown. My arms and legs all seem to be where they should be and somewhat functional. I can't exactly jump up and do a backflip, but I can wiggle my fingers and toes. That's got to be a good sign, right?

But how did I get here? And where is here? Am I close to home? My mind flicks to Darren and especially Jayden. Why aren't they here by my side to reassure me everything is okay?

I try to speak, to ask the most basic of questions, but my mouth feels like it's been stuffed with cotton wool balls. I try to lift my head up again, but I only manage a few inches before a wave of dizziness and nausea shoves me back down. My skull hits the thin mattress of the bed, slamming against it as if I had fallen from a ten-story apartment.

"Take it easy, darlin'," the man pushing me around says. I still can't see his face, but I can smell his aftershave drowning out the room. His scent only adds more swirling sensations to my brain, urging the contents of my stomach to come up against my will.

I give up my pathetic attempts to gain control of the situation and try to remember what brought me here in the first place—wherever here is.

I push my brain to recall my last memory. What was the last thing I saw? It feels like I'm trying to get an old film projector to work inside my head as flashes of things that don't make sense hit my mind all at once. I start to see something: two impossibly black eyes staring into my soul, ready to feast upon me.

"No!" I yell out loud as I try to shake the thoughts in my head. I thrash about, left and right, trying to regain control of my body. That's when I realize my arms and legs have been restrained. Why didn't I notice this a second ago?

The discovery only serves to provoke me more, spurring me to fight back harder, yell even louder. I feel my body lift up and slam down in place as I try to escape those eyes. They won't stop boring down into my being, drilling through my skull like it's made of paper.

The hospital bed stops moving, coming to a sudden stop. The lone man pushing me hovers above, his face upside down. All I see is the sneer of a person in his late thirties with slicked-back hair and the kind of mustache you might find on a police officer.

"You need to settle the fuck down, darlin'," he says to me.

I shake my head and jerk my body up and down on the squeaking bed, making it move a fraction. What kind of professional talks to their patient like that? I get my answer when two strong arms pin me down by the shoulders. The man calls for some assistance, leaving me to wonder who else is nearby.

Several more arms attach themselves to my body and forcefully clasp me down so hard I can only move my neck. The throbbing pain in my head triples, filling me with more fear than I knew to be possible. Are these people going to kill me?

"Please don't hurt me," I say.

The voices above argue back and forth, ignoring my words like I'm a wild beast that needs to be appropriately restrained. I see a needle out of the corner of my eye, in the hands of one of these people forcefully keeping me still. The sharp tip only aggravates me further, urging my body to find a way out of this situation. What's going to happen if that needle gets stuck into my body? Will I be knocked unconscious, or worse?

Either way, I can't stop them. The prick punctures through the skin in my arm. A second later, a substance warms my limb and floods my system. After a few more attempts to escape, I finally begin to forget what caused me to freak out in the first place. The world seems to shrink back down and let go. I feel their power loosen and fall away.

I stare up at the man's mustache again and see the sick satisfaction he got in doing that to me. I want to hide from the sight of his face, but I have nowhere to go. All I can do is roll my head to the side and wait for the inevitable.

"Take it easy, darlin'," the man repeats. "It'll all make sense soon enough."

CHAPTER 5

Three weeks later

I don't sleep anymore. Then again, being forced to live inside a psychiatric hospital tends to do that to a person.

As I lie on my appointed bed, eyes wide open, staring at the cracks in the ceiling, I think about what has kept me awake every night since I arrived here. Is it the inescapable hours of endless wails, which never let up for even the briefest of moments? Is it the thought of the robotic daily routine enforced upon every lessened individual that is niggling at my brain? Or is it the constant threat of a migraine slowly edging its way from the back of my head to the front of my pupils?

None of those things help, but the answer is simple: whenever I fall asleep, I have horrible nightmares of a night my mind has blocked out; a night I never want to remember.

For three long weeks, I've been stuck inside Hopevale Psychiatric Hospital. Three drug-addled weeks of pills, therapy sessions, and long conversations wrapped in clichés like, "How does that make you feel?" and "Tell me about your father."

I don't know why I'm here or what needs to happen so I can leave and be with Darren and Jayden again.

For some, three weeks of this might not sound like much compared to the permanent guests of the hospital—the ones who will never return to the real world again. But to me, a conscious person, this is hell.

I came into the involuntary ward of the department on a stretcher with both arms and legs strapped down tight. The staff practically diagnosed me on arrival. The doctors said I was suffering from a psychotic breakdown brought on by post-traumatic stress disorder. The head shrink, whom I have spent hours each day studying from opposite his comfortable swivel chair, determined my illness in less time than it took for a pizza to arrive. Without a second opinion, the man decided my fate in a heartbeat and set my weeks of pain into motion.

There's nothing I can do to leave. No amount of groveling or telling the man in charge what he wants to hear will remove the array of red flags from my file. There's nothing in my dwindling arsenal of feminine charms that can convince Doctor Felix Gaertner that I am fit to be discharged.

It feels strange to accept it, but I've been admitted to a psychiatric hospital. I never once thought in my entire life that I would find myself in such a place. The worst part is not knowing why. All I can remember is that something terrible happened, something so life-changing it has devastated my memory of a certain night. Doctor Gaertner tells me that my brain is trying to protect me from the truth, but that my memories will all come back with time. Do I even want those damaging memories back, though?

The thought, the only thought I ever produce anymore, stirs me from my bed to the floor of the cold, sterile building. I sit on the ground and sense a beast brewing in the back of my head. It's dying to get out and send me into an anxiety-fueled spiral of panic. Two black eyes stare at me with a sting of hatred, but I cannot determine to whom they belong.

"Here we have patient 90153, Emma Turner." The voice of Doctor Felix Gaertner breaks into my thoughts as he approaches the reinforced door to my room. I jump back up to my bed and face away before anyone has a chance to witness me on the floor. Odd behavior like that is frowned upon and punished.

A few seconds later, the stoic professional is gazing in through the small observation window as if viewing a dozing tiger at the zoo. I don't need to see him to confirm he is there, judging me with his stare.

A second voice speaks beside the doctor's, indicating to me that at least two people are watching. Their words are not muffled to protect my nonexistent self-esteem. Instead, Gaertner speaks about me like he is a custodian introducing a new employee to a row of toilets that need daily cleaning.

"Mrs. Turner is under a strict watch after suffering a mental breakdown," Gaertner says, his voice still audible. He only lowers it slightly, but I can always hear the contempt the man holds for me.

"I strongly suggest reading her file in full, Doctor Shaw. The acuteness of the trauma she suffered is the very cataclysm of her admission to the ward."

There Gaertner goes again, speaking about the event like an emotionless news anchor announcing the death statistics of a natural disaster. I want to fight back and give him a piece of my mind, but any rage I muster is quickly replaced by fear. Instead, I retreat back into myself, shrinking down as much as I can. I fight back the tears instead of arguing with my doctor.

After a few moments of crippling dread, I turn over on the creaky mattress enough to see their faces. I want them to know the impact of their words, but instead I notice the expression of the person Doctor Gaertner is introducing to my room. Doctor Shaw stares in through the glass with something I have not seen in my entire three weeks here: genuine sympathy. The young woman stares into my eyes in a way that suggests she might give a damn if I live or die.

I remove some of the fear from my mind and lock my eyes on Doctor Shaw's until she gives me a slight wave. Gaertner breaks our silent connection by ushering Shaw along to the next patient in the row of wailers and moaners.

I find myself climbing out of bed and scurrying to the door to try to examine the new doctor before she continues her tour of the hospital. Of course, I am too late, despite pressing my face against the grimy film of the window.

I let my body fall backward and down to the floor again. The beast lurks behind. It always strikes at the worst of times, never passing on an opportunity to feast on my suffering. I get closer to the ground and find some comfort on the hard surface.

All I can think about is Gaertner trivializing the last moments of my life before I stopped being Emma Turner and became the husk of a woman I am today.

I lie there wondering what this new doctor will be like. The thought takes me back to a conversation I had with Gaertner the previous day. His words didn't seem real, but he promised me that, with enough time and progress, my family would be able to visit me.

I had too many questions in response to the idea of Darren and Jayden seeing me. I know I did something to make them lose all faith and love in me. It's the reason they haven't been in yet to see me. I can only guess it's something to do with my lost memories. What did I do to lose their respect? How could my family despise me so much that they haven't come to see if I'm okay?

All I know is that the truth will come out with enough therapy. But I'm not sure I want the doctors to help me face reality. If they do, I will be forced to know what landed me in a building full of mentally unstable people, and more importantly, what has torn my family apart.

Once again, two cold, dead retinas stare at the back of my head, burning a hole in my mind where those memories once lived. I don't know if Doctor Gaertner can repair the damage that has been done. All I know, beyond a shadow of a doubt, is that I want to see my family again.

CHAPTER 6

The next few hours crawl by at the same agonizing pace of every minute spent in this hospital. My concrete room is devoid of anything to occupy my time. A single window sits high above my bed in the form of a thin horizontal panel, letting in dust-filtered light. There is no TV, no books to read, not even a real mirror in the attached bathroom. In its place sits a fixed piece of metal, a precaution meant to stop people from harming themselves. I'm not one of those patients, but I get lumped in with them all the same.

The thought of suicide sends a stabbing pain to the pit of my stomach. Even in this place, I value being alive. I could never leave this world behind, not when Darren and Jayden are out there. I need them now more than ever before. The hospital, however, is killing me slowly with solitude and boredom. If I were suicidal, how would it help to lock me away in a cage?

An interruption breaks my thoughts. It's the sound of my door unlocking. A stiff, uncaring orderly named Tom pushes his way inside and gives me the usual up and down stare that tears right through me. The slight sneer at the corner of his mouth raises his sleazy mustache, reminding me of our first interaction on the night I was brought into this place. I cringe at the thought and feel any strength I had in me vanish.

His eyes reconfirm what I already knew about the creep: he is trying to figure out what's underneath my disheveled gray sweater and white cordless pants. Tom is the typical snake these places attract.

"Time to go, Turner. You've got a session," he says with a southern drawl. The man gives me his best impersonation of a professional orderly as he gestures for the door. "Come on. I've got other people to process."

"Sorry," I say in a croaky voice. It has been ten hours since I last spoke a word to anyone, myself included. Tom continues his stare as I move past him, both of my arms wrapped tight around my body. I can sense his pupils on the back of my neck. At any moment, I swear he is going to lash out and grab me by the throat. I close my eyes whenever he is near.

As Tom escorts me out the door and along the ward beyond the other patients of the hospital, I can't help but overhear the conversation he is having on the radio. The scumbags of the place mainly use the communications network as a means to update one another on the day's findings.

"Wait till you see what's happening in the east wing," a voice brags over the speaker.

"I'll come see for myself. Just need to finish escorting this little patient of mine down to the shrinks." Tom's hand presses slightly against my back, lingering for a moment. A crippling jitter runs down my spine as I inevitably cringe away.

"Now, don't be like that, darlin'. I was simply helping you along."

I shake off the temptation to run away and hide in a closet. He isn't worth the fresh hell that would come my way if I tried to escape his authority, though.

This man has total control over me, and he knows it. If the doctors were to sit down with Tom and his buddies for a few minutes, they'd realize they all do indeed belong in a facility like this, only on the other side of the cell doors.

*

Our slow walk eventually brings us to the row of doctors' offices in a section patients aren't privy to, behind a few secured checkpoints. Gaertner's office is the first room. Every day I have two sessions with the man, for one long hour each. Depending on my mood, this can feel like an eternity.

Tom walks me beyond the first door without stopping.

"I thought I was seeing Doctor Gaertner?" I ask.

"Not today, darlin'. You're meeting with someone else instead."

"But, I always—"

"Zip it," Tom shouts. "Not my problem, understand? Now shut the hell up and walk." He grabs me with a firm squeeze by the bicep, handling me like baggage at the airport as he raises a fist to knock on the door of the fifth doctor's office.

A moment later, Doctor Shaw opens the entrance.

"Doc, Turner's here for her session," Tom says as he guides me inside like a lost puppy. I almost don't know what to think once I realize my meeting will be with Doctor Shaw. She gives me a calm smile that seeps into my brain the way it had only hours ago. Despite her kind appearance, part of me wonders if I will receive more than hollow empathy from her, the latest person in my life upon whom I am meant to unload my darkest, most profound thoughts.

I stare around the half-empty room as Tom nudges me farther inside. I've never had the pleasure of seeing any other office besides Gaertner's. Where he has plaques and certificates on the wall, Shaw has dust outlines of the framed documents of a previous occupant. She's moved in today, I assume. The only thing I see on her desk is a stack of papers I recognize as my file.

"Thank you. That will be all," Shaw says to Tom. He nods, eyeing her up and down, giving out his creepy assessment before he leaves with half a sneer still covering his face. I turn to Doctor Shaw and realize she must have noticed Tom leering at her by the slight trace of disgust in her eyes.

I let a breath of air escape me when the smell of his aftershave begins to diminish. His odor lingers, though, helping to keep me on my toes and ready for the world to explode.

"Take a seat, Emma," Shaw says, gesturing with an open palm as she settles into her chair on the other side of the aging oak desk that dominates the room. I sit down gently and wrap my arms tightly around my body as I huddle into the chair.

"My name is Doctor Eva Shaw, and I will be taking over your case from Doctor Gaertner."

I nod, trying to hold the panic in my brain while my eyes dance around Shaw's face. "May I ask why?"

The corners of her mouth tighten with a smile I am yet to classify as genuine or not. "Yes, of course. As you know, Doctor Gaertner is the head of the department and ultimately responsible for all thirty-nine patients in this ward. Based on his time spent with you over the last three weeks, he has decided that you are ready to move out of his immediate care to someone like me for the next phase of your treatment."

I mumble my understanding to Shaw. "So, you're saying I don't need to see him twice a day anymore? I've been downgraded, so to speak."

"That's one perspective. Think of it more as progress. Yes, I am still a qualified and experienced psychiatrist, like Doctor Gaertner, but I am not the head of this department."

Just the next cog in the machine, I think. I give her a forced smile before I speak. It will fade into an absent gaze soon enough. "Okay."

"Don't worry, Emma. With time, we will come to understand each other well enough for there to be a genuine comfort between us."

I nod as I think about Gaertner saying those same words when I first started with him. I will never forget the ever-present icing-sugar spots that stained his suits during our sessions. It was as if he had been forced to fit me in between doughnuts.

Doctor Shaw, on the other hand, doesn't seem the type to let a single piece of her appearance allow you to believe she is anything other than a professional. Appearing to be in her late twenties, the brunette wears thick-rimmed designer glasses, a tailored suit jacket with a white business shirt underneath, and matching pants to complete the look. I feel like an ugly slob just being in the same room with her.

"Why don't we start. Would you like to take a seat on the couch?"

I half turn toward the therapy setup in the corner, which Doctor Shaw must have insisted upon having. Gaertner always made me speak from the discomfort of his guest chair. I often wondered why he required me to sit on that seat. Maybe he didn't want his patients to relax. The thought keeps me from replying to Doctor Shaw. It's a habit I am starting to develop.

"Emma? We don't have to move over there if you're not happy with the idea."

"No, I am. I just wasn't expecting it, sorry."

"Perfectly fine. Take your time." Shaw waves her hand toward the couch. I get up, arms still around myself, and walk over to the sofa. I sit on the edge as if I am covered in mud, not wanting to ruin the doctor's furniture.

"Get comfortable, Emma. I want you to think of this space as somewhere you can relax and be yourself."

Myself? I doubt the doctor is ready for the current version of myself. It's taking everything I have not to be the new me every minute I spend in the hospital.

Once Shaw settles into her armchair opposite with a pen and notepad, I ease back into the couch. Its absorbent padding lets me melt back into the soft material as the weight of my body sinks me into the depths of comfort. It is the first time in three weeks I relax my tense muscles. The reaction evaporates the second Shaw speaks again.

"Emma, I want you to understand that I have read your file in full. I know everything: the event, the aftermath, every session spent with Doctor Gaertner. But those are words on a page. What

I want is to listen to you tell me everything again from the start as you remember it."

It feels as though my eyes double in size as I shake my head. An image flashes into my mind of that night. The two black eyes stare at me through the light snowfall. "No, please, I don't want—"

Shaw holds up a palm toward me. "Take a deep breath, Emma. I don't want you just to go back to the event and force out that horrible night. I want you to go back to the days leading up to that time and tell me what was going on in your life."

My heart begins to slow down a little as I allow the tiniest slice of calm to wash over me.

"That could take some time," I say. "We only have two one-hour sessions each day."

"Actually, you will be cut back to a single one-hour session each day. We feel you are ready to dial back your time spent in therapy. But please know that we will get there, no matter how many sessions it takes."

I thrust my body back and press my skull tight against the surface of the couch. The pressure relieves me for a moment. I pull my hair and close my eyes before opening them back up. I stare right into Shaw's eyes and say, "Are you sure you want to hear this?"

The doctor nods as calmly as a person can. "Yes, Emma. There's a horrific story locked away in there that needs to come out into the open. It's not going to be an easy task, by any stretch of the imagination, but I want you to tell me what happened, the way you remember."

My hands find their way to my face and begin rubbing my eyes and forehead. The doctor's request is going to kill me, but for some reason, I feel compelled to comply.

I don't know if it's Shaw's questioning stare that is about to make me open up, but every hidden memory wants to come out, whether I want them to or not.

CHAPTER 7

Before

The warnings flowed in. Threatening texts to Darren's phone had plagued our night. I had picked up Jayden from his friend's house several hours earlier, after we abandoned our dinner plans. It was now close to one in the morning, and I was still awake.

"Fucking Victor," Darren muttered as we lay in bed. The blue light from his cell bathed his angry face as he haphazardly scrolled through the threatening words sent anonymously to his number.

"How do you know it's him?" I asked as I placed my e-reader down.

"Who else could it be?"

"I couldn't imagine Victor doing this, though. Does he even have a cell phone?"

"Yeah, a basic one, but he also has an angry family. I know this is them. They think they're doing him a favor, but I'm saving all this crap for court. Maybe the whole case will be thrown out."

I stroked Darren's arm in an attempt to calm him down a little. "Why don't you turn that thing off for the night?" I could feel the stress pouring through him. He flinched at my touch and tilted the screen away.

"No, I can't. I want every text recorded and backed up. I'm not letting them destroy everything I've busted my ass to build.

These asshole family members of his are just trying to force me to settle for a payout."

I shook my head. "It's so stupid. How could they possibly think this will help?"

He shrugged. "You understand more than anyone how people are when it comes to family. It brings out the best and worst in all of us."

Where did that come from? Darren wasn't usually so flippant with my past. We didn't often talk about my brother, James, and the strained relationship between us. I decided it must be the stress and agreed with the side of his head before rolling over to a more comfortable position. Darren continued to scroll manically through his phone. I didn't want to be the one to tell him that there was no way those texts would hold up in court without proof Victor's family sent them. I allowed him to funnel his anger into the task, hoping it would calm him down a little.

As I began to drift off to sleep, a loud crash outside pulled me into an alert state. Darren responded twice as fast as me and was already up.

"What the hell was that?" I asked. My heart pounded in my chest so hard I could almost hear it.

"Victor," Darren said without looking back to me as he got up and put some clothing on. A moment later, he grabbed a baseball bat from the side of my dresser.

"What are you doing?" I whispered.

Darren kept his focus forward as he gripped the weapon tight. "I won't let them intimidate me."

Before I could talk him back down, he headed for the door.

"Darren," I called after him. He continued his determined pace and exited our bedroom, heading for the stairs.

With no choice but to follow, I leaped out of the bed and went after him. The noise had come from outside, next to our bins.

Darren would be moving down a level to the side door where we kept the garbage, so I stayed back a little.

In the dark of the night, I stood directly behind him with one hand on his shoulder. I wanted him to identify where I was and not to mistake me for the intruder. The last thing I needed was to be struck over the head with a bat.

As we moved toward the door, another clang made us stop in our tracks.

"Come on, assholes," Darren whispered as he continued to creep up to the door. I let him get a few steps ahead, the reality of the situation freezing me in my place. The handle began to jiggle as Darren came to within two feet of the door. He raised the bat, turning the piece of sports equipment from a fun object to a deadly tool.

The door sprang open. Darren reached out and grabbed at the intruder, pulling them roughly inside.

"Whoa, Dad, it's me. Put down the bat!" Jayden yelled as Darren pressed him up against the wall, knocking over a lamp in the process. I quickly found the nearest light switch and flicked it on.

Darren lowered the bat and slapped the makeshift weapon down on a small table kept by the door. "What the hell are you doing out there?" he asked. "I thought you were trying to break into our house. I could have hurt you."

Jayden's brow twisted up as he shook his head. "Nothing."

"Nothing?" Darren yelled as he got closer to our son. "Bullshit. You've got about three seconds to tell me."

"Whatever," Jayden muttered, glancing away from his father.

"Don't you 'whatever' me, Jayden. This is serious. Now tell us what you were doing sneaking into the house at one in the goddamn morning."

Jayden let out a sigh as he continued to avoid his father's gaze. "I was hanging out with some friends, okay?"

"On a school night after I just picked you up from seeing them?" I asked over Darren's shoulder. Jayden had been home since nine. Now we discovered he had crept out once we'd all gone to bed.

"With who?" I asked.

"None of your business."

"Is that right?" Darren said. "Well, son, I think you'll find that it is entirely our business. Consider yourself grounded until further notice."

"What?" Jayden said as Darren grabbed the bat and walked away from him. "That's not—"

"I don't want to hear it. You're grounded. Now go to bed." Darren didn't wait for a rebuttal and headed back up the stairs.

"How long has this been going on?" I asked Jayden with crossed arms.

He shrugged. "I don't know. What does it matter, anyway?"

I resisted the temptation to fall into another argument with him. "Well, it stops now. Your father is going through some tough times at work and doesn't need this nonsense on top of everything."

"Tough times?" Jayden asked. "What do you mean?"

I let out a huff as I debated how much to tell him. We were usually upfront about most things with our son. I stared him in the eyes. "Your father lost his big contract after Victor broke his spine on site due to a fall. He is now suing the business."

"Holy shit," Jayden said.

"Hey, watch the language. You're in enough trouble as it is. Don't make things worse."

"Sorry," he said. I'm not sure if he was apologizing for the cursing or the late-night sneaking. Either way, the conversation could wait until morning.

"Go to bed. You've got to go to school in the morning, in case you forgot."

"I'm going," he groaned, heading for the stairs.

I shook my head with a smile and remembered stealing back into the house when I was his age. My father only caught me once. Never again did I try such a thing.

Before I headed back upstairs, I fixed up the lamp and checked that the side door was locked. As I reached for the knob, I heard what sounded like an idling car. For whatever reason, the noise prompted me to open the door a touch and spy outside.

Out in the snowy night in front of our house, I saw an old sedan from the seventies idling away with a lone driver inside. It didn't belong to anyone in the neighborhood, nor had I seen it before. A figure inside put the vehicle into gear and drove off in hurry without any lights on.

"Jayden," I muttered to myself, wondering who'd dropped him off at this time of night. I shook my head and shut and locked the door. I headed up to the bedroom and ran into Jayden as he was brushing his teeth. I waited for him to finish before I asked about the car.

"So, who was that dropping you off in the middle of the night, huh?"

He wiped his mouth as a crease formed across his brow. At that moment, he looked exactly like his father. "What are you talking about?"

"Don't play dumb. I won't add anything to your punishment or tell your father if you spill the beans right now."

Jayden shook his head. "I didn't get a lift home. I rode. I swear it. You can ask anyone—or check my bike, even. It's got snow on the tires."

I crossed my arms, using my limited range of mom poses, but he didn't budge on his stance. A sudden prickle of fear ran down my spine when I realized something: Jayden was telling me the truth.

CHAPTER 8

The next morning, I stirred awake from a disturbed slumber feeling worse than when I'd gone to bed. Through the night, I had woken up every hour and pretended to go to the bathroom so I could peek out the window of our bedroom to the street below. I didn't spot any more idling cars, but the thought never escaped my mind.

I rolled in my bed and realized Darren had gotten up earlier than usual. I'd been waiting until morning to tell him about the car I saw last night. He had a lot on his mind, and the business never let him take a minute off.

I headed downstairs to see if I could make Darren some breakfast or fix him a coffee, but he was already rushing out the door.

"Honey?" I called out to him. He had his keys in his mouth, his hands overloaded with paperwork, coffee, and his bag. He saw me calling and placed enough items down on the small counter by the front door so that he could spit out the car keys. With raised eyebrows, he waited for me to speak.

"Were you going to say goodbye to me?"

He closed his eyes with a wrinkled brow and lowered his head. "Sorry. I've just got so much to do today. I didn't mean to take off without a word."

"It's okay," I said as I walked across to him. I placed a hand on his chest and leaned up to kiss him on the cheek. He looked at me with tired eyes, and I realized he had somehow aged by several years over the last week.

"We'll push through this," I said. "One day at a time."

He smiled at me half-heartedly, lifting only one corner of his mouth. "What if we don't? What if we lose everything? The business, the house. It could all go if this gets ugly."

"We won't let it get ugly. Maybe we need to reach out to Victor and talk to him without any lawyers or family members in his ear. He always seemed like a reasonable guy to me."

Darren nodded. "Yeah, he was. He was like family. Out of all the guys I've hired, he was the last one I'd ever expect to do this, but I guess losing your livelihood will do that to a person."

I forced a smile. "Just work through today, honey. We'll talk more when you come home tonight. I'll make you something nice for dinner so we can grab a head start on a relaxing weekend."

He wrapped his spare arm around me and pulled me in tight. "That sounds perfect." He kissed me on the cheek and held me for a moment longer. "I'd better go," he said. "I'll be home by six."

I watched, standing in the front doorway, as he gathered his things again and headed out to work. His cell rang before he reached his truck, forcing him to juggle the phone out of his pocket and fumble his way into his work vehicle.

I shut the front door and turned the knob to push the deadbolt into place. Normally, I didn't worry about locking every single door in the house, but after seeing the threats sent to Darren's number and the creepy driver in the middle of the night, I was starting to become quite paranoid.

I let out a huff, knowing I still had to go to work today. It would probably be a good distraction, but I was less than motivated to head back upstairs and prepare for the day. I still had an hour before I needed to leave, so I thought about going to the gym once Jayden took off to school.

Of course, I would first have to face the loathing my teenage son would no doubt direct toward me when he came down from his room.

*

Breakfast with Jayden was more awkward than usual. Whenever Darren grounded him, I was the one who had to enforce the punishment, meaning Jayden's anger would be directed at me.

"So, did you do your homework at all last night? Or were you and your friends too busy sneaking around?"

Jayden muttered something under his breath as he ate his cereal. I moved closer to him and leaned down to his lowered eye level. "Well?"

"I'll do it before I leave, okay?"

I let out a sigh. "That's not how homework is supposed to be done."

"What's your problem? I'm doing it at home before I go to school."

"After going to bed in the early hours of the morning. Should be your best work to date." I couldn't help myself. I knew I was only making him resent me more than he already did, but someone needed to get through to him, and it sure as hell wasn't going to be Darren.

Within a few days, the two would go back to being great buddies again, like the grounding never happened. Before the punishment had time to sink in and take effect, Darren would drop it and let Jayden go back to doing whatever he wanted. I was always left to be the bad guy.

I stood back while Jayden slid out his homework from his backpack and haphazardly worked on it one-handed while he ate his breakfast.

"Do you need any help?" I asked.

"No, I'm fine," he grunted back. "Don't worry about me, Mom."

I let out a sigh through flared nostrils and left the room to grab my gym gear. I used the excuse to get away from him before I escalated things. I headed upstairs and walked into my bedroom, shutting the door behind me. The day felt like it was getting to me, and I hadn't even left the house yet.

After taking a moment to scream into my pillow, I found my gym gear and changed in the bathroom. When I saw myself in the mirror, I felt frustrated as hell with the bags under my eyes. My blonde hair was a mess and needed a good wash, but I didn't feel like spending any time sorting it out. I just wanted to hit the gym and burn off some of my grievances.

Before I had a chance to finish covering up my face with makeup that I'd sweat right back off, my cell beeped in the bedroom. I had forgotten to take it off charge when I woke up.

I left the bathroom and sat down on our bed to pick up my phone. A message was staring back at me on the lock screen from an unknown number.

If you value your family's safety, open this link.

I clicked the link and my cell loaded up a website I'd never seen before. It contained an array of images and nothing else. I dropped the device on the bed and watched as it bounced and fell to the floor. Both of my hands flew up and covered my mouth.

I slowly bent down and picked up the phone as if it might bite me. I had no choice but to look again.

There, staring back up at me was a whole bunch of photos of our family. I studied each one with my mouth open. I saw Darren in his office, me heading to work from the parking lot, Jayden around the schoolyard.

"What the fuck?" I said out loud. There was more: a photo of Darren working on site behind the security fencing; a picture of me looking out the window last night. The last one was of the front of our house, taken this morning as Darren left for work. I could see myself standing in the doorway, watching my husband go.

My hands shook as a single thought popped into my brain and came out of my mouth. "Jayden."

CHAPTER 9

I charged down the steps and ran to the kitchen to find Jayden still sitting by the counter doing his homework. I moved behind him and glanced out the front window. I held up my phone for reference and realized the photo had been taken from our neighbor's house, where a line of small bushes sat. Had one of Victor's family members been hiding in those shrubs, waiting for Darren to leave for work just to scare us? Was it the same person who had been in that car last night, taking photos of me as I gazed out of the curtains? How did I not see anyone?

The thought of a creep watching our house pulled me back and away from the door. As I spun around, I bashed into Jayden, and he dropped his half-full cereal dish to the tiled floor. The bowl made a hideous sound as it shattered into what seemed to be a million pieces.

"Whoa, Mom. Watch out," he said, almost shouting.

I grabbed hold of his wrist with one hand and stared into his eyes with two wild pupils.

"Mom?" he asked me, realizing something was wrong.

"You can't go to school. You can't leave the house. I have to call the police."

"What? Is this because of last night?"

I shook my head. "You don't understand. Someone is watching us. There's no time to explain, but your father has been receiving threats. We think it's Victor's family."

"The guy that broke his spine?"

I nodded as I swallowed. My throat suddenly felt dry.

"What kind of threats?" Jayden asked, his voice cracking a little.

I still had the phone in my hand, and debated whether to show him. The pictures could freak him out even more than me, so I kept them hidden. "That doesn't matter right now. We need to stay put. I'm calling the police and your father. Please don't move."

He nodded his head quicker than was necessary as his eyes continued to focus on mine. There's nothing like an emergency to get your teenage son to listen to you for a change.

I dialed 911 and got straight through to a dispatcher, who asked me which service I was after. I tried to remain calm and responsible as I asked for the police. I needed to be the strong parent now and not allow the thought of a stranger breaking into our house upset me.

After a slight delay, I was transferred to the police department. I explained everything to the operator and then had to go through the frustrating process of giving her my details. Why couldn't they use some fancy technology to work out who I was and where my house could be found in an instant? I'd be all for the invasion of privacy if it meant the police could stop someone from harming my family before it was too late.

The operator instructed us to hide somewhere in the house with a locking door. I instantly thought of the basement and took Jayden by the hand like he was three years old again. The dispatcher told me to keep my cell handy, as the police would be calling it the second they arrived.

Jayden and I charged down to the basement. I locked the door behind us at the bottom of the stairs and pulled him farther around behind the back of the stairwell. We had a small storage section there, behind which we could hide if someone ventured this far into the house. I also took the opportunity to grab one of Darren's old hammers, which we kept stored away under the stairs. At least I wasn't unarmed.

"Mom," Jayden whispered.

"What?"

His eyes darted around in his head. "What are we going to do?"

"We're going to stay put and keep quiet until the police arrive. Got it?"

Jayden eased back. I remembered to breathe and took the opportunity to call Darren. The call went straight through to his voice mail. I left a panicked message and hoped he got it sooner rather than later.

In the dim light from the dusty bulb that hung low in the storage area, I saw Jayden quietly retreating into himself. I could only hope that the police arrived before our house got broken into.

✽

Twenty minutes later, my cell blared out loud, startling us both. A blocked number came up. I assumed it was the police, so I answered. "Hello? Officer?"

My words were met with some muffled sounds, as if someone was covering the microphone.

"Hello?" I asked again. "Are you calling from the police station?"

The line went dead with a solid crack, sounding almost like a call from an old landline. Before I had time to understand what happened, my cell rang again, but this time with an actual number on my display.

"Hello? Who the hell is this?"

"Ma'am, my name is Sergeant Cole, I'm with the CHPD. We received a report that you believe someone is trying to break into your home."

"Did you call just call me a second ago?" I asked. "My son and I are in the basement with the door locked, as instructed."

"This is the first call I've made to you, ma'am," the officer said. "We are parked in your driveway now. We will check out the exterior entries to your home and try to determine if anyone has broken in. Just stay put. I will call you once we have the all-clear."

"Thank you, sir," I said. "The back gate is unlocked. Our Labrador, Bessie, is in the backyard, but she's harmless."

"Not a problem, ma'am."

The line went dead, allowing me time to let out an extended sigh of relief. I found myself leaning back into an old pile of bedding we'd we never got around to hauling to one of the charity drop-offs around town. I felt guilty about that, but I was also enjoying the comfort of the material, despite its fusty smell.

"So?" Jayden asked.

I slapped my head, feeling stupid for not relaying the current happenings to him. I filled Jayden in and took a moment to reassure him everything would be okay. Then my cell rang again. Cole asked if we could come to the front door. He and his partner couldn't find any evidence of a break-in. I had no idea whether that was a good thing or not.

We climbed back upstairs and headed to the main entry. I asked Jayden to stay behind me for his own safety while I slowly unlocked the thick door. I opened it only enough to let my head poke through. An officer in his fifties was standing in front of the house, with a younger partner. The two men both had their hands close to their pistols.

"Mrs. Turner?" the first man asked.

"Yes, that's me." I saw that the two officers were standing not far from their white cruiser, the slogan "Justice with Honor" written on the side.

"Sergeant Cole here," he said as he put one hand on his chest. "This is my partner, Officer Jordan. Is everything okay? May we come inside?"

"Yes, I think so. Please come in," I said as I opened the door the rest of the way.

The two men took their hats off as they entered. They were wearing black uniforms that rattled with the numerous tools of the trade as they moved into my house.

"You reported a potential break-in. Would you like us to search your home for anything suspicious?"

I thought about it for a moment. "No, that's okay, sir. If there is no sign of someone trying to break down the doors or windows, then everything is fine for now."

Cole stared at me with pursed lips and nodded. "Very well. Is there anything you would like to report? We were told you received some threatening photos."

"Yes. I called you here today because I got a few aggressive photos, sent to my cell from an unknown contact." I told them about each photo and how recently they must have been taken, especially the one from this morning. I could hear Jayden's reaction to the description of each image sent to my phone. He was breathing faster than average.

"Okay," Cole said, without sounding too concerned. He'd probably seen it all, based on his age. He walked toward me, both hands holding his overloaded belt. "Can you show me these photos?"

I nodded with half a smile. "Yes. They're on my phone." I pulled my cell from my pocket and navigated to the messages. I found the most recent one and opened the link inside. The website tried to load up, but I saw nothing but an error message saying there was a problem reaching the server. I didn't quite understand what I was reading. I tried the link again, making sure I had an Internet connection on my cell.

My stomach filled with concrete. "Wait, it's not working." I continued to try again and again, closing everything down and opening it all up again. My phone should have shown me the website, but all I got was the same error over and over. "This can't be right."

"Let me have a look," Jayden said, sounding a little embarrassed. I handed it over and watched him go through my phone with absolute efficiency. He opened apps I didn't know existed and searched everywhere. No photos came up.

"I don't understand," I said. "They were there, plain as day, on this website sent to me from a link."

"Did you save the photos? Did you send the link to your son, by chance?"

I shook my head. "I never thought to." I turned to Jayden, realizing he hadn't seen the photos. No one had.

Cole cleared his throat as he exchanged a look with his partner. "Unfortunately, ma'am, some criminals are now using technology that allows a website to automatically delete itself after a short time. If you did receive this link, it was most likely sitting on an untraceable server from Russia or China. Unless you saved those images, they are long gone."

"I did receive a link, thank you. I thought…" I trailed off as a wave of embarrassment greater than I believed possible grabbed me. I could sense their doubt.

"It's fine, ma'am. I'm not saying I don't believe you. Just that this happens all the time. Regrettably, this means we have nothing to write in our report other than your statement. And I'll be honest, that is not going to be a lot to go on."

The officer continued to tell me the futility of it all. He could send the link on to one of their techs, but he doubted it would turn up anything of use. All he could suggest was that I keep the doors locked and consider having some security cameras installed. I wanted to kick myself.

Once Cole finished warning me about how little the CHPD could do given the situation, he took my statement, including what I had seen last night after Jayden went to bed.

When the police finally left, I locked the front door and fell in a heap, sliding down the doorway. I covered my face with both hands, knowing Jayden was sitting in the kitchen, seeing it all.

CHAPTER 10

After

Doctor Shaw looks at me with laser focus as I finish telling her about the first time the police were called to our house.

"That's all the time we have for today, I'm afraid, Emma," Doctor Shaw says. She closes her notepad and straightens her outfit. "Each day, we will pick up where you left off and build up to that moment where everything changed."

I nod my head. "Okay, doctor," I say, hiding within myself. I stand from my seat and wait for Shaw to show me back to the secured ward I belong to.

"It's okay to be unsure, Emma. I realize that this will not be an easy thing to relive. I could never begin to understand what you went through, but gradually talking about it openly, more so than you ever have before, will be a positive step forward."

I scratch my head for a moment as I think about what might have made Doctor Shaw choose this job over any of the million professions she is smart enough to thrive in. Why would anyone want to hear what I have to say, especially knowing the ending in advance? I disturb myself daily without even knowing the full truth. Now she expects me to be happy to work my way up to speaking about the very instant my life stopped. The instant I killed a piece of myself in a single blow.

"I'm ready to leave," I say, not wanting to spend another second in the room. My hands begin to sweat. A continuous feeling of dread hangs over me. I swear a truck might burst through the walls and kill us both in a heartbeat. It's a disturbing feeling of fear that I've come to live with.

"Right this way, Emma. I can take you back to the ward."

"Thank you," I say, relieved to not need one of the orderlies to escort me.

We walk past the other offices and slowly move down the corridors of the hospital until we are back through the checkpoints, surrounded by the noise of the other patients. The absence of this racket is the only good thing the therapy sessions provide.

Doctor Shaw stands by the final checkpoint, one arm gripping the frame of the magnetically locking door. "Emma, before you head back inside, I've got a bit of news for you."

My stomach knots itself up. Hearing the unknown now makes me want to shrivel into a ball and die in the corner. My brain can't handle anything new. I cower away from Shaw, as if that might stop her words.

"Nothing bad. In fact, it's something positive. Your brother is coming for a visit. We thought it would be helpful for you to lay eyes on a familiar face for a change."

My mouth falls open as I try to respond. Despite being twins, I haven't seen my brother in eight years. The last time we spoke, we were disagreeing over James's falling-out with my father.

"Have a good day, Emma. I'll see you tomorrow for the next session. Rest up."

With that, the doctor leaves without revealing any other bits of information regarding my brother. Either she doesn't know about our strained relationship, or she didn't think to ask how close we were. And why is James coming in for a visit and not Darren and Jayden? If I am ready to see someone outside of these walls, what is stopping my husband and son from coming to see me?

Rationalizing the whole thing to be a mistake, I try to ignore the thought and carry on through to the ward under the watchful eyes of another orderly until the image of my brother enters my brain again. I can't avoid it.

"Why is James coming to see me?" I ask myself out loud. It's the only thought I will have for the rest of the day.

CHAPTER 11

I spend the rest of the day in a numbed state in the day room, as I have every day of the last three weeks. I have the option to go outside into the winter sun, but the thought of natural lighting makes me sick.

The blur of the day room buzzes all around. I feel like the other patients and staff are all set to ten while I run at one. They move around me with urgency while I sit motionless, waiting for the day to end so I can go back to failing in my attempts to sleep.

There are moments, a precious few hours each night, when I actually fall asleep. Those are the best minutes of my current existence. More than anything else, I want to rest in an endless gray void free from activity—free from this place. It's not until the monsters in the back of my mind seep into that private space and rip me from my slumber that I wake up with sweat soaking my clothing.

That night, one of the beasts pulls me from sleep at around one in the morning, dragging me to the floor in a heap. I can hear myself screaming as I attempt to claw my way under the bed, but the extra bars that run down the sides stop me from venturing under and into the safe space. I am apparently not the first person to try to escape the room beneath the bed.

After a minute, I calm down and remember where I am. My screaming has set off the patient across the way. His moaning then follows on to the next lost soul, until the whole ward is ripe with activity.

The interruption to the rare quiet prompts the orderlies to rush into my room with a syringe full of suffering to dull my sense of self into oblivion, silencing my future cries for at least six more hours.

"No!" I yell out as they grab my arms and legs. I kick and claw at what I can, not wanting the concoction of chemicals to flood my system. It will help me rest, but I won't be asleep. I'll be trapped inside my brain all night long.

The needle goes in after my failed effort to stop the two hulking orderlies from doing what they have done a thousand times before. The sting of ice crawls up my veins and grabs my mind, forcing me into a stupor somewhere between awake and anesthetized.

The two heroes of the night toss me back onto the mattress and place a strap across my chest for good measure. I'm not going anywhere and have no choice but to gaze at whatever section of the wall my eyes land on.

This is going to be another long night.

I try to fall asleep while I stare at the walls and sense my brain cells dying from inactivity. To avoid speculating about that night, I transition my thoughts to James. I think about the last time I saw him.

*

I had just gotten back from my mother's funeral. The day was draining for all involved, but my father felt the most significant impact when James decided to skip the funeral entirely. All day long, Dad complained and reiterated his disgust with James for not showing up to pay his respects to his dead mother, ranting and raving about the countless sacrifices she had made for him over the years, even when diagnosed with breast cancer. My father's feelings were reflected onto me, as I had guaranteed James would be present on the day. I had promised Dad that his son would be there no matter what.

When I pulled into our street after dropping Dad off at his home, I spotted James's old pickup sitting in our drive.

I pulled up to the curb and stormed inside to find Darren and James in the lounge sharing a beer. I could see the awkward look plastered on Darren's face as he tried to be a good host in my absence. He was still wearing his black suit from the funeral.

"Hello, honey," Darren said to me the second I entered. It was as if he was trying to warn me who was in the house. I didn't need a warning, though.

"Hi, Emma," James said from the couch.

I didn't respond or smile. Instead, I stared at my brother. Darren took that as the perfect time to leave. "Good to see you again, James," he said. He stood from his favorite armchair and hurried into the kitchen.

"What are you doing here?" I asked James.

"Seeing my sister. What else?"

"Don't give me that bullshit. Where were you today?"

"I was busy."

"Busy? It was Mom's funeral. How could you have been busy?"

James placed his beer down on the coffee table and held up both palms. "You're upset. I get that, but I had a good reason for—"

"What possible reason could you have for missing her funeral? Do you have any idea how angry Dad is? I promised him you would be there. You promised me too."

He waved me off, casting his eyes away. "You don't understand."

I scoffed as loudly as I could. "I don't understand? Tell me then, what is it I don't understand?"

James scowled at me for a moment. His casual approach was slowly beginning to fade. "I couldn't do it," he said.

"Do what?"

"The funeral. It was all too much, you know. Reminded me of her."

I stared into his eyes and saw memories stabbing into his heart. James's fiancée, Sarah, had died two years ago after committing suicide. My father had tried to help my brother rebuild his life, but James wouldn't accept his support.

"I knew it was going to be tough for you. That's why I was going to be the one to get you there and help you through the day. We all would have—you know that. But you missed Mom's funeral, James. This wasn't some co-worker you barely knew; it was Mom."

"I know!" he yelled. "You don't have to keep saying it. I screwed up. I can't change that."

I let out a huff and walked farther into the room. I sat on the arm of one of the recliners with crossed arms. "So where were you today?"

James played with the beer on the coffee table, keeping his eyes from mine. We had been so close once, always with one another, through it all. No one could ever come between us. But these past few years had changed James, ever since Sarah had died. I felt like I didn't know him anymore.

"I was at a bar across town."

"You were drinking?"

"Yeah, so what? I'm not allowed to have a drink now?"

"That's not the point and you know it," I said. I could hear myself getting riled up, disturbing the house, but I didn't care. He needed to understand what he had done.

"What is the point?" James asked me. "Why go to a funeral? That person is dead and gone. They don't know if we've come to see them off or not. It certainly won't bring them back."

I huffed as I gripped the bridge of my nose with my fingers. "That might be true, but we were also there to support each other and to support Dad."

"Dad, huh? It's all about him, isn't it?"

"What do you mean?" I asked, standing.

James stared at me like I was crazy. "You wouldn't get it, Emma."

I moved toward him. "Try me."

I watched as James leaned back on the couch with a smirk. "You don't see it, do you? You never did."

"What is there to see? Dad has always been there for you, especially when Sarah died. And what do you do when he needs your help? You let him down."

James shook his head. I saw tears forming in his eyes. "I tried, Emma. I really did, but you don't know what it's like. Dad thought he was helping me back then; you all did. I just wanted to be left alone and not reminded every three seconds that she was gone and it was all my fault."

I frowned as I sat back down on the arm of the chair, my mouth agape. "It wasn't your fault, James. She was suffering from depression. In the end, there was nothing you could have done. She made her choice."

James's eyes darted up to mine. "Don't feed me those bullshit lines again, Emma."

"I'm not—"

"I don't want to hear it," he said cutting me off. "You have this perfect life here. You would never understand what it's like to lose the person you care about more than anyone else in the world."

I opened my mouth to speak, but no words came out. I focused my eyes on his, taking a moment to think. "I get that today would have been tough on you, James, but the simple fact is that you let us all down at the worst possible time. If we can't rely on you for big things like today, then how can we ever trust you again?"

James stood from the couch and grabbed his beer up with one hand. He finished it off in one gulp before walking out of the room with a scowl on his face.

"I'll see you around, Emma," he said to me without making eye contact.

I didn't say another word to him. There was nothing left to discuss. James went through the front door and left. Moments later, he drove off in his pickup.

I hadn't seen James since.

CHAPTER 12

The next morning, after yet another restless night, I am placed down in the visiting area and told James will arrive any minute.

It's been eight years. And not just any eight years. Life as I knew it has changed beyond recognition. I don't want him to discover what I've become. I don't want anyone to see me now, but I have no choice, do I?

My fingers shake underneath one of the fixed tables found in the visitors' room. I do what I can to hide my jitters, but it's impossible to conceal what is written across my face.

I think back, beyond the last time I saw James, to when we were kids. We were inseparable. When we were teenagers, we hung out in the same circle of friends and got up to the same mischief together. If one of us got into trouble, we both did.

We continued to be close beyond high school and beyond college. I'd see him multiple times per week. He'd come to dinner with Sarah, and we'd visit them whenever we could. But when Sarah passed, a piece of James went with her.

He left town after Sarah's funeral. I tried to see him every chance I could, but he was always busy. Or so he said. It was like I no longer had the brother I once knew.

James strolls into the room like it's an everyday occurrence for him to visit his twin sister in the nuthouse. He doesn't seem nervous or too concerned for his safety given the number of other lunatics who are present in the limited space.

He comes straight toward me once he spots me—the husk of his sister, trying to look as small as possible at the cold metal table. His confidence evaporates the moment our eyes meet. A wrinkle creases his forehead, as if the reality of visiting a family member in the psychiatric ward finally hits home.

"Emma?" he asks, double-checking he is staring at the right person.

I am half tempted to pretend I don't remember him. Seeing my brother after eight years in a place like this is more than I can handle, but I also am aware the doctors are observing me during this entire interaction. They wanted this meeting to occur.

"Hi, James," I say, after a long delay.

He steps closer, not taking his eyes off me. "May I sit down?"

I give him a shrug. "If you want." It's been eight years since we spoke, and all I can muster is a teenager's response.

I realize he is wearing new clothing: designer jeans, a leather belt, a tucked-in white business shirt with the top two buttons undone, and a watch that appears expensive at a cursory glance. His brown hair is wavy but neat, and he has a finely maintained bit of stubble. He is holding a thick brown sports jacket, neatly folded in one hand.

I have never seen him like this. My memory of my brother is of a man who takes the least care of his appearance possible.

James pulls out the chair opposite me and sits down with the jacket across his lap. He places both hands on the table and interlaces his fingers. His thick watch chinks against the surface of the table.

"Emma," he says, his expression pleading. "The hospital tracked me down and told me you'd been placed in here. I jumped straight on the next plane. That was a few weeks ago. I wanted to visit you sooner, but the doctors wouldn't allow it until now."

The words coming out of his mouth don't seem right. The James I know travels by bus. The James I know wouldn't drop everything to visit the sister he'd fallen out with. Had my breakdown motivated him to find me?

My thoughts are pushed aside when he leans across the table and pulls me in for a hug. The sudden action takes me by surprise. I can sense genuine compassion and warmth coming from his body. I resist at first, but it doesn't take long for me to give in and wrap my arms around him. This isn't a forced exchange; we are two siblings holding each other tight to fight off the demons of the world. I start to sob.

"It's okay," James whispers into my ear. "I'm here for you."

After the longest hug I've ever received from my brother, I let go of him and fall back into my chair. I immediately start to wipe my tears with the sleeve of my gray jumper. I sniff uncontrollably and notice James has also been crying.

"Why are you here?" I blurt out.

"That's a fair question," he says, leaning forward. "And I understand your confusion. The last time we spoke wasn't exactly pleasant."

"No, it wasn't," I agree, staring at the table.

James clears his throat. "It's stupid. After we had parted ways that day, all I wanted was to be angry at you and Dad, but something else eventually happened instead: you motivated me to get my act together."

"What?"

"Yeah, hear me out, Emma. You probably won't believe me, but I realized something that day—about you."

"You did?" I ask. I feel my heart skip a beat.

"You were trying to be there for two people. Even though Mom had just died, you were trying to support both me and Dad at the same time, without any regard for yourself. I wanted that same strength. I was finally able to appreciate your sacrifice and I wanted to be that person too."

I stay silent for a moment as my eyes dart around the features of his face. I can't maintain eye contact for long these days. "I wanted to help you," I say. "I didn't want to fight."

"I realized that after some time. Of course, my ego got in the way, so I figured I had no option but to do you a favor and stay out of your life."

"I never wished for that," I say, reaching a hand toward him. "I called you a few times, sent you emails—letters, even—but you never responded."

"I know. I'm sorry. I was in another place back then. No excuses, but at first it was for the best. I needed to get my head right before I was worthy of your attention. I guess I let that doubt carry on for too long."

"Eight years too long."

James gives me a warm smile. It feels odd to see it. Whenever I have thought about him, I only ever pictured a sour, angry face. Was I getting the brother I loved so dearly back? The world had a strange way of working.

"Enough about me," James says. "I'm not here to ask for forgiveness or to give you excuses. I'm here for you." He places his hand over mine and gives it a gentle squeeze.

At that moment, all I can think about is the time we have lost, and for no good reason. I tore myself apart after the fight, feeling so stupid. I should have been a better sister, but I was also trying to be a good daughter. The two had become competitors. James pushed me away, and I let him.

"Is there anything that you need?" he asks.

His question brings me back to the present. I glance around the room, as if the answer will be written on the walls. I find it hard to process the easiest of thoughts now. Is it the drugs they give me that create this constant haze of confusion, or have the repressed memories of that night crushed my ability to think?

"Emma?"

I shake my head and look away. "No. I don't even know why I'm really here. All I remember is something horrible happened, and it's all my fault."

James lowers his voice. "Hey, listen to me. You don't deserve any of this. Just remember that, okay?"

I force in a deep breath with closed eyes. When I open them and exhale, I focus on James's stare and take a few moments to reach out and grab his hand. "Have you seen Darren and Jayden?"

He shakes his head. "Have they not been in to visit you?"

I slump into my seat. "No. I don't know what I did, but they must hate me."

"I doubt that they hate you. Whatever it is that's happened, I'm sure the three of you can reconnect and move forward. You, Darren, and Jayden are the strongest people I know."

I lean back and away from James, wondering if the staff coached him on what to say. Is this just another session disguised as a visit?

I refocus on James as he tells me what sounds like a rehearsed bit of therapy. Are the doctors operating him like a mouthpiece, studying my reactions to his every word?

After a few more minutes of it, I don't know how long I can sit on the thought. I need to leave.

"Thank you for coming, James, but I'm starting to feel tired."

"Oh, I'm sorry. I can come back another time that suits. You rest up and take it easy." He stands and moves around to give me another hug. "I'll be staying nearby. I've given my number to the staff. Call me any time, day or night. I'm here for you, Emma. We'll fight through this thing together."

I have nothing to say apart from my thanks. My eyes follow him as he leaves the room to fade out of my life again. Part of me wonders how real he is. Has the stress of the facility finally broken me? Am I now officially crazy?

As if timing things to perfection, Tom shows up out of the corner of my eye and grunts something about my next session starting a bit earlier than usual. He escorts me along to Doctor Shaw's office and drops me off like a disinterested parent.

"Take a seat," Shaw tells me as the door clicks shut.

I take a quick glance at the clock on the wall. One hour won't be enough therapy after today's visitor.

CHAPTER 13

Before

Darren rushed home from his office across town after receiving my message. There was a good hour's delay before he knew there was a problem at home. He burst through the front door and wrapped his arms around me the second he could. I hadn't felt him embrace me like that in God knows how long, but there was no time to savor the hug.

"What happened? Why were the police here?" Darren looked to Jayden, who was standing in the kitchen. He had questions. I couldn't describe everything over the phone, but now that he was here, I explained why I had called the police out to our home.

"After you left for work, someone sent me a link to a bunch of pictures."

"Pictures?"

"Yes. Pictures of us. Pictures of you at the office, me walking into work, Jayden at school, and even one of the front of our house."

"The front of our house?" Darren asked as multiple creases lined his forehead.

"Hear me out. This wasn't simply a photo of our house; it was a photo of our house as you were leaving this morning. I was standing in the doorway seeing you off. From the angle, it looked like it was taken from the bushes across the street."

Darren got into his signature worried pose: right hand scrunching the hair above his forehead while his left gripped the side of his jacket on his hip.

"Jesus," he said.

"It freaked me the hell out," I cried, tears forming. I fought them off, but I couldn't hide how much I was struggling.

"Come here," Darren said, pulling me into another hug. He then offered an arm to Jayden, who reluctantly accepted the family support. We stood there in a rare flash of unity. I realized that this was what it took for the three of us to share a moment together.

"I can't believe this," Darren said.

"That's not all. Last night, after we caught Jayden sneaking in, I spotted an old sedan idling out the front of the house. As soon as I opened the door to look at it, the driver took off. So, you can see why I called the cops. Someone is stalking us."

Darren shook his head. "No, not some unknown creep. I'm positive I know who it is."

I pulled back. Jayden took the opportunity to let go too, but he wanted to know his father's thoughts. "Who?" he asked.

Darren's eyes moved left and right before settling back on me. "I'm pretty sure Victor's cousin, Karlo Liberda, is behind all of this threatening shit. According to a few of my most trusted guys, this Karlo is a real piece of work."

"In what way?"

"The ex-con kind of way. He's done time for all sorts of violent things, from what I've heard. And he's not some moron criminal, either. Word has it he used to work for the Czech mob."

"Jesus."

"Could be some BS rumor, but he's still not someone to mess with."

I shook my head with closed eyes at the thought of some ex-con taking pleasure in getting back at the family that had supposedly wronged his cousin. People like that used the whole family honor thing to act out their natural tendencies toward violence. It was the perfect cover to justify being an asshole to total strangers in a situation that hadn't reached anywhere near such a boiling point.

"He's not getting away with this, especially if he's dumb enough to send photos. You gave copies to the police, right?"

I let out a sigh. "Here's the thing: the images on the website are gone. Whoever sent me the link deleted it before I had time to save them."

Darren's face turned to a mixture of anger and confusion. "What?"

"The police told me that there isn't much we can do about it. They most likely used an untraceable server."

Darren waved me off. He'd never been a big fan of technology and cringed at the first mention of it.

"I swear I received those freaky pictures this morning. I didn't think to save them because I genuinely thought Jayden and I were about to be attacked. I'm so sorry." The tears flowed for real this time.

"It's okay," Darren said as he pulled me back in. "Karlo knew what he was doing. He's been told to be as careful as possible not to leave any evidence. The bastard must be experienced, unfortunately."

I sniffed into Darren's chest for a few moments before attempting to pull myself together. I couldn't explain why, but I suddenly realized that this was how Victor's family wanted us to react. I shook my head, feeling stupid again for falling into their trap.

I stood tall and thought to myself that those pricks wouldn't stop me from living my life. I wiped away my tears and headed for the front door.

"What are you doing?"

I grabbed my keys and my handbag. It wasn't my primary bag, but it held enough items to get me through the day. "Jayden is late for school, and I'm going to be late for work."

"You're going to work after all this? You're still in your gym gear."

"I have to. We can't let these people run our lives."

"But—"

Darren started to speak, but I cut him off. "I'll be okay. So will our son. They are trying to scare us. I won't let them. Come on, Jayden," I said, ushering him along.

My son complied, possibly not knowing what else to do. He probably wanted to be away from the house as soon as possible.

"Emma, I understand what you're saying, but we need to be careful. This guy shouldn't be underestimated."

"Why? He's just some asshole taking the opportunity to be himself. I'm not going to let him terrorize us to satisfy Victor."

Darren shifted into his worried pose again, keeping his focus on me. At that moment, I realized how much stress he must have been under with the business losing a massive contract while simultaneously being sued by an injured worker. Me adding my stubbornness on top of the pile couldn't help.

"I'll be careful," I said, moving back toward him while Jayden waited by the door. Darren shook his head and muttered to himself. I placed a hand on his forearm and rubbed it up and down. "I'll make sure to leave the university and walk to the parking lot with someone else, and I'll call you on my way home. Jayden can stay at a friend's house until one of us are free to pick him up."

Darren groaned, signaling his acceptance of defeat. "Fine," he said, "but I'm going to buy you something to defend yourself with."

I waved a palm at him. "I'm not carrying a gun in my handbag."

"I know," he said. "I mean like pepper spray or a stun gun. It'll make me feel better knowing you at least have one thing to defend yourself with."

I wondered if Darren had gone and purchased a weapon of his own. I resisted asking him about it right then, but I kept the thought in the back of my mind.

"Okay," I said. "I'll be happy to carry one of those things. For today, I'll be extra cautious and make sure I'm always with another person. That goes for you too, Jayden."

Jayden nodded.

I faced Darren again. "Can we go now?"

"Yes, but I'm following you until I can see you're safely out of the area."

"Fine by me."

Letting out a sigh, Darren scratched his head. "What are you going to tell the school about Jayden being late?"

"I'll think of something," I said as I headed for the door. Darren followed Jayden and me outside and locked the door as soon as we left. To reach my car, parked under the detached carport to the side of our driveway, I had to pass Darren's truck. Without being obvious, I peeked inside and spotted a bag from the local gun store sitting on the passenger seat. I shook my head and reminded myself to speak with him about it later.

"I'll see you tonight," he said as we reached my car. I turned back and stared him in the eyes, giving him a look that only he could interpret. Without saying a word, I told him to stay safe and not do anything stupid.

CHAPTER 14

Darren followed us to the school in his truck and continued to his office, apparently feeling okay enough to let me drop Jayden off on my own.

As I pulled into the empty drop-off point, a single teacher spotted my car approaching. "Oh, crap," Jayden said, when we both realized the teacher was Miss Cantin, one of the school's counselors. I'd had run-ins with her before over Jayden's grades. Needless to say, she didn't like me as a parent.

Miss Cantin was in her late fifties, unmarried, and was dedicated to the education system. Wearing something a professional businesswoman might wear to an office job in the city, she approached my car without any prompting. A steely look clouded her eyes as she held her head higher than was required while maintaining her scowl. I almost shuddered just glancing at her.

"I'll see you later," Jayden said in a hurry as he exited the passenger seat.

"Text me whose house you're staying at this afternoon," I yelled as he stepped past Miss Cantin without making eye contact. She stared him down as though her eyes held enough power to stop him cold.

I saw my opportunity to slip away despite being required to sign Jayden in for his lateness, but Miss Cantin struck with her lightning approach.

"Mrs. Turner," she said, with a refined voice that always seemed out of place in such a small-town middle school. "Is there any particular reason Jayden is so late this morning?"

I let out a sigh as I reminded myself not to become angry at the teacher, who was only trying to do her job. I refocused on Miss Cantin. "We had a family emergency, sorry."

"A family emergency, you say?"

"Someone tried to break into our house this morning." I decided to go with something close to the truth, hoping it would shut her up. It didn't.

"I'm sorry to hear that, Mrs. Turner, but break-in or not, we expect a phone call to the office when a student is going to be late or away for the day."

"I understand, it's just—"

"We can't have students showing up whenever their parents feel like bringing them to school."

"It wasn't like that, Miss Cantin," I said. "We had the police at our house this morning. I didn't think at the time that the school needed to be involved in the matter."

She stared me down, making me feel like I was back in school and powerless. "Well then, next time you'll understand what to do, won't you?"

"Yes, Miss Cantin, I will."

The old hag smiled at me, baring her teeth, satisfied with the strips of dignity she'd torn from my carcass. How did a person reach such a point in their life that they needed to dress down parents to feel happy about themselves? She didn't know what it was like to raise a child, no matter how many kids she'd taught or offered counsel to. I let the thought evaporate as Miss Cantin straightened her long dress.

"Is that all?" I asked, waiting for permission to leave. I could have driven away, but the old battle-ax would have chased after me.

"No. Do you have a moment to talk inside? I would like to discuss a few things with you."

I couldn't help but sigh. "I can spare ten minutes," I said. I had already called work to let them know I was running late due to an emergency. It wasn't a particularly busy time at the university, so my absence wouldn't be a huge burden.

"I'll see you inside," she said, knowing full well that I would have to park my car somewhere else first. She probably delighted in the minor inconvenience she'd caused me.

As the counselor walked back toward the school, I fought off the temptation to hit the gas and head to work.

＊

After finding a spot to park in the visitors' zone, I rushed inside to Miss Cantin's office. I'd been called in enough times now to know where it was. I first needed to sign in at the front desk before I could access the old crow's lair. I took the opportunity to sign Jayden in too, despite him already having run off to class.

"Take a seat," Miss Cantin said, gesturing toward one of the two chairs opposite her. Countless posters covered the walls of the cramped office with all kinds of school propaganda. I studied the warnings about taking drugs, being a bully, cheating on exams, and even the dangers of cell phones. There was not one positive thing in her office; it was a shrine to teenage shame.

I sat carefully in one of the visitor chairs and placed my handbag down on the seat next to me. I thought back to that morning's conversation with Darren and started to see the benefits of firearm ownership as I stared back at Miss Cantin.

The counselor gave me a faint smile for a brief second, but it didn't extend up to her eyes. "So, Mrs. Turner, why are we here?"

I scrunched my brow. "You asked me in here."

"Yes, I did. And why do you think that might be?"

I didn't have a clue, but the curse word out of Jayden's mouth when we arrived to find Miss Cantin greeting us started to make sense now. "What's he done now?"

"It's not what he has done that is concerning us, Mrs. Turner. It's what Jayden hasn't done that has forced me to call you into my office today."

I leaned forward, waiting to hear what she was going to say.

"For the last three months, there has been a steady drop-off in the quality and promptness of Jayden's homework. His teachers have informed me that, each week, he is handing in work that is mediocre, at best. That is, of course, when he decides to hand in his workbook at all."

Homework? Is that all the old bat wanted to talk about? Normally, this sort of thing would have concerned me, but with everything that had been happening, it didn't seem like such a big deal. For a second, I thought she was going to say Jayden had started a fire. I fought the urge to stand and leave.

Miss Cantin continued, "Frankly, Mrs. Turner, we are concerned at this gradual decline your son is demonstrating. We have cause to believe that the problem may be coming from some issues your son is having at home."

"Issues?" I asked, defense cluttering my voice.

"Yes," Miss Cantin said, with her stern, unwavering voice. "We can see Jayden is not getting the proper support needed to maintain the level of excellence we expect from our students."

"Level of excellence? This is a public school, not some private, overpriced academy."

"Mrs. Turner—"

"What?" I asked, cutting her off.

"Mrs. Turner," she said, louder than before, "I am well aware of this school's limitations. And believe me, I've worked in worse establishments, but the fact that we are a public school does not mean that standards should slip."

I slumped back in my chair. Half of me wanted to fight her and defend Jayden, while the rest of me wanted to break down for letting my son's homework become such a shambles. I didn't know which option was better, so I just sat there and allowed Miss Cantin to continue her lecture.

Once she was finished pointing out the areas Jayden needed to make improvements on, I shuffled forward again and thanked her for her concern. "My husband and I will look into this, I promise. Jayden's homework and overall grades will improve from here on out."

"That's good to hear," she replied, "but until I believe that this newfound motivation isn't just talk to shut me up, I will be monitoring the situation closely. I don't want to see a promising boy like Jayden slip through the cracks of our weakening system."

My mouth dropped open, but I stopped myself from reacting to her remarks. Instead, I stood, thanked the counselor for her time, and left.

As the school became a distant object in my mirror, I rushed to work feeling more overwhelmed than I had in a long time.

CHAPTER 15

My slightly shorter day at the university passed by like any other. Everyone checked in with me throughout the day to see if everything was okay. Word had spread that I had been late due to a family issue. All I'd said over the phone was that there had been an emergency, but naturally my co-workers wanted to find out what that was, so I told them the first thing that came to mind.

"Darren's truck broke down, so he needed me to run him around briefly for a few hours while the mechanics got it working again."

"So, nothing too dramatic," Heather said. She was the office gossiper, always having to know everyone else's business. I often wondered whether it was because she had very little going on in her own life or if it was boredom egging her on.

"Not really. Just the joys of business ownership. Darren can never take a moment off when things go wrong."

"Well, good thing you were there to save his bacon," Heather said as she removed herself from the corner of my desk, where she was sitting. With a smile, she turned away to head back to her station.

I breathed out a sigh after she'd left. I wasn't the best liar in the world and hated having to tell the same lot of garbage to each person as I interacted with them throughout the day. I kept reminding myself that it was safer than getting anyone involved in the real problems we were having at home. The less other people knew, the better. I couldn't stomach the embarrassment of someone like Heather having a loaded gun's worth of gossip on me. I didn't want to be the subject of water-cooler hyperbole.

Darren checked in with me throughout the day with a few texts. We rarely communicated via text, unlike our son, who sent hundreds of messages per day to his friends, as if they hadn't seen each other in years. I'd never understand why kids today felt the need to be in constant contact with one another.

I replied to the third text from Darren with much of the same, and asked how he was doing. He gave me the same one-word response I'd given him all day: fine. Neither one of us wanted to get into how we were handling things at the moment.

I finished up for the day ten minutes after the rest of the office had cleared out. As I grabbed my things to leave, I spotted the new Emma muttering to her computer. She appeared to be distraught about something, so I assumed that fake boyfriend problem of hers was still giving her trouble. I shook my head at the thought of staying in that sort of relationship. Darren and I might have drifted apart in recent years, but he'd always, for the most part, been a supportive husband and father. He would never harm Jayden or me physically or emotionally.

I attempted to creep out on my own, despite the promise I'd made to Darren that I would leave work safely accompanied by one of my colleagues. I doubted Karlo would bother following me all the way to the city for his cousin. I figured his harassment would be kept local.

"Why does this keep happening?" I heard Emma say as I stepped past her. I froze in place and realized that I couldn't ignore the young woman.

"Everything okay?" I asked.

I was met with two eyes that were ready to spill over with tears. "No," she said.

I pushed out a huff of air and sat down at the next desk, placing my bag on the floor. "Maybe you should think about ditching this boyfriend of yours. He seems to be more trouble than he's worth."

Emma fluttered her head with a forced grin. "I don't have a boyfriend," she said.

I knew I was right, so I played along. "But I thought—"

"I lied. Sorry. I could tell you were in a rush the other day, so I didn't want to annoy you with this problem I'm having."

I thought about my flow of lies earlier today and nodded with a smile. "It's okay. I understand. Sometimes it's easier just to tell people something simple—throw them as far away from the truth as possible."

"Yeah," she said, agreeing with furrowed eyebrows. "Exactly."

A moment of silence passed between us. "So, what's actually troubling you, if you don't mind me asking?"

The other Emma closed her eyes for a moment, as if to concentrate. When she opened them again, a torrent of words flowed out of her mouth.

"I didn't want to tell anyone about this and cause a bunch of trouble so early on in my time here, but I keep getting threatening emails sent to my work account. Each day they're becoming worse and worse. Most of them don't seem to make sense. I tried blocking the emails, but the person just sends another message from a new email account, mocking my efforts to make them stop. It's gotten to the point that I can't stand the thought of turning this computer on."

I sat forward, a bit stunned by Emma's ability to talk so fast. "Wow," is all I said in response at first. "That is not ideal. We need to report this to the university and the police, right away. Do you think you know who might be sending you the emails?"

She shook her head. "There's no one I can think of. I don't have enemies or people who hate me. I'm always nice to everyone I meet. I even donate to charities."

"Whoa, slow down. This is probably just some random sicko with nothing better to do. Would you mind showing me one of the messages?"

She took a breath, apparently not wanting to look at the emails unless necessary. She wiggled her mouse and activated her screen.

"I've saved them all to a local folder in case the system crashes."

"Good thinking," I said, silently wishing I had managed to save the photos sent to me this morning. The thought broke my concentration until Emma turned her screen in my direction. I rose and stepped toward her desk to study the email she'd brought up.

I read and reread the message as the pit of my stomach twisted itself tighter than I ever thought possible.

"No," I said, as I stared at the words haunting me.

You won't get away with what you did to our family.

"Show me another one," I demanded. Emma brought up the next message with shaky hands.

You will pay for the damage that has been done.

"Next," I requested, my voice rising as my panic mounted. Emma clicked.

Your time will come. I will take back what is mine.

The emails continued. All were only one line, and threatening in a non-specific way.

You will know what it means to suffer.
You will know what true pain is.
You are going to wish you were dead.

My mouth hung open, and I couldn't read another word of it.

"It's so messed up," Emma said. "Why would someone send this to me? I haven't done anything to anyone."

I found myself drifting away from her and the computer as I located the edge of the next desk and half fell on its top. Emma span around and saw my face. Her eyes almost popped out of her head at the sight of me. "What is it?" she asked.

"Those emails," I muttered, "were all meant for me."

CHAPTER 16

After

Doctor Shaw stares at me with her usual level of concern. No other person in this place manages to do that. I almost believe she cares about my well-being.

"How did you know the emails were meant for you?"

"It was obvious," I say. "The idiot who emailed them had accidentally sent the threats to the wrong Emma at the university. We don't use family names in the directory, so he had sent the messages to an Emma in a different department."

Doctor Shaw nods, urging me to continue.

"The more I read those messages, the clearer my theory became that they were supposed to go to my inbox and not to that sweet young girl's."

"You felt sorry for her?"

"Yes, why wouldn't I?"

Shaw clears her throat. "Typically, when faced with immediate danger, we tend to only think of ourselves or our close family. You took a moment out of your own desperate time to think about the impact thrown upon this young girl because of threats intended for you."

"Maybe it was just maternal instincts or something," I say, waving her off. The thought reminded me of Jayden and the things I'd do to keep him safe. If only he and Darren were here with me now to get me through these never-ending conversations.

"Maybe." She scrawls away in her notebook.

"The threats were directed at my family and were a warning. I should have taken those messages to the police straight away or reported them to the university."

"Why didn't you?"

That question rattles around in my head on repeat every day. Why did I wait? Part of me thinks fear was a significant component, but I also have my doubts about what use it would have been anyway. The police didn't believe me when I told them about the photos. I saw it in their eyes the first time they came to our house. Calling 911 seemed like the smart thing to do at the time to prevent any harm from coming our way. The thought of someone wanting to harm my family angered and scared me beyond control.

"Emma?" Doctor Shaw asks, reiterating her question.

"I thought I knew better, I guess. Stupid, right? Not that it really made a difference."

"It wasn't stupidity holding you back, Emma. It was fear. You were concerned, not only for you and your family's safety, but for what people might think of you calling the police every five minutes."

I nod my understanding as Shaw continues. My mind drifts away to the sound of her voice. Why am I bothering with any of this? Something happened that cannot be undone. No amount of talking will change that.

I give the doctor what she wants by pretending to agree with every word out of her mouth. She doesn't appear to be convinced in any way. She can see right through me.

"We still have some time left today, so I wanted to ask you about your brother."

"James?"

"Yes, James. He visited you earlier this morning. Is that correct?" Shaw studies me carefully, not allowing her eyes to leave my line of sight.

"Yes, I saw him today for the first time in eight years."

"And how was that for you? It can't have been easy."

"No, it wasn't. Honestly, I'm surprised you people let him in here, given my current state."

"Doctor Gaertner and I both agreed it would be good for you. We received word from James after the funeral that he wanted to speak with you and make things right again."

I think for a moment. "I thought you contacted him?"

Doctor Shaw flips through her notes for a moment. "Maybe we did. I can check with Doctor Gaertner if you'd like?"

"It's not important," I say, shrugging.

She studies me for a moment. I hate the way she does this.

"So, did you manage to patch things up at all with James?"

"You might say that. We're not exactly close again just yet, but some issues were brought to light. With enough time and effort, we could be brother and sister again, if that's what he wants."

"Do you want that?"

I shrug. "In my heart I do, but I'm not sure if I'm capable of fully trusting anyone."

Shaw nods as she jots something down in her notes. "What is holding you back at the moment from trusting him again?"

There are too many things to consider. Trust can't be forced after eight years. Plus, I don't want to think about James. Instead, my mind drifts to Darren and Jayden. Will they ever trust me again? They are more important to me right now than mending a broken relationship with my brother.

"Emma?" Shaw asks. She won't let me escape the question. "What's stopping you?"

I scoff. "He took off after my mother died. He never showed up when my dad died either. I guess I haven't forgotten that just yet."

"It's not about forgetting, Emma; it's about forgiving." She stops speaking and glances up at the clock as it ticks over to the hour. "That's all we have time for today. We'll pick this up again tomorrow."

I stand and head for the door. Doctor Shaw follows. She has to escort me back, as per usual. Before the door opens, she places one hand lightly on my shoulder.

"Emma?"

"Yes?" I answer, doing my best not to cringe away.

"If you are uncomfortable with your brother visiting, just say the word, and we'll tell him that now is not the right time."

I think about it for a moment. Seeing James was hard. It added more stress to my crumbling mind, but at the same time, it felt good to reconnect with my brother, even if it was only on a small, manageable level.

"It's okay," I say. "If he wants to see me again, I don't mind."

She smiles at me. "That's great to hear. I believe James will be a great help to your recovery. Oh, and before you go, I wanted to tell you that we are slowly making progress toward that night you are struggling to remember. When the time comes, you will be ready to face what happened."

I can sense my thoughts darting around in my head as my breathing quickens. I remind myself to calm down and take a breath. I try my hardest to look into Shaw's eyes and nod, not knowing how else to react.

Whether I want to face my demons or not, they are coming for me. It's only a matter of time.

CHAPTER 17

After my session, I decide to go outside for the first time. The ward I am forced to stay in has a small, snowy garden attached to it, to allow us some time out in the winter sun and fresh air. Of course, most patients in the hospital are too paranoid to go outside, fearing invisible threats.

As I open and step through the double doorway that leads out to the courtyard, a howling wind pierces me in an instant, reminding me how cold the tail end of this winter has been. The hospital, despite its flaws, possesses reliable central heating.

The chill is nothing compared to the sting of daylight. The clear sky above allows the sun to punch straight down into my retinas, and I must take a few moments to adjust.

"First time's a bitch, isn't it?" asks someone off to the side of the courtyard. I glance around for the source of the words and see a blurry patient wearing the same drab colors as me. I blink a few times and see an older woman, maybe in her late forties, leaning against a tall brick wall that no person could scale. She's smoking in the corner like a teenager skulking behind the bleachers, even though smoking is allowed here.

"I didn't think it would hurt this much," I say as I stumble toward her. My eyes start to refocus as I come within an acceptable social distance of the woman. She swaps the cigarette into her left hand so she can extend her right out to greet me.

"The name's Andrea," she says, a cloud of smoke billowing out of her mouth.

I accept her hand and give it a weak shake in return, not wanting her smoke-damaged fingers to stain me with their foul odor. When I pull back, I can sense the transference of stench onto my skin. I'll need to scrub my hands clean the first second I can.

"Are you going to tell me your name? Or are you one of those patients?"

"I'm sorry," I say, shaking my head. "It's Emma."

"Well then, pleased to meet you, Emma. What they got you in here for, if you don't mind me asking? You don't seem the type to be locked up in the loony bin."

"Why's that?" I ask without thought. I want to know how screwed up a person needs to look to belong inside this place, and how I can avoid reaching that point.

"Can't explain it. You just sound like you're visiting or something. It's like you're waiting for the day to be over so you can go home."

"Well, thanks, I guess. But I'd rather not talk about why I'm in here."

Andrea shoves the cigarette into her mouth and throws up both hands in defense of her question. "All good. No one ever answers that question—well, not truthfully, that is. I'm always told what they think is the reason for their incarceration. It's usually a bunch of gibberish, but it gives me the truth one way or the other."

Andrea takes a long drag on the dwindling stick between her fingers and snuffs out the butt on a fixed metal bin tucked away to the side of the courtyard. So much for the fresh air I had in mind.

"So, why are you in here?" I ask with crossed arms. The question surprises Andrea, as her eyes almost pop out of her head. I wonder why she didn't expect me to ask this in return as she fumbles for an answer.

"Well, it's kind of hard to pinpoint any single reason. I mean, yes, I did start that fire, but it wasn't my fault, you know?"

I hold up my palms with a tilted head and half-closed eyes. "It's fine, Andrea. You don't have to tell me. I can barely focus on my own problems, let alone hear someone else's."

My words bring a smile to her face. "That's an interesting thought," she says. "See, most people in here want to forget why they've found themselves locked inside a nuthouse. Hearing the problems of others tends to help me forget my bullshit."

I look away for a moment, my mind drifting to things that sit on the edge of my memory. "Every second I spend talking to a patient, an orderly, or a doctor only reinforces in my head that I'm not out in the real world." I turn back to Andrea and give her a long moment to stare at my cold dead eyes. It's more than I can usually stand to maintain eye contact. "On top of that, I'm awake most nights with crippling nightmares. I can't remember the last time I really slept."

Andrea smiles at my statement. Her voice lowers down to half a whisper. "Nightmares, hey? If you need some help taking the pain out of your sleep, I can hook you up with the right kind of medicine to do the job."

My brow screws tight. "What are you talking about?" I ask, wondering what crazy answer I'll get in return.

Andrea checks the area sharply for anyone who might be listening. We are the only two patients outside, and no one is keeping an eye on us. She focuses back on me and whispers as she pulls out a blister pack of pills. "Take some of these. They'll help to relax you."

I see two rows of tablets in her hand and ask, "What are they?"

"Diazepam. Ten milligrams. Take enough of them and you'll forget your troubles. You'll feel like everything is as it should be."

I reach out to grab some without thinking, but pause just out of reach. I've taken diazepam in the past, but from a packet purchased with a prescription. These possibly expired pills are from the pockets of a person with a mental-health condition. Despite the multiple red flags staring me in the face, recent times have lowered my standards, and I find myself actually considering taking them.

"Go on. These are yours."

"Are you sure?" I ask, staring up at her.

"Trust me," she says. "I got your back. None of these assholes in here give enough of a shit to want us to feel better. Let old Andrea do their jobs for them."

I gently grab the tablets and shove them into my waistband. "How did you find these?" I ask.

Andrea chuckles. "Best not to know, my dear. Let's just say that some of the orderlies can easily be bought off, if you catch my drift."

I nod, understanding, as I think about Tom and his mustache. The thought sends a shudder down my spine that I can't shake off.

"Don't take all of them at once. Otherwise the docs will realize they have a problem on their hands." Andrea pulls out another smoke from her packet and lights up. "Anyway, if I were you, I'd save those pills for overnight only. That's the worst time."

"Yeah," I say with a forced laugh. Each night is more challenging than the last inside this hospital. The walls start to close in as the hours wear on. Every morning, I'm clawing to leave the tiny locked space.

"Anyway, best you move along, Emma. Don't want the doctors getting too suspicious." She gives me a wink as she takes another drag on her cigarette.

"Thank you," I say.

"Don't mention it. I'll see you around." Andrea turns away from me, signaling that the conversation is over. I take the hint and leave. The entire time I walk, I keep one hand on the tablets in my waistband.

I head back to my room. Knowing it has already been cleaned for the day, I shove the tablets into a gap between the lumpy mattress and the metal bed frame.

At that moment, I'm almost too excited to go to sleep, but I hope the tablets will do what Andrea promised.

CHAPTER 18

After dinner, I sit on my bed waiting for lights out at nine. Time seems to be dragging on longer than usual, until finally the automated lighting system turns off. Dim hallway lights allow us to see enough to be able to reach the bathrooms attached to our rooms, which is where I head the second it's dark. I bring the pills along with me and set them on the countertop.

There are twelve tablets in the packet, and I don't know how many I should take. The pills look larger than the ones I'd had at home, before arriving at the hospital. As a guide, I try to think back to how many I would take at a time. I guess I'm just a bit nervous.

After some thought, I settle on swallowing four hits of diazepam, figuring that I need the extra dosage to handle my current frame of mind. At the same time, I don't want it to be painfully obvious I've taken something when the orderly comes in the morning. With a mouthful of water each time, I gulp down four pills, one by one. My throat feels thick and dry as the tablets slide down, and I realize how little water I have drunk during the day.

I head back to bed and settle in for what I hope is going to be a calm night. My expectations are met with a relaxed buzz that no amount of therapy could produce. I can sense myself floating through the bedroom, a smile coating my face. I could kiss Andrea if she were in the room with me. She has given me a gateway to a kind of freedom I could never aspire to achieve.

By the time morning comes around, I have fallen into the deepest sleep of my life. Tom has to shake me vigorously to rouse me from my slumber.

"Jesus, Turner. I don't have time for your lazy ass. Get a move on."

I pull myself out of my blissful rest and realize what he is carrying on about. I have a session first thing this morning. His brutish arms haul me out of bed and to my feet.

"I need to pee," I say in a hurry as I lean toward the bathroom. Tom lets me go while muttering away.

I rush into the lavatory and take a minute to splash some water on my face. When I stare into the greasy metal of the fixed mirror, I realize that both of my pupils are dilated and are too enlarged to ignore.

"Shit," I mutter, realizing too late that I overdid it. Doctor Shaw will only need half a moment to figure out I've taken something that hasn't been prescribed to me.

"Hurry up!" Tom yells.

My eyes dart left and right, searching for an answer as a sweat prickles at my forehead. I have no idea what to do.

Tom doesn't give me a second longer as he heads into the bathroom. "What the fuck is taking you so—" He stops cold when he sees my eyes. "Well, look what we have here. I see you've been hitting the pharmacy a little too hard."

I shy away, but he grabs my shoulders with his thick hands and turns me back. "No, let me see them." He uses one hand to tilt my head back. "Yep, just as I thought, missy. Someone has been taking a few tranquilizers."

"No, I haven't. It must be the new pills Doctor Shaw has me on."

"Bullshit. You're still on the same crap you've been on since day one. You, darlin', have been dipping your toe into something that's going to land you in hot water."

My stomach drops. I have no idea what this will do for my recovery. The doctors might place me in an even worse facility. I can't let that happen.

"Please, Tom. You can't say anything."

"Are you trying to tell me how to do my job?" he asks.

"No, I would never—"

He silences me with a single finger held to his mouth. "Keep your voice down, missy. I'll hold onto your little secret. Hell, I'll even delay your session to give you enough time to sober up. But, know this: you owe me. Big time."

I nod, knowing I am now at the mercy of this asshole. "Thank you," I muster up.

Tom gives me a wink that I can almost sense on my skin. I wonder at that moment if I would be better off letting Doctor Shaw find out about the diazepam, but it's too late now.

"Follow me," he says.

We leave my room and head to the medical supply closet a few corridors away. He ushers me through a door to an area I'm not allowed to go into and selects a small bottle of liquid from the shelf. He pushes my head back as he distributes some eye drops into each of my pupils. The substance stings, but I do my best not to let it show. Tears fall down my cheeks as a result.

Tom puts the bottle back and then pulls out a small penlight. "Keep 'em open," he says as he grabs my forehead again and brings the flashlight up close to my left eye. He turns it on and holds my head tighter. "Don't blink. Just need a few seconds in each eye."

I'm blinded by the time he finishes tricking my pupils into shrinking back down to a regular size.

"That should cut down the time your eyes need to go back to normal by a good few hours. Now get the hell out of here while I find Doctor Shaw and tell her you're not feeling well enough for a morning session."

"Thank you," I say. As I go to leave, I feel Tom grab me from behind. He swings me around and cups my ass with one hand.

"Don't mention it, missy," he says. I cower away. I know what he wants. How am I supposed to stop him if I need his help? I think about Darren and how angry he would get if he saw this. Tom would be flat on his back after the punch my husband would give him. Again, I think about Darren and Jayden and wonder why they haven't come to visit me yet.

Tom releases his grip on my butt and sets me free. "Go along now. I'll find you for your afternoon session. Don't make eye contact with the other orderlies."

I nod and leave the room, shaking off the disgust that has overtaken my body.

＊

When the afternoon comes, Tom silently ushers me along with a tilt of his head. I follow him through to Doctor Shaw's office, knowing my eyes will no longer betray me.

"Okay, Emma," the doctor says. "Let's pick up where we left off."

I force a smile as the memories hit me again. The tablets helped me to sleep, but there's little they can do for me while I'm awake and aware that I am in this place.

I settle in for my next session with the doctor.

CHAPTER 19

Before

I didn't want to tell Darren about the emails, but I knew I would. He'd had enough crap dropped on him for one day, and most of it had come from me. How did I always manage to be the one to make his day worse? Even when it was Jayden who was acting up, I found a way to add to Darren's stress levels.

I was about to head home after walking to my car with the other Emma by my side. She asked me over and over if I was okay, apologizing for the emails as if she were somehow to blame for everything.

"You've got nothing to be sorry for, Emma," I said. "You didn't write those messages. If anything, I owe you an apology. It's obvious this psycho mixed up our email addresses."

"It's so messed up," she said. "Why do you think this person was trying to send you these kinds of messages?"

I didn't feel like getting into the truth with her. "It's complicated. Let's just say you're better off not knowing the whole story."

"Okay." She unexpectedly hugged me goodbye and told me to get home safe. "Are you going to take the emails to the police?" she asked. We had made copies of every message and downloaded them to a USB stick I now had in my bag.

"Soon. But I want to discuss things with my husband first." I was thinking about this Karlo guy who wanted to see my family in ruins. It just seemed all too easy for any idiot these days to threaten someone from behind a computer screen. The police were near powerless when it came to this kind of activity. Technology would always continue to outpace the law.

"I hope they find the guy soon. Try to take it easy," Emma said to me as she climbed into her car, parked only a few spaces away.

"I'll try. And thanks for walking me out here."

"Thank you, too," she said. "I'm pretty freaked out about all of this. I think I'm going to need a full bottle of wine to deal with today."

"Sounds like an excellent idea," I said. The thought of drinking myself stupid seemed like the best cure for the nagging ideas that were rattling around in my head. I'd give anything to be able to leave my brain for a minute, but I couldn't. That voice in the back of my mind wouldn't let me relax.

"Bye," Emma said as she rolled out of the lot.

I opened my car with my key fob and climbed inside. I took a deep breath and locked the doors before starting the engine. A local radio station came on louder than expected, making me jump back. It was just some annoying advert designed to grab my attention. I slammed the off button and clutched at my face with my free hand.

I thought I was so smart coming to work, that I could beat these people by not letting them intimidate my family. I was wrong. It didn't seem real before. The photos, the police, the look in Darren's eyes when I said I was still going to work. But now it was.

"Get it together," I said to myself. "Just make it home in one piece." My own words sounded like a load of crap as I fought the urge to scream. How was I going to make it to the house in one piece?

The drive home seemed to take longer in my mind than it should have. Typically, the road was a blur of the same old landscape I'd seen a thousand times before. But I was desperate to be somewhere, to be with my husband, to tell him the psycho stalking his family had now taken things to the next level by harassing his wife at work, and it was like seeing the world for the first time. I took in every lamppost, every embankment, and every red taillight.

Shadows came to life as the light faded. I swore I could see figures lurking in dark places, but the shapes swirled into everyday objects the closer I got to them. All I could wonder was why there wasn't enough street lighting around.

When I rolled into the driveway, I spotted Darren's truck already there. The external lights were on, along with almost every other bulb in the lower level of our house. I breathed a sigh of relief that he was home, while also dreading the conversation I needed to have with him.

Darren emerged from the front door, having heard my car. He stretched his arms out and shrugged. I parked the car, shut off the engine, and opened my door. Before I climbed out, he stormed up to me.

"You didn't call. You said you'd call me when you left. God, Emma. I was starting to think the worst."

I shook my head. "I forgot, sorry. Had a lot on my mind."

He wrapped his arms around me and pulled me in tight. "It's okay," he said. I could feel the stubble of his chin scratching against my forehead. The sensation felt good on my stressed-out brain.

I climbed out of the car with my bag and locked up, wondering why Darren was hugging me. He was never this affectionate. The events of the morning must have rattled him.

"Come inside. We'll get changed and go pick up Jayden together. Whose house is he staying at?"

Darren's words made my eyes bulge in my head. I'd forgotten to ask my son where we could find him after school. Jayden had apparently done the same thing, as I realized I hadn't received a text from him after school finished. I'd been so swept up in my thoughts that I'd failed to keep track of my own son. What kind of parent was I?

"Jesus," Darren said, without me needing to utter another word.

"I forgot to organize it."

"Emma, we can't be this careless," he said as he pulled out his cell. "There's some asshole out there taking photos of us."

"I'm sorry. I screwed up, okay? I'm sure he's playing video games with one of his friends right now."

Darren held up a finger to silence me as he shoved his cell to his ear and turned away. He paced around, trying to get through to Jayden. After the tenth ring, it went to voice mail.

"Shit," Darren said as he listened to a recorded message of Jayden muttering out a few words. He waited for the prompt and spoke. "Jayden, it's your dad. Where are you, buddy? Your mom and I are coming to pick you up. We'll head around to Douglas's house first and try there. Call your mother or me back as soon as you get this."

I released my held breath as I attempted to shove the horrible thoughts crowding my brain down to the depths where they belonged. I focused on Darren and worked up the courage to speak. "He's probably too busy to notice we called. I'll send him a text. You know what kids are like these days." I smiled nervously at my husband, like I was a manager trying to deal with an angry customer. It worked about as well as expected.

"He knows we need to come pick him up. Why hasn't he left his cell out with the ringer on loud?"

"He's a teenager, Darren. They don't think straight all the time."

"Maybe, but he was here this morning when you called the cops. He should be as alert as we are." Darren shook his head while he rechecked his phone and mumbled something under his breath. He looked across at me as if something had suddenly occurred to him. "Did anything else weird happen today?"

I instantly felt for the USB stick in my bag, feeling like it was about to pop out and leap into Darren's hand. I didn't know whether to tell him about the emails or not. My mouth hung half open, making me look suspicious as hell. "What do you mean?" is all I could think to ask.

"You know, like something threatening or out of the ordinary. Nothing to make you think Jayden might be in any danger?"

"Well…" The single word betrayed me in a heartbeat.

"What? Did something happen?"

I lowered my eyes, trying to remain calm for my husband. I fiddled with a zipper on my clothing. He was about to freak the hell out. "I was going to tell you about this later."

"Tell me about what?" Darren stomped toward me.

I backed up. "I've been getting some threatening emails sent to me at work. Well, more specifically, a new girl also named Emma has been, but it's pretty obvious the messages were meant for me."

His hand flew up to his forehead. "What the hell? Are you sure they were for us?"

"Positive."

"Jesus. How long were you planning on keeping this from me?"

"I was going to tell you tonight. I only just discovered them today, by chance. As I said, they'd been sent to a different Emma at work."

Darren paced around, rechecking his phone. "How far back do they go, the emails?"

I thought about the oldest message I saved. "About three days."

Darren muttered. "Assholes don't mess around." He headed to his truck. "Come on," he said. "We're finding Jayden. Then we're going to the cops."

I followed without question.

"Text Jayden on the way." Darren reached the truck and yanked the door open. "If anyone has hurt our boy—" He slammed the door behind him.

As I ran around the front of the vehicle with my handbag, I fumbled for my cell. I looked up to see Darren messing around with the same bag from the gun store I had seen sitting in the passenger seat earlier. I wanted to say something, but at this point, I was too rattled to speak. I could barely work the phone in my hand as I messed around trying to force the door open.

Darren hopped out and stuffed the bag into the trunk of his truck before moving back to the driver's seat to fire up the engine.

As we started moving, he glanced sideways at me. He looked as though he could kill the next person who crossed our family. I sent a text to Jayden with shaky thumbs.

CHAPTER 20

By the time we reached Douglas's house, Jayden had texted me back. "He's not here," I said to Darren from the passenger seat. He turned to me with raised brows.

"Where, then?"

I cleared my throat. "The mall."

"What?" Darren spat out. "After all that crap today, he decided it would be a good idea to hang out at the goddamn mall?"

I grabbed Darren by the forearm. "It is Friday. He probably wanted to be with his friends."

"I don't give a shit," Darren said. "He's grounded, and he knows it. Going to a friend's house was only happening because of this morning." He continued to mutter away, shaking his head.

I tried to be as neutral about this as I could. "Go easy on him," I said. "He's just as freaked out as we are with all this. Maybe it's his way of dealing with everything."

Darren ran his fingers through his messy hair, over and over. "Fine. He gets this one for free. But from here on out, he does what I say without exception."

"Sounds fair to me, honey," I said, trying to please him. Darren had come to despise it when either Jayden or I went against his wishes. It wasn't like Darren was an overbearing control freak on purpose; it was just the byproduct of being the boss of ten guys.

As we headed to the mall in the next town, I thought about everything that'd happened over the last few days. I felt the weight of it all pressing down on me, and with every new bit of crap that hit us, the feeling only got worse. I tried not to let everything get to me, but I didn't know how much more of it I could take.

*

When we arrived at the mall, we spotted Jayden where he said he'd be. Darren pulled right up to him, despite the three other teenagers who were there. I could almost feel the heat of the flush in Jayden's cheeks as he gave us a look through gritted teeth. The embarrassment he was suffering by allowing his friends to comprehend our existence was palpable.

"Get in the truck," Darren barked.

Jayden opened the rear passenger door of the twin cab and tossed his backpack across to the spare seat. I glanced at Darren and recognized he was about to unload. I gripped his wrist to remind him what we had agreed. Darren closed his mouth and focused on driving out of the mall parking lot.

When we hit the main road again, Darren couldn't help himself. "What the hell were you thinking, coming all the way out here?"

"Nothing, okay? I wanted to see my friends."

"You're grounded, remember? That means unless we say otherwise, you're stuck at home or a friend's house. Nothing else."

"I didn't think it would be a big deal."

"Not a big deal?" Darren's voice continued to rise as he unleashed his anger. "We had the police at our house this morning because someone is harassing our family. That sounds like a big deal to me."

"Whatever," muttered Jayden. "You guys are overreacting. I doubt they're serious threats. They want us to be scared, so we cave and settle with Victor out of court."

My eyes popped wide open. I was impressed by my son's ability to dismiss the warnings so logically. What he had just said sounded entirely plausible and made me feel a little more relaxed about the whole thing—but then I remembered the emails.

"That's your theory, son," Darren said, his voice a little calmer. "But you could be wrong. They could be serious about these threats. One of us could be attacked at any moment. There's no point in testing out that possibility by hanging out at the mall. Got it?"

"Yes," Jayden mumbled.

I could see him staring out the window via the side mirror. The scowl on his face could turn permanent if we said one more thing to upset him.

The rest of the trip passed by in silence. We kept our eyes away from each other. I checked on Jayden every so often and saw him gazing into the distance, his chin resting on his palm. Darren was leaning on the driver's door with his hand half covering his face. We were all tired and annoyed.

When we arrived back home to our well-lit house, I spotted something strange out front. Bessie was sitting by the main door as if waiting for us to come home. She saw Darren's truck and jumped up, excitedly wagging her tail.

"Why is Bessie sitting at the front of the house?" Jayden asked before any of us could say a word.

"No one leaves this truck," Darren said with a stern face.

"Okay," I replied. Jayden nodded. We both sat still while Darren slowly exited the vehicle and moved over to Bessie. The Labrador ran up to meet him and almost jumped into his arms with excitement. With ease, Darren commanded her to sit and told her to stay as he approached the front door.

"What's going on, Mom?" Jayden asked.

I heard his voice crack, though I could tell he was trying to sound brave. "Nothing," I said with my own failed version of a confident voice. "Your father is making sure the house is safe." I turned back to Jayden and smiled at him. "He'll be back in a minute." My son saw straight through me. My eyes, no doubt, gave me away.

I refocused on Darren as he tried the front door. It was locked, the way he left it. Before I could catch his attention, Darren disappeared down the side path that wrapped around the house, completely vanishing from sight.

"Jesus," I said, as panic set in. I could hear myself breathing louder than normal as every second of Darren's absence compounded into more anxiety. "What the hell are you doing, Darren?"

Unable to take much more, I opened the car door and told Jayden to stay put.

"But Dad said to—"

"I know what he said. I'm just going to do a quick check to make sure he's okay. I'll be back in a second. Keep the doors locked."

Jayden nodded quickly. I could see how much he didn't want either of us to leave his sight, but I knew he'd be safer inside the truck. It's where I wished I could remain, but I had to be courageous for my son.

After a few small steps, I suddenly felt exposed and vulnerable. I tried to call out to Darren, but my voice wasn't loud enough to sound like more than a whisper. I could sense the fear around me, closing my windpipe. Someone was about to attack.

I edged up to the corner of our house and half closed my eyes, not wanting to run into some stalker who had been waiting to lure us into his trap.

As I rounded the bend, a figure emerged and crashed right into me. I fell back as two strong arms grasped my forearms.

"I told you to stay in the truck," Darren said as his face reached the light of the front driveway.

"You vanished down the side. I wanted to make sure you were okay."

Darren breathed out a frustrated sigh as he looked away, releasing me from his grip. "Sorry," he said.

"Did you find anything?"

He shook his head. "Bessie got the gate open. The police mustn't have closed it properly. Nothing to worry about."

I wanted to slap myself in the face for not checking the gate after they left. Everything had happened so fast; I hadn't had time to think clearly.

"I should have made sure it was okay. I'm sorry," I said, deflated.

"It's fine. Let's just head inside, have some dinner, and go to bed. It's been a long damn week."

I found myself falling into Darren's arms at the suggestion. "That sounds like the best idea I've heard all day."

Darren called Bessie over and took her back through the gate. He shut the metal door with a slam and locked it. We walked to the truck and collected Jayden with smiles on our faces, attempting to laugh off the situation. Once we all made it inside, I realized I'd left my phone in Darren's truck. I had just stepped back out to retrieve my cell when I heard the sound of a car starting up in the distance. The vehicle rolled away a moment later. It was the same sedan that had been out the front of our house the night before.

Someone had been watching us the entire time.

CHAPTER 21

That night, I couldn't fall asleep. The photos, the emails, and the sight of Bessie sitting at the front of our house kept me wide awake. No amount of reading or trying to focus on my breathing was able to pull my mind away from it all. After half the night disappeared with me staring into the darkness till my eyes began to ache, I gave up and headed for the medicine cabinet in our bathroom.

I ignored the various surfaces in desperate need of a clean and opened the mirrored cabinet. I fished around and found a bottle of diazepam that I kept in case of nights like this. I took one small 5 mg tablet with a mouthful of water and swallowed it down. In about fifteen minutes, I'd feel a calm wash over me, as though I didn't have a care in the world. Before long, sleep would claim me.

I headed back to bed and felt the effects of the magic tablet start to kick in. It took everything I had to not take more pills. I understood the risks of getting hooked on this stuff, but during such a time, a fistful wasn't enough of a dosage.

＊

Morning came. I didn't remember drifting off, and I was shocked to see the time on my bedside clock: 10 a.m.

"What the hell?" I couldn't remember the last time I'd slept past seven in the morning, let alone ten. I span around and realized Darren was nowhere to be found. I almost panicked at the sight of his empty side of the bed, but tried my best to find a reasonable explanation instead of freaking out.

I threw on a dressing gown and hurried downstairs. I spotted Jayden in the living room, playing video games. I was only slightly surprised to see Darren reading the paper at the kitchen counter while his grounded son enjoyed himself in the background.

"Morning, sleepyhead," Darren said.

I breathed a sigh of relief while Jayden half turned from his game and said hello to me.

I paced straight over to Darren with a twisted brow. "I thought he was grounded. That usually means no video games as well."

"I know," Darren said as he placed the newspaper down. "I thought he could use a break after yesterday."

I smiled at my husband and ran my hand over his bicep. "You're such a softy," I joked. "Can I make you some breakfast?"

"Already taken care of, honey," he said as he gestured toward the bacon and eggs sitting on the kitchen counter. "I was about to come wake you up with it."

I leaned down and kissed him on the forehead. "Thank you, baby." I couldn't remember the last time I'd called him that. I was briefly reminded of the carefree weekends we used to while away together at the end of a long week, spending half the day in bed watching TV and making love. I stayed back in that time for a few seconds until the smell of the food drew me to the present. I wolfed it down in about five minutes.

"Someone was hungry."

"I didn't end up eating anything last night. I couldn't wrap my head around the thought of food with everything that's been going on."

Darren nodded away. "I understand. Concentrating at the moment is hard. Speaking of everything that's been going on, can you show me the emails? I think we need to take them to the police as soon as possible."

I nodded back. "I'll grab the USB." I headed over to my handbag and pulled out the stick. I loaded up the emails on the laptop we kept in the kitchen for paying bills and online shopping. I swiveled it toward Darren and showed him the messages.

He read through each one slowly, as if he would be able to recognize who wrote them by concentration alone.

"Mean anything to you?" I asked him. I felt the pit of my stomach twisting and writhing.

"Not really. Just similar junk to what I've had sent to my phone. Still, we should take everything in this morning and have the police add it to the file. It'll show the cops how serious we are. Maybe they can run some security checks on these accounts and trace down where they came from."

"I doubt they'll find much. There's a new email account associated with every message. It takes three seconds to make one these days."

Darren's mouth turned down into a frustrated grimace. "Why do we need this fancy technology? It just makes things easier for these assholes."

"I know," I said. I thought about the kinds of problems Jayden's generation would have because of the constant flow of new technology.

We sat in silence for a minute, each lost in our thoughts. Darren spoke first. "Take a shower and get dressed. We'll head out straight after and go to the police station. We'll drop Jayden off at Douglas's and meet him at the game later today. I'm sure his parents won't mind."

"Shouldn't Jayden come with us?" I asked, concern lining my eyes.

Darren shook his head. "He'll be safer at a friend's house. Trust me."

I agreed and thanked Darren again for the food. He had been so amazing. I never got breakfast made for me unless it was a special occasion. I silently wished it didn't take this kind of situation for me to receive some attention in the house.

I enjoyed a long shower and dressed for the day in some casual wear. My hair took the usual time to dry and style. Darren bugged me a few times during the process, as per usual, asking when I'd be ready. I gave him my typical line of "Soon."

Once I was satisfied with my appearance, I headed downstairs and saw Jayden and Darren eager to go. Jayden had a full gym bag and was wearing his basketball gear, ready for a game his team had lined up at the middle school later in the day. I realized he had also packed some overnight clothing. I gave Darren a quick look.

"I thought he could stay the night at a friend's house—be away from here, you know?"

"Okay," I said as I crossed my arms. "I guess this grounding you laid down is on hold, then."

"For now," Darren said with a sideways glance at Jayden. "When this stuff with Victor calms down, we'll think of a suitable punishment to give him."

"I'm right here, by the way."

"Don't push your luck, son," Darren said with a chuckle. "Think of this as an opportunity to do the right thing and not give us anything else to worry about."

Jayden agreed. There was nothing else he could say without risking his freedom, so he kept his mouth shut.

"Anyway," Darren said, turning to me, "it's time you and I got out of here too and had a night off from this crap. I thought we could go to the movies. I can't remember the last time we did that."

I was almost left speechless. "Yes, please," I said, knowing how desperate I sounded. With the business, Jayden going to middle school, and me working full-time, Darren and I rarely had time off alone together. We felt more like roommates than husband and wife.

"I can't wait," I whispered to Darren as we walked out the door.

"I heard that," Jayden said without looking back.

For a few moments, I wasn't thinking about the problem our family was facing with Victor or his family. It was the best feeling, short of a handful of diazepam.

CHAPTER 22

After

The day before seems like a blur when I wake from only a few hours of disturbed sleep. I decided to take two pills overnight, hoping to avoid waking up with dilated pupils. The halved amount didn't work the way it should, so I ended up wasting the tablets. I guess under normal circumstances the dosage would more than do the trick. The discovery makes me realize I'll only sleep properly overnight with the help of Tom. I still have no confirmation of what he'll want in return for his discretion, but I can guess. I shudder to think of the possibilities.

I feel like a dead weight in the shower. The hot water only lasts about three minutes on average, and the pressure is weak. I scrub myself as clean as the hospital will allow.

After, I put on fresh clothing and wait for my door to unlock at the hands of Tom. As much as I cringe whenever I see him, his familiar face calms me when it appears in the small viewing window. There's something positive to be said about the hospital's strict routines.

Tom arrives on schedule and strolls in with a straight back and a stiff upper lip, his mustache twitching.

"On your feet, Turner," he says as he scans my clean room. I keep the empty area dust-free using a small hand towel and water. Not for the orderlies or the doctors, but for myself.

"Shaw tells me you've got a visitor."

"Probably my brother," I reply.

"Brother, huh? So that's who came to see you yesterday. I was starting to get jealous." Tom laughs out loud at his terrible joke. "Has he come to visit his sister in the nuthouse? Poor bastard. If any of my family members ended up in this shithole, they'd be lucky if I came to see them once a year."

I give Tom a fake smile that quickly fades. He knows how to grind the patients just enough, winding them up without leaving himself responsible for any slippage in their behavior. How can a man like this be allowed to work with people in such a sensitive environment? Do they not run personality checks when they hire these meatheads? I figure the problem might be the job itself. Who would want to work in such a profession?

Before I realize what's going on, Tom is escorting me along the ward as if I'm a lost child at the mall. It's like being dragged around by an underpaid security guard who had his doughnut break interrupted by some rowdy teenagers.

Tom runs his mouth to everyone we pass, patient or staff. He struts through the ward like he's the mayor of Crazy Town, USA. I smile at the thought.

"Something funny?"

I shake my head, losing the brief second of enjoyment. No patient is ever allowed to find the smallest piece of happiness when Tom is around.

He reminds me of a guy I knew in high school. He had a crush on me that quickly deteriorated into a burning hatred the moment I turned him down. Jeremy Peters was his name. I still remember it to this day.

I was in my senior year of high school, eagerly anticipating the end of the year, when Jeremy asked me out. We'd hung out a few times as friends. I got the impression after a short time that he wanted to be more than just that. He wasn't my type, though. Plus, I had the biggest crush on his friend, whose name I've since forgotten.

We'd been hanging out after school outside the mall, just the two of us, after our other friends had taken off home. I was arguing with my mom and didn't want to face another night of it, so I stayed out as late as I could with Jeremy. He seemed all too pleased with the idea.

"Emma, I was wondering," he said to me through a cracking voice, rubbing his sweaty palms together.

"Yeah?" My response threw him off his rehearsed lines, and he began to awkwardly stutter.

"Look, Jeremy," I said, "I know what you're going to say next, and I just want to say that I like you as a friend."

"But not as more than a friend?" he asked, both eyes sunken.

I nodded. "You're a wonderful friend. I just like someone else. Do you understand?"

He didn't say a word and instead closed his eyes. He raised his palm for me to stop talking. I swore he was crying, but he kept every tear hidden from me.

"You stupid bitch," he said.

My eyes popped out of my head. I was so surprised by his reaction.

"You think you're so much better than me, don't you?"

"Not at all. I don't know why you would think that. And don't call me a—"

"I'll call you what I want. You don't get to tell me what to do."

I frowned at him and turned to leave. He grabbed my wrist and pulled me back.

"Where the hell do you think you're going, huh? I didn't say you could go."

"Jeremy, please," I said in a whisper. "You're hurting me. Stop."

He shook his head with a grimace. "No, you don't get to ruin things between us and play the victim."

I felt his grip tighten on my wrist. How had I not seen this anger underneath the surface, so eager to come out?

"I'm sorry," I said. "I didn't mean to offend you."

"Offend me? Emma, I'm trying to bare my soul here, and all you're doing is spitting in my face. You don't get to apologize for that. No one treats me like—"

Jeremy never finished his sentence. His words were silenced by James's right hook as it struck his jaw and sent him flying back to the ground. Jeremy's grip on my wrist gave up, leaving painful red marks where each of his fingers had pinched me.

Jeremy rolled around on the ground, confused and disoriented. He moaned and tried to stumble away, but James kicked him in the ribs.

"Don't you touch my sister, you piece of shit!"

I backed away from the two as another of my friends appeared and asked if I was okay. I tried to speak to her, but I couldn't remember how to talk.

James hovered over Jeremy as he struggled to breathe. "Get up, asshole. I dare you."

Jeremy heaved for air as we stared at his pathetic display on the ground.

A security guard came up to us, having seen the commotion. "What the hell is all this?" the old man yelled. He looked like he was ten years past retirement.

James backed away, leaving Jeremy on the ground.

"Get up, kid," the old man said.

James came straight over to me and put his arm around my shoulders. "Are you okay? Did he hurt you?"

"Only a little, thank you."

"Bastard," James said, glancing back to Jeremy as the guard struggled to get him on his feet. "He can't touch you now. Sorry I wasn't here earlier."

"You've got nothing to apologize for. Thank God you came when you did. He was an animal. He…" I couldn't even finish my thought before tears spilled out of my eyes.

James took me home straight away. As soon as Mom saw my bruised arm and James's swollen knuckles, she forgot about whatever it was we were fighting over.

James had saved me from a psychopath that day, sparing me from an unknown fate at the hands of Jeremy. Should I tell him now about the asshole who is leading me toward the visitors' room as we speak?

Tom directs me to the entrance and takes the opportunity to grab me on the ass again. "I'll see you later, sweet cheeks." He chuckles to himself as his saunters off.

If things get any worse with Tom, I won't have a choice but to tell James everything.

CHAPTER 23

James is already sitting at an empty table in the middle of the visitors' room. He appears uneasy with the noise of the patients around, constantly checking over his shoulders, waiting for an attack. I understand the feeling he's having. You never want to become used to a place like this.

James spots me and brightens the room with his warm smile. I'm still trying to force my head around the fact that he is here and happy. The image I have carried of my brother over the last eight years becomes almost unreal given the way he now carries himself. It's not just the way he dresses or his new hairstyle: there's an aura about him I can't explain. He looks complete. I wonder if I'll ever feel that way again.

"Hi, Emma," James says with a quick wave as I arrive in front of him. He places both of his hands forward on the table and interlaces his fingers, keeping a straight back.

"Hello," I say as I sit down.

"How have you been?"

I shrug. "You know. Same old. Nothing's changed since your last visit, if that's what you're asking me."

Both of James's hands fly up in defense. "Just a question, Emma. Probably not the best one to ask you, though. I meant no offense."

"I'm sorry," I say. "I'm just trying to wrap my brain around all of this, you know?"

"It's fine," he says. "Don't stress."

"So, how have you been?"

"I'm good, but don't worry about me," he says, dismissing the question as diplomatically as possible. I can see from the excitement in his eyes he has something he wants to tell me.

"Why are you here again?" I ask.

He exhales loudly and closes his eyes for a second. "I'm here to support you, more than anything else."

"That's fine, but what brings you here right now? Surely you're not going to visit every day?"

"I can, if you want?" he asks, a little too eagerly for my liking.

"Trust me: you don't want to do that. You'll end up in here with me."

James doesn't laugh at my terrible joke. Instead, he lowers his head slightly. "Emma, I'm here to see if you know what happened."

My heart almost jumps out of my chest. "What do you mean?"

"I mean what got you thrown in here in the first place. Have they told you why you're here?"

I look around to see if there is a doctor silently watching me, as if James might have been coached on what to say. "No, they haven't. They also told me that I need to remember on my own and not have someone inject a false memory into my brain."

"Okay," he says. "That's good. I just wanted to be sure."

"Why do you want to know if the doctors have told me anything? Is this some sort of sick joke?"

"No," James says, his eyes wide. "I would never come here just to see you suffer."

"Then what is it? Why do you want to know?"

James sighs and leans back in his chair. The metal creaks and groans. He gazes around the room at the other patients, studying their very existence.

"James?" I ask him. I need to know.

"Okay. The thing is, I know what happened that night."

"You what?" The words catch in my throat. "How?"

"A police report. I had a friend get it for me. The doctors weren't telling me anything. I needed to know and…"

I shake my head. "How could you?"

"I'm sorry, Emma, but I wanted to know what got my twin sister thrown into a psychiatric hospital. I was concerned that you had been put in here against your will."

"I have been, but for a good reason. I did something, something so fucked up I can't even remember doing it. Whatever I did is so screwed up, you are the only one who has come to see me. Not my friends, my colleagues, not even Darren or Jayden. And now you're telling me you know what it is that I did."

He nods at me, eyes lowered to the cold, metallic surface of the table. "I wish I didn't know, but I do."

"So why are you here? Just to rub it in my face?"

"No. Never. I wanted to make sure they were treating you right in here. I also want to help you come to terms with what happened. I want to be there for you when you remember."

I strain to see through my tears. I wipe them free and try to see again. "This isn't some damn game, James. It's my life."

"I know it is, Emma, and I want to make up for the past eight years and help you fight through what happened. I owe you that much."

I don't know what to say to him. I want to hate him for violating my privacy, but at the same time, after eight long years, I miss my brother.

"James…" I can't finish my sentence. Tears and pain choke me into a blubbering mess. My head drops to the table as my hands cover my face.

"It's okay," James says. "I'm here for you, Emma. We'll get through this. I promise you."

CHAPTER 24

The next morning, I don't wake up. It's kind of hard to do that when you haven't been asleep.

Doctor Shaw was away yesterday, and I had no replacement doctor to help me through the day. James's visit left me so confused that I forgot to take any pills. Now, I'm paying for it, and I promise myself I'll swallow the remaining six tablets at lights out, too many hours from now.

Like a zombie, I shuffle to the bathroom and shower. I wait for the hot water to run out as I huddle inside the cramped space. The warm liquid gradually turns so cold that it could wake the dead. After a full minute of standing in the freezing stream, I shut the taps off.

I dry off as fast as I can and dress for the day. The cold has jolted me awake, but it has also left me shivering. With limited blankets and sheets on my bed, I'm forced to layer up as much as possible with extra clothing found inside a small cupboard to the side of my bed. Half the reason I don't sleep well in here is due to the simple fact that they won't give me enough bedding out of fear I might use it to kill myself. I'm not one of the suicidal patients that will use any object they can find to end their suffering, but I'm treated the same nonetheless. The thought makes me shake my head. If I were going to end it all, it wouldn't be with a rope twisted out of cheap bed sheets.

After the usual blur of activity, I find myself out in the courtyard again. The area is free of patients, allowing me a moment of calm before a yell in the distance reminds me where I am. I try to block out the noise of a patient arguing with an orderly as I stare up at the leaves of the silver maple in the courtyard.

After a few moments, the smell of the tree hits my brain. I instantly think back to when James and I were about ten years old. We'd spend our Saturdays lazing about in our parents' backyard by the silver maple my father was so proud of. The tree was taller than any I'd ever seen, especially to my youthful eyes. We'd sit under the tree and hang out for hours. James would play with his handheld video games, while I read my way through the classic Nancy Drew series. We couldn't be separated.

Our parents would always tell us both that we'd forever have a friend for life, being twins. I would never have thought otherwise until Sarah died. Mom's funeral was the final cut that severed the bond we once shared. Was it possible we were going to reconnect again in this place?

I think about the irony of James now being a success while I am a withered mess in a psychiatric hospital. Maybe the years of hardship after he lost Sarah built him up into the resilient man he is today. Maybe my cushy ride up until this point had set me up for permanent failure.

I come back to reality when Andrea walks outside.

"Emma. What brings you out here?"

"Nothing," I reply. "Just thought I'd find some peace, you know?"

Andrea laughs. "I don't think that's even remotely possible in this hellhole." She walks over to me and ushers me out of sight of the doorway. "So, how did you go with your new friends?"

"New friends?" I ask, my face a blank canvas of ignorance.

"The pills, dummy."

My eyes widen as I realize what she means. "Good the first night. Not so good the next."

"What went wrong on night two?"

I explain to her about underdosing and the need to rely on Tom. She nods but comes in close to me. "You gotta take enough to do the job. Otherwise there's no point."

I show my understanding as something painfully obvious hits me again. "I only have six left. Do you think you can find me some more?"

Andrea shifts. "Without question. Except they're going to cost you."

I was expecting this. "How much?" I ask.

"Twenty."

A reasonable price, I think to myself. "I should be able to secure that without hassle." I have around eighty dollars stashed away in my belongings at the front desk—everything I had on me when they hauled me in here. I just need to collect it somehow.

"Not twenty for the sleeve; twenty per pill."

My mouth falls open as I resist the urge to scream. "Are you kidding me? I'm not paying two hundred and forty dollars for something I can buy from the pharmacy for a lot less."

"Be my guest," Andrea says. "You're here voluntarily, right?"

My brows lower into a scowl. "You know I'm not. Besides, I don't have that kind of money on me. Not here, anyway."

Andrea crosses her arms. "Then find it. Ask someone to bring it in for you. I saw that guy who visited you yesterday. He looked like he could spare some cash."

"This is stupid. I'm not going to ask my brother to front me money to supply my drug dealer. The doctors will find out in a flash."

Andrea starts to walk away. "Not my problem."

I throw my arm out and grab at her shoulder. "Wait, you can't just—"

She lashes out and slaps me clean in the face. I spin away from the blow and check my cheek for blood. I find none. What I do find is a steaming Andrea staring back at me.

"Don't ever touch me like that again, bitch. Got it?"

I nod.

"Either bring me the money or fuck off."

I go to respond, but I choke up. I say nothing and watch Andrea leave. She gives me one last stare as she heads back inside.

I step away and fall into the corner of the courtyard. I hear myself crying as I realize how stupid I was to trust someone who hands out free drugs inside a psychiatric hospital. It's another failure to add to the list. I sit there for another twenty minutes in the cold, feeling sorry for myself. Tom soon locates me.

"There you are. Time for your session with Doctor Shaw." He leans down and hauls me up with one hand. There's no thought or care about his approach. I'm a problem that needs relocating.

He gives my eyes a fixed stare, possibly looking for some dilation in my pupils. He seems almost annoyed when he finds nothing. "Come on," he grunts.

We move through the facility at a fast pace, buzzing past other patients. The usual mindless conversations fill the air, all things I've heard a thousand times before. It's like some of these people forget the previous day and wake up each morning as if for the first time.

We arrive outside Shaw's office. Before Tom knocks, he pulls me aside. "Heard about your cash-flow problem."

I try to ignore his statement as I shake my head. I should have known he was involved in this black market.

"Just an FYI: I can get you more pills. We could work on some kind of payment plan if you know what I mean." He grabs my ass and gives me a firm squeeze. I cringe at his touch but say nothing. We both know he could land me in a world of trouble without much effort.

"Enjoy your session," he says as he lets go and knocks on the door. He starts to walk off before Shaw answers. "Think about it," he says over his shoulder.

Once he clears the hall, the door opens. Shaw is reading through some notes as she greets me. "Come on in, Emma. I'll be with you in a minute. I just have some paperwork to process. It never ends in this place."

I walk inside, holding one arm with the other as I take small steps straight toward the couch and sit down. I can still feel Tom on me. I take a deep breath in, preparing for the session. I can't let Doctor Shaw see that something has got me rattled. It will only make things worse. Thankfully, the paperwork in her hands holds her full attention.

After a few minutes, the doctor shoves her work to the side and pulls out my file. "Sorry about that. I'm determined not to have to stay late tonight."

I smile to be polite. I don't care if she needs to stay a few hours later. I never get to leave this place for a single second.

"Now, where were we?" Shaw asks out loud. She goes through her notes and taps something with her finger. "Right." She glances up at me and interlaces her fingers. "Today, we are going to focus on something new that I would like to try with you."

My heart almost leaps out of my chest at the very mention of the word "new." I can barely handle my routine as it is and she wants to try something new.

"What is it?" I ask.

"Nothing major. I simply want you to keep one thought in the back of your head the entire time we are doing this: a deadline for you to reach the event."

"A deadline? Why? I thought I had as long as I needed to come to that point?"

"You do, Emma. Without a doubt. But I want you to put one on yourself in the hope that it will stop you from delaying the inevitable. Eventually, you will have to relive that moment. The longer we take to arrive at that point, the harder it's going to be for you to process it. But, if I can see that you are not ready to go down the final stretch of the journey, then we will slow right down and take as long as you need."

My eyes flutter as I try not to tell her to forget her deadline. I instantly think of James's words from yesterday. Part of me wants to remember the event so I can begin to make amends to Darren and Jayden. I'd give anything to see their faces come through the door of the doctor's office to tell me that this has all been a big misunderstanding. But I know that's not going to happen anytime soon. They still haven't forgiven me yet. I look to the doctor. If the pain of that night can bring them back to me, then I can stomach the thought of facing it.

I begin to wonder why Doctor Shaw is placing this sudden timeline on me. All I can guess is she is getting pressure put on her by her superiors. They want me dealt with and shoved through the system.

"Are you okay, Emma?"

"Yes," I say, my voice a whisper. "Let's just get this over with."

Shaw nods at me and writes down a long note. No doubt I've made things worse for myself in less time than it took for Tom to harass me.

CHAPTER 25

Before

"Good luck, son," Darren yelled from the window of his truck. "We'll meet you at the game later today."

We both sat there, waiting for Jayden to go inside his friend's house without anyone harassing him. I tried to shake the sensation that someone was following us, but it was a constant presence in the back of my mind.

"Okay," Darren said. "To the police station. You've got the USB, right?" This was the third time he'd asked me.

"Yep, right here." I clutched it tight. There was no way I was losing this evidence the way I'd lost the photos on my phone. The cops would have to take me seriously this time, instead of assuming I was just another crazy person slowing down their day.

We drove along toward the small police station in town. It wasn't often that I had to go to our local department. With my hand holding up my chin as I leaned on the window of the truck, my mind drifted back to the last time I walked inside the Clearwater Hills Police Department.

Five years ago, Darren and I had taken Jayden to our local county fair. We hadn't done anything together as a family in weeks. Between my income from the university and the multiple jobs Darren irregularly worked, we were struggling. A day out for some fun with our son was both a relief while at the same time a terrible way to add more pressure to our lives.

The county fair, while being a reasonably priced way to spend a day, was an expense we could not afford. The mortgage was overdue along with several utility bills. But Darren was expecting a decent enough check to come in the mail in the next few days for a house he'd helped a friend build a few towns over.

"Hey, Mom? Can we go on the pirate ship? It's only five dollars."

Darren and I looked at one another. It was a ride we both knew Darren would have to take him on, doubling the cost. But we couldn't say no, could we? How can you take a kid out to such a place and not be prepared to spend a few dollars?

"Have fun," I told them, as they ran off to join the short line for the pirate ship. Watching the ride in action, I knew it was something I wouldn't appreciate.

After a few minutes of waiting, they got to jump on board. I moved to the side of the ride, watching my husband and son sway back and forth. The ship gradually swung higher and higher, until they were both holding on for dear life while yelling out with joy.

I stared up at the smile on Jayden's lips, which had spread to Darren. I'd missed seeing that on either of them. We'd had a hard few months of trying to get by on as little money as possible so we could keep our dream home. Darren would need to be pulled out by a small army before he'd ever sell our house. His blood, sweat, and tears were literally cemented into its foundation.

With his stubbornness came an eagerness to earn more money, which had seen Darren take a few questionable jobs around town. He was asked to use his license to sign off on some construction work I knew wasn't up to his usual standards. I tried to ask him about it, but he refused to discuss the issue when the work was bringing in money we sorely needed.

My phone had buzzed in my purse. Those were the days when a phone was just a phone, metal and plastic, and not something I craved more than almost anything else. I flipped the device open after seeing a number I didn't recognize. Darren often gave people my cell number along with his own whenever he applied for jobs, so I had to make sure I answered every call.

"Hello, Emma Turner speaking." I sounded a bit formal for my own liking, but I wanted the caller to know my surname.

"Hello, Mrs. Turner. This is Deputy Ken Irvin with the Clearwater Hills Police Department. Do you have a moment to talk?"

"You're from the police station?"

"Yes. I'm afraid there's no other way for me to say this, but there has been an accident."

"An accident?" I could feel my heart thumping harder in my chest than it ever had. I glanced toward Darren and Jayden, foolishly double-checking they were okay.

"Yes, an accident. I'm afraid that—"

"Who is it?" I demanded to know as my mind tried to decipher who it could be. Jennifer from work, my friend Tammy, one of Darren's friends? I was way off.

"I'm sorry. It was your father."

The officer's words hit me hard, swatting me down with ease. I reached out for something to grab onto, expecting Darren to be there when I needed him, but my hand found nothing. I dropped to the grass on my knees, keeping the phone glued to my head.

I choked the next words out. "What happened? Is he okay?"

A brief moment of silence filled me with dread. No person has ever left a lull like that for any reason other than to avoid the inevitable.

"He's dead. I'm sorry for your loss."

The phone fell away as I tried to process what the officer had just told me. I crawled around, trying to find something to grab hold of for support. I stumbled upon the edge of the wooden decking that surrounded the pirate ship and pulled myself up. I could hear the officer trying to grab my attention on the other end of the line.

"Mrs. Turner?" he called out, his voice faint. After a few seconds, I lifted the phone to my ear, unsure if what I'd heard was real. It had to be some kind of terrible joke someone was playing on me, right?

"Mrs. Turner?"

"I'm here," I said, my voice barely louder than a whisper. "I'm here."

The officer went on to explain what had happened in detail. Apparently, Dad had been coming home from the university after heading in to do some extra work for some of his students. It wasn't uncommon for him to do such a thing. He came to an intersection he'd passed through a million times. On this occasion, though, he wasn't paying attention and drove straight through at the exact moment a large truck came barreling along. The heavy vehicle hit the driver's side of the car and killed my father on impact.

Just like that, a life was over. It took only one brief second and a decision made during a moment of fatigue.

The police officer asked if I could come down to the station and confirm that some of the items pulled from the crash belonged to him. There wasn't a body to identify, as the truck had destroyed Dad's hatchback beyond recognition and the remains had caught fire. They thought Dad had filled up the tank a few minutes prior.

I acknowledged the officer's words, not knowing what else to say. I thanked him for his time and snapped my phone shut. It felt as though a thick fog had swept in from all angles to consume me. I gripped the metal barrier that surrounded the pirate ship with both hands until my knuckles turned white.

I had to stand and wait for the ride to come to an end. Darren and Jayden were enjoying themselves while my world was falling apart around me.

As the rocking of the ride gradually slowed, Darren caught sight of my face and gave me a gesture to ask what was wrong. All I could do was shake my head. How else do you communicate that your father has died in a car crash?

Time slowed down as Darren and Jayden approached me. I remembered speaking the words I had to say to Darren, but the rest was a blur. He rushed the three of us away from the relaxing day we had planned, back to his aging pickup.

He whisked us across town to the Clearwater Hills Police Department, leaving the fun we were supposed to be having behind in the rearview mirror.

CHAPTER 26

I identified Dad's wedding ring at the police station, along with a few other pieces of jewelry he had been wearing during the crash. I could see where the fire had damaged each item. Scorch marks covered the metal, but it wasn't enough to melt the pieces.

I was given everything in a sealed container and asked to sign a few documents. I had no idea what I was signing, nor did I care. I now had a dead father, and a funeral to plan. But how do you send off one of the greatest men you have ever known? It was a task I didn't want to face alone.

I sat by the phone at home the next day, trying my hardest to summon up the courage to call James. I hadn't spoken to my brother in the three years that had passed since Mom's funeral. But our father was dead and he needed to know. He also needed to be here and do his part in all of this. Just because we'd all had a falling-out didn't mean he got to ignore the previous sixty-three years of our father's life.

I called James on the only number of his I had. His home phone had been disconnected not long after he took off, so all I had in my possession was his cell number.

It rang out and went to voice mail. I tried to say the words I needed to say, but I couldn't speak. I hung up the phone again after leaving three voiceless messages that would sound creepy at best.

"Dammit," I yelled as I tossed the phone into the cushions on the couch. "Why is this so hard?"

Darren was nearby. He had to be. "Take it easy, honey. You'll do it when you're ready."

"I need to do it now, though. We have to organize this funeral as quickly as possible. I'm already getting a few calls about it."

"Jesus, really? Damn vultures couldn't wait a few minutes to let us breathe?"

"It's not like that," I said, waving off Darren's theory that a lot of people would be after Dad's money. It was no secret he had been sitting on a sizable nest egg he was keeping in reserve for when and if he ever decided to leave the university. The matter of his will, however, would have to wait until after the funeral.

After another day of stress, I managed to leave a message on James's voice mail. I could have made Darren do the dreaded task, but I knew it had to be me. Words were not coming out of my mouth the way they usually did. I explained what had happened and said that I needed him to help me with the funeral. I gave him my number in case he had lost it on purpose.

A few minutes later, my phone rang, James's number flashing up on the caller ID display. I answered straight away.

"James? Hello?" I said. "Are you there? Can you hear me?" I listened as he breathed down the line. I swore I heard the faint sound of tears or sobbing being muffled by his hand over the microphone, but he hung up before I got another word out.

I tried calling him again and again, leaving several messages, but he never called back. By the next day, his number stopped working. Had he disconnected it on purpose? Part of me tried to rationalize that perhaps he had just forgotten to pay the bill, but I knew that was a lie. He didn't want to see me, let alone talk to me. His position was clear.

With the help of Darren and a few close friends Dad had known in and around the area, we got through the funeral. I remembered standing in the church, glancing back to the doors of the packed building, hoping James would show up. Even if he just kept to the back and never said a word to anyone I could have forgiven him, but he never showed.

I spent the rest of the day explaining why James hadn't made it. The relatives all knew the truth, but felt the need to bring up the touchy subject anyway. It was the last thing I needed to deal with.

The funeral came and went in a haze of tears, anger, and confusion. Why hadn't James shown up? Surely he could have used this as the perfect time to reconnect with his twin sister, even if he and Dad were never going to see eye to eye again? Instead, James had managed to miss both of our parents' funerals. It was another day that I'd needed him there, another day that he hadn't shown.

Would he ever be there for me again?

CHAPTER 27

I was named as the executor of Dad's will. After the funeral had taken place, I immediately got to the task of filing his will through the court. I wanted the grim job over with. I couldn't stand Dad's few relatives whom I hadn't seen in years asking me what they were getting, like they'd won some prize and were waiting to collect.

I hadn't read his will in full. I simply completed my part of the legal process. As far as I was concerned, nothing could replace Dad.

We'd have Sunday dinners at his house after Mom died. I'd help him prepare it all, giving him the connection he so sorely needed to our small family. With Mom's passing and James's absence, our dinners weren't anything too grand. The four of us tried to make do and keep each other strong.

When Dad died, it sent a rip through our family that continued into my marriage. Darren and I fought and complained more than ever before, as our financial troubles became so severe the bank had scheduled a meeting to discuss our plans for the future.

"What the hell are we going to do?" I asked Darren. It had been one month since Dad had died.

Life continued along as our various problems gathered pace. My father had offered us money on more occasions than I could remember, but Darren always refused to take a single dollar of it. He wanted to earn his money and owe nothing to anyone. I could respect that to a certain degree, but when the wolves are at your door, you take what help you can get.

I got the shock of my life when I found out Dad had left me a considerable chunk of money in his will.

Darren thought it was amazing, suddenly changing his tune on handouts. Was the fact that it was inherited enough for him to write it off in his mind as not being charity? Some people deserved their parents' fortunes after the years of suffering they'd had to endure, but I never felt that sense of entitlement. I'd loved Dad more than anything. If he'd decided to leave the entire fortune to his pet cat, I wouldn't have cared.

Darren's eyes lit up like dollar signs when he saw our bank account increase in three months to a level it had never seen before. We settled our immediate debts and went about paying off the house in full, like we'd won the lottery. There was plenty left over but not enough to retire. We would still have to keep working, but things wouldn't be as hard as they had been. That's when Darren came to me with his plan.

"I know I could pull this off," he said as he pitched me his idea for starting a construction company. He went over all the pros while I went over all the cons, until, in the end, we agreed. He started the paperwork the next day.

A few weeks later, I was thinking about Dad and everything that had happened in the last few years. Could I really blame James for not coming to Mom's funeral? If it had been me in his position, with Darren dead and buried, would I have behaved any differently? I shuddered at the thought and tried to think how I could mend the relationship with my brother.

I had most likely pushed back any chance of reconciliation with the tone of the message I left on his cell when Dad passed. I didn't mean to be that way. I just wished he could have put aside our differences and come forward during a time when I needed my brother. It would have meant so much.

It felt strange to have the house paid off in full. But it didn't take long for our new problem to become Darren's business. The first six months got off to a decent start as he slowly ramped up the company he had built out of thin air. Most companies could say things like "family owned for twenty years" or "established in 1975". Darren had to be upfront and tell potential clients that the business was new, but he didn't.

We settled into a new rhythm that somewhat matched the old. I handled the house, worked full-time, and sorted Jayden out. Darren took care of his business and nothing else. If I ever asked him to do anything outside of that, he would complain about not having the time.

I didn't bother to argue and accepted what had to be. Part of me wished that we had invested the extra money that was now tied up in the business, but neither of us understood the first thing about that side of life. Instead, we stuck to what we knew.

Before I realized, a year had gone by, and we were still a functioning family. Jayden was transitioning into a teenager, Darren was beaming with confidence as he tried to grow his business, and I remained the same. It suited me. I wasn't one for drastic change. I still felt surprised that Darren had been able to convince me to fund his dream. But I loved him more than anything. How could I say no?

Things were looking up for the Turners. Despite the difficulties of the previous few years, we were pushing forward and not looking back. But James always sat in the corner of my mind. He always would, but I stopped letting our failed relationship control me. If he wanted to be back in our lives—or in my life, at least—he knew where he could find us.

He had to be the one willing to come forward and put himself on the line.

CHAPTER 28

After

"That was the last time I ever felt that way," I say.

"What way?" Doctor Shaw asks.

"You know, optimistic. Ever since that moment, I'm lucky if I can feel half as good as I did back then."

Shaw studies me with thick worry lines over her brows. "Do you believe you will ever be happy again?"

I stare at the floor and wonder the same thing. It doesn't seem possible, given my current standing. I don't speak and let the silence give her an answer. She writes something down about my lack of a response, as if she can interpret my every thought.

"We'll pick this up again tomorrow," Shaw says. "In the meantime, I want you to focus on one thing for me."

I shrug. "What?"

"The thought that you will be happy again. I understand the concept might feel impossible after waking up in a place like this, but one day, you will find happiness."

I don't respond. Instead, I focus on her words, which only increase my anxiety. I know I'll never be happy again. If there's one thing I've come to understand and accept in this confusing mess, it's that I will never be the same. My good years are behind me, ticked off as completed by the stroke of a doctor's pen.

Shaw walks me back to my ward. The hour of peace away from the wailing and moaning isn't lost on me. I'd pay a small fortune for a decent pair of noise-canceling headphones to drown out the madness.

The thought reminds me of my current issue with securing more diazepam from Andrea. Despite the nervous feeling I get when I think about her, she's my best source of the pills I need to sleep. And after being awake now for over thirty hours, I realize I will drop the remaining six tablets tonight whether I get any more or not. The only other person who can get me the medication is Tom. I don't want to think about the cost involved if I have to rely on him.

I head back to my room and ensure the sleeve is still hidden in the mattress. Thankfully, the staff here are not thorough enough to check such an obvious hiding place. It makes me wonder what else I could stuff in there.

I leave my room and head for the day area, where we are supposed to be when the sun is out. I find a seat in a corner no one has taken yet and try to ignore the noise of the dozen or so patients filtering in and out of the room. I never see everyone in here at the same time. It's as if the orderlies can't stand the thought of our collective annoyance. I don't blame them.

I think back to the yoga practice I once enjoyed and try to meditate. Tom blabbers away in the background, being his usual self to one of the patients. I block out his voice and the feeling of his hand on my body as best I can, but there is only so much my limited knowledge of meditation can achieve.

"Well, well, well," Tom says as he steps up to me. "Never figured you for one of these spiritual clowns."

My eyes snap open with a shudder. I stare up at him from my seat. He doesn't wait for me to bite back.

"Given my proposal some thought?" he whispers as he squats down to my level. "Because, darlin', I can make your time here much easier." His hand, hidden by his body from any other members of the staff, runs over my leg. I shy away the second his fingers touch me. I can't help the gag reflex.

"No need to be like that," he says as he stands straight with his sly grin. "Because I can also make things far worse for you." His smile turns into a sneer. He gives me a wink and walks away, checking over his shoulder as he moves on to his next victim.

I let the tremble that's been dying to come out of me run down my spine. My breath quickens as I shake my head and mutter to myself, quiet enough so that no one else will hear me. I stop after a short moment and realize I've become one of them, one of those crazy people who spend their days talking to themselves in the corner.

I push away the image of Tom touching me for the second time that day and try to get back to my meditation. I know it's a waste of time, but I have plenty of it to kill.

*

A few hours pass. In that time, I eat lunch, take my prescribed medication, listen to a patient argue about the government, and find out my brother will be in soon for another visit. He seems to be dropping in a lot. As much as I value his time, I don't know if I can take it.

Reconnecting with him is taking up all of my available energy. It's not that I don't want to see him or that I don't feel like rebuilding the bond we once shared; I just want to see Darren and Jayden more than anyone else in the world. Would I ever look upon their warm faces again? I'm not in a good place right now.

I wait in the visitors' room and try not to think about anything, but it's impossible. A haze of memories cloud together and stab back at me. I snap to the present and realize my face is stained with tears. Even though I can't remember the event, it's there, waiting for me to remove the wool from my eyes and relive it.

Tom's smug face interrupts my haunting thoughts as he leans down in front of me, hands placed firmly on the table.

"Yes?" I ask.

"Oh, nothing. Just thought you should know that your brother is here. I suggest you keep the conversation light. Nothing too dramatic. We don't want any trouble coming our way, do we?"

I catch Tom's less-than-subtle suggestion and nod. "I won't say anything. I promise." I have no idea if I can indeed keep quiet, but part of me knows I can't get James involved without making things worse.

"Good girl," Tom says.

I ignore his attempt to shape me into his pet and smile as best I can. I'm not convincing anyone with my bullshit grin, least of all Tom.

As my brother enters the room, I focus on his sparkling demeanor. He appears to be chirpier than before. I shake my head, suddenly annoyed by his happiness, though I should be pleased for him. A slight flush of shame washes over me.

"Hey, Emma," he says, bending down to give me a quick hug. I lightly squeeze him back, still not comfortable touching another human being. Tom's advances have only made me more sensitive than before.

"How are you today?" he asks.

It's a question I hear more than any other, and I hate answering it. I can't tell him how I really am today. He doesn't need to listen to it, as much as I would like to unload all of my pain upon him.

"I'm okay. You?" I say after a delay.

"I'm fine. Better than fine." He bends in close to me. "I've been doing some thinking about everything."

His words startle me. I don't know why, but a slap of angst hits my brain as to what he will say next. I have no reason at all to think he is about to tell me something terrible, but I can't help this new way I think.

"You know that I've read the police report. You understand that I know what happened that night."

I feel my body collapse in on itself as I try to shrink down to half my size. Why is he talking about that night? If he says too much, it could trigger something within my core that might explode.

"I can see that the very mention of it is hurting you, but I have an idea that might help bring it all out in one cleansing motion."

My heart feels like it is about to break through my chest and fly off the table. My eyes dart left and right as I try to escape his stare. What am I supposed to say?

"Emma," James says, reaching a hand toward me. "I think we should take you there, to the place where it all happened."

CHAPTER 29

I stare at James as if he has just asked me for a kidney. "What?"

"You heard me. We take you to that place so you can confront what happened head on."

I shake my head as my gaze darts away. My mouth is half open and my brows twist tight.

"Emma," James says, "listen to me. You can do this. I can take you out of here this weekend. I looked into it. As long as your doctors agree, you can be released into my care. They don't need to know where we're really going. We can face it together."

"I don't…" I trail off as my eyes close. A migraine is coming. This is all too much for me to face, and James can't see that. My eyes pop open as I search the room for Doctor Shaw. She will be able to read my thoughts and sense the situation I'm in.

"Take your time. This is a lot to take in, I realize. If you're not up to the idea, it's fine."

My head starts to spin. I can sense the beast behind me, waiting for me to fail. I bury the dark thoughts in the back of my skull and push the table away from my body, startling James and the rest of the room. I need space to breathe.

"No," I whisper, trying to keep quiet. "I am up to this. I want to know what happened. I won't let these memories slip away. I can't."

James nods with both eyes narrowed in on me. "You can do this. I know you, Emma. You're the strong twin, the one who always helps everyone else. Let me help you through this."

"What if I can't? What if I fail?"

"You won't fail. I won't let you."

We stare at one another while the rest of the world continues to spin around us.

"Okay," I say.

James grins at me. "I'll make the arrangements and pick you up Saturday morning. In the meantime, I want you to spend every day until then preparing yourself for this. It's not going to be easy."

I nod as I think about what might be ahead. All I will be focusing on is reliving that night. I don't even know if the doctors will allow James to do what he is proposing. But what if it works? What if I remember it all and accelerate my recovery? I'll finally feel safe again and, who knows, maybe get the chance to see Darren and Jayden again. The thought of their faces blocks out any dark images from my mind, as if nothing bad ever happened. Could the recovered memories grant me the courage to leave this place once the doctors clear me?

I stare back at James. I can see how satisfied he is to be helping me, as if making up for lost time.

I lean forward and touch the table in front of him. "Thank you," I say. "Thank you for not giving up on me or our relationship."

"I never did, Emma. I know it might seem like I had, but deep down, I've always wanted to be there for you. Instead of being a burden in your life."

"You were never a burden, James. You were lost, just like I am now."

He smiles and opens his arms wide for a hug. I accept the offer and we meet in the middle.

"We can do this," he says. "We can get you out of this place together."

*

After James leaves the visitors' room, I am ushered back to the day room for the remainder of the afternoon. The usual chaos is unleashed and I sit back and watch the orderlies struggle with the patients. I almost feel a sense of calm wash over me as my mind drifts to what James said. I want to go through with his idea, no matter how much anxiety it might cause me. If Doctor Shaw had come to me with the same suggestion, I doubt I'd feel compelled to comply. Things are just different when it comes to family.

Andrea sits down beside me, as if our rough exchange this morning never happened.

"Vultures, the lot of them," she says, watching two orderlies handling a patient who has just thrown food in their faces. I'm unsure whom she is referring to, and I don't bother to seek a clarification.

"So, did you speak to your brother?"

I turn to face her and wonder what she means. Does she know about the weekend trip I am planning with James? Not that it should matter to a drug dealer. I try to stall for time, but I can't think of a distraction.

"Well?" Andrea asks.

"Speak to him about what?"

Andrea huffs. "The money. What else?"

"Oh, not yet. It didn't come up."

She laughs at me. "Oh, it will come up. Trust me. You'll be begging me a few days from now. I can see you haven't slept in a long time. How are the nightmares?"

"I don't need your precious pills."

"Whatever, honey," she says, standing up. "You let yourself think that, and we'll see who's right and who's wrong."

"We will," I say, with more confidence than I should have on the topic. Whether I can admit it to myself or not, I am about to run into a wall with the diazepam. Sleep is calling me, but my brain has too many dark thoughts stored in it to allow me the simple pleasure.

"I'll see you soon," Andrea says with a chuckle as she walks away.

I resist saying any more as she leaves. This isn't her first time pushing drugs, nor will it be her last.

After dinner, we are sent to bed for the last portion of the day. We have two hours alone in our rooms with the doors open before the automatic lights cut out and the staff comes around to seal us in for the night. For most, it's the worst time. Isolation is about to surround each of us in ways only we can understand.

I stare at the ceiling as I debate in my head what to do with the precious tablets sitting beneath my pillow. I pull them out the second I can and leave them hidden in my fist for easy access once I decide what to do.

I have a few options: I can take half now and half tomorrow to force some scattered rest. Or, I could down the whole lot and sleep like there's no tomorrow.

I try to come up with the answer as I listen to the buzzing light overhead. The bulb fills the room with a dull yellow and acts as a white noise machine. I wonder how long it'll be until it burns itself out and has to be discarded as trash.

An orderly startles me as he grabs the door to lock me in.

"Lights out in three minutes," he says.

I nod. A three-minute warning isn't enough time to sort myself out, so I remain on my bed.

I listen to the sound of my door closing and locking. Until an orderly opens my door in the morning, I'm trapped in here like an animal in a cage.

The light overhead clicks off a few minutes later, allowing me to pull out the packet of six tablets. I stare at the array, deciding exactly what I'm going to do with them.

CHAPTER 30

I stand over the toilet with the tablets. All I have to do is pop them into the bowl and flush. I've gone a day without taking any and feel okay. I haven't ingested enough for an addiction to form, but Andrea is relying on my lack of sleep to get me hooked.

I can't let that happen.

"Come on," I say to myself for encouragement. My hand starts to shake and rattle the pills. I steady my wrist with my other arm, locking it tight. Never have I been racked with such indecision. Or have I?

Darkness swirls in my head. I can't face the nightmares that take me back to that moment, but I also can't keep myself awake any longer. I will fall asleep tonight, one way or the other, but only the diazepam can block out the pain and give me the rest I need. I might as well have one night free from suffering.

I stumble back and turn away from the toilet. I toss the sleeve to the counter that wraps around the stained sink. I stare at the piece of metal on the wall that serves as a mirror. I look awful. I've looked this way for a long time now. I have no makeup, and no straightener to deal with my out-of-control hair.

I am the classic crazy patient. How did I end up in this place?

Both of my palms are planted on the counter, and I lean closer and closer to the mirror, until my nose touches the surface. I see the person in there behind her dead eyes and realize she isn't me. She can't be. I would never let this all happen. I would never have allowed myself to fall this far down.

But the mirror doesn't lie.

Tears streak my face as I pick up the sleeve and unleash each tablet into my left hand. I can hear myself sobbing as I start to swallow them one at a time, until all six are gone. I let the empty packet drop into the sink and close my eyes. I know I'll need to get rid of it somehow, but that seems like a minor problem compared to the one I've now made for myself.

With a swimming head and the tablet sleeve in hand, I head to bed. The last thing I'm able to do before the chemicals claim me is stuff the evidence away.

I fall asleep without a care in the world. I don't worry if Tom is the one who opens my room tomorrow and spots my eyes. I don't worry about my next session with Doctor Shaw. No one can make me feel guilty or force me to stress about my past or future.

For a fleeting moment in time, I am free from the nightmares, and I am free from my life.

*

Tom stands over me with both hands on my shoulders. He had shaken me awake the way Jayden used to when he was just big enough to climb into our bed and give Darren and me an early morning hello. Tom, on the other hand, isn't a cute young boy but a middle-aged jerk.

"Time to wake up, darlin'," he says while rocking me.

I blink several times to break through the crust in my eyes. Through my confusion, I realize that it is indeed morning. The night felt like it lasted only a few minutes. I slept the entire time.

"Well, well. It looks like someone gave themselves a warm glass of milk last night." Tom stands upright and adjusts his belt. "Looks like you took a hefty dose too. Let's take a gander, shall we?" He bends back down, leaning in close to my face. I can taste his breath on me and can smell the coffee and cigarettes that stain his teeth.

I squirm away as his hand slides down into my mattress and pulls out the empty sleeve. He didn't even need to search for it.

"So, it would appear that you are fresh out," he says as he stands back up tall and studies the packet. He crumples it up and shoves it into his pocket. "I'll dispose of this for you."

I'm tempted to say thanks, but I know exactly what he's doing.

"Got any plans on how you're going to secure your next batch?" His right eyebrow lifts as he tilts his head in anticipation.

I shrug. "I don't have any money. None that I have access to."

"Well now, darlin', don't let that stop you, because I can guarantee after last night, you're gonna want some more pills whether you like it or not."

My heart thumps against my chest. I know he's right. I'll want to sleep like this again. Without the drugs, I can't stop the terror entering my mind in my dreams. Perhaps this one good night has motivated my brain to stop torturing me the way it does, but I doubt it.

My fleeting hope is stomped out when Tom shows his displeasure at my lack of response. "Time to get up," he orders. He pulls me out of bed, directing me toward the bathroom. "Get your shit together so I can take you to the medical supply room again. Your eyes are like two neon signs that say 'drug addict.' It's not a good look to have around all of these judgmental doctors."

I hear him chuckle to himself, taking amusement at my suffering. "Asshole," I mutter as I go inside the bathroom. He continues to rant away while I try to zone him out.

In the mirror, my eyes are bloodshot and my pupils are huge. I attempt to help the situation by splashing water on my face. It makes a slight difference, but not enough to hide the truth.

"Hurry up, Turner!" Tom shouts.

I shudder at his yelling and run my fingers through my hair. They won't even supply me with a comb in here. How am I supposed to gain some control of the frizzy mess on top of my head? At this point, I'd be happy to shave it all off.

Tom gets impatient and stomps into the bathroom. He drags me away and walks me out of my room. "We have to go now," he says, "before the doctors arrive, understand?"

I nod as I feel my shoulders tense up. He takes me the usual way through the checkpoints and guides me with confidence through to the medical supply room. He walks me into the back and finds the eye drops again.

We go through the same agonizing routine as last time, leaving me half blind. I find myself standing in the small closet space alone with Tom while sunspots fill my eyes.

"Much better. Now you don't look as fucked up, darlin'."

I don't say a word.

"Where's the gratitude, huh? I just did you a huge favor. The way I see it, you owe me again." He creeps up to me and wraps his arms around my waist. His hands head straight for my ass like magnets. He pulls me in close to his groin as I attempt to shy away from him. Every time I feel him near, my body flinches away, but it doesn't stop him.

"Now, are we going to work out some sort of payment for these services rendered? Or do I need to get the docs involved?"

I gulp, not knowing the right thing to say. I'm convinced he's going to do what he wants to me no matter what. Then I wonder what would happen if I came clean to Shaw about the pills and Tom. My thoughts are rendered void as the orderly forces himself upon me.

Tom tries to kiss me, pulling my resisting head in tight, his mustache brushing my face. One of his hands runs over my breast and squeezes, sending a jolt of pain through my chest. It takes every ounce of strength I have left in me to push back and say "No," but he doesn't listen. He kisses my neck like it's going to make some difference to my resistance.

I try with everything I have to fend him off, but I have no power, and he's made up his mind. He spins me around and presses me into one of the shelves.

"You're mine," he says into my ear. "We'll continue this later. I've got other patients to sort out, darlin', but I'll find you to resume our conversation. Sound good?"

I nod with closed eyes and a wrinkled forehead. What else can I do? He has total control, and he knows it. My mind flashes back to that night—to Karlo. I feel him on me as if he were in Tom's place. The memory has surfaced at the hands of this disgusting orderly. Why did Karlo have me in a similar position?

Tom releases me.

The thoughts in my head spin and swirl as I try to remember where I am. What am I going to do?

I could come clean to Doctor Shaw, but then James wouldn't be allowed to take me away for the weekend. I'll be put on a stricter watch than I already am, and the chance of me getting any real sleep again will die. On the flip side of the coin, I know without a doubt that Tom will keep doing this until he gets what he wants. I'm not sure my brain could process that if it ever happens.

I shudder as I straighten my clothing and wait for him to open the door. He makes himself presentable again before opening the exit a touch so he can see who else is around. After he is satisfied with his findings, we leave the closet.

I'm taken to the day room and told to sit. "I'll be back at three. I just need to change your appointment again with Shaw so we can really hide those eyes of yours. You sure do get sick a lot," he says with a chuckle as he strolls off.

When Tom leaves my sight, I rub at my skin and find the nearest bathroom to clean myself. No amount of scrubbing seems to do the trick, though. I can't wash off his stink.

*

The rest of the day trickles slowly away until I find myself in a session with Shaw. Once again, she is finishing some paperwork, oblivious to the fact that her patient had almost been raped by an orderly. I wonder how many lives Tom has made significantly worse in his time here. I doubt I'm the only one.

"So your brother has put in a request for some weekend leave into his custody. How do you feel about that?"

The question catches me off guard. James wasn't messing around. "Excellent," I say. "I think it would do me good to be out of here for a few days." Away from Tom, I think.

Doctor Shaw nods as she writes my every utterance down. "At this stage, the decision is still pending. I want to see how things play out for you over the next few days before we can commit to something that major. It's not going to be easy for you to head back out into the real world again."

"I know," I say, "but I want to spend some time with James, away from here. We've got a lot to catch up on. We've wasted too much time over the last eight years."

"Of course. Family is important. I do believe he will have a great impact on your recovery."

Me too, I think. He will help me bring what happened to light. As terrifying as that sounds, I think it will be the thing that saves me from this place. I just have to be willing to rip that Band-Aid off in one go.

"Okay, Emma. Let's pick up where we left off," Shaw says as she studies her notes. "You were at the moment you believed to be your happiest. What happened next?"

CHAPTER 31

Before

The Clearwater Hills Police Department was only a short drive away from Jayden's friend's house. I thought about the reaction the police would give us. As much as I hated to admit it, having Darren with me would make a huge difference. Even though the email harassment had only been directed at me because I was his wife, it still felt like a personal attack.

I shook off the thought before I became paranoid. I shifted my brain in a positive direction instead and asked Darren about tonight. "What movie should we see?"

He stroked his stubble with his free hand, the other on the wheel. "How about something light and funny? Nothing serious. I think we need a distraction from everything."

"Sounds perfect," I said. In all honesty, I didn't even care what we saw. I just wanted to be with my husband and feel safe again. The week of hell was starting to get to me.

We arrived at the police station. The building was an old brick colonial house that had been converted into a government facility. We parked in one of the limited visitors' spaces and stepped out of the truck.

"Are you okay?" he asked me as I stared at the building.

"Yeah, fine. Let's just get this over with."

We headed inside through the double doors and stepped up to a tall counter, where a weary-looking officer was nursing a steaming coffee cup in his firm grasp. The middle-aged man didn't look up from his paperwork as he took a hefty sip of the hot liquid. It was then that I saw a sign behind the counter that read "13 officers serving a community of over 7,800 people." I allowed the thought to sink in before we interrupted.

"Hello," Darren said to the officer. According to his badge, his name was Officer Peterson.

Peterson sighed and placed his pen down. "How may I help you, sir?"

Darren scratched at his head. "My, uh, wife called you out to our house yesterday because of a few threatening photos someone sent her."

"And?" Peterson said as he grabbed his pen back up and started tapping it against his paperwork.

"Well, the thing is, at the time, the photos kind of deleted themselves."

"Deleted themselves?"

"Yes. It's hard to explain, but—"

"Is this your wife?" he asked, jutting a finger in my direction.

"Yes, she is. But the thing is—"

"Can she talk for herself? Maybe this would sound better coming from her."

Darren threw up his hands in defeat and passed an imaginary ball to me. Now it was my turn to speak with the impatient man.

"Officer," I said as I stepped forward, "yesterday I received a link to a website containing photos of my family."

"What kind of photos?"

"The creepy kind. One of my husband leaving for work while I waved him off, one of him at his office, one of our son at school, and one of me looking out of our curtains at night."

The officer raised his brows and rubbed his chin.

"Darren's company is about to face legal action from a former employee who injured himself on site. We've been receiving threatening text messages and photos ever since, and I have been getting further threats sent to my email at work."

With as little emotion as possible, Peterson turned and started tapping away at a computer. He didn't say a word as he entered commands into the system one finger at a time.

"Turner?" he asked out of the corner of his mouth.

"Yes, we're the Turners."

Peterson pursed his lips with a slight grunt as his eyes scanned what appeared to be a report by the officers who had come to our house the day before. "I can update the file with the threatening emails and the text messages. Do you have copies?"

I pulled out the USB and held it up to him.

"I can't take that. It could have a virus or anything on it. You're going to need to come back with some hard copies."

"Jesus," Darren muttered, both arms crossed over his chest.

"Is there a problem?" Peterson asked, leaning forward.

"No, Officer. Everything is just dandy."

The two men stared each other down until I put myself between them. "Thank you, Officer. We'll come back with the hard copies."

Peterson slowly took his gaze away from Darren's. "I'll be honest with you, ma'am, these photos and emails won't get you very far. We have a backlog of crimes to investigate and not enough officers to make a dent in the pile. I'm sorry to be so blunt, but there's little we can do at this stage. Is there anything else I can help you with today?"

"No," Darren answered for me, and stormed for the exit. I followed him, giving the officer a brief smile in the process. Darren was halfway to the truck by the time I jogged up to him.

"Asshole," he let out. "What is with that guy?"

"Don't worry about him," I said. "He's probably just over-worked, you know?"

Darren shook his head. "We're all overworked. Doesn't mean we can be like that."

I said nothing, just listened as he got some more things off his chest. The officer's honesty was a gut blow to us both.

*

Over the next few hours, we grabbed some lunch and decided to leave the hard copies for another day. They wouldn't make an ounce of difference to the police, anyway.

With food in our systems, we made our way to Jayden's school for his game. When we arrived, I thought about the conversation I'd had with Miss Cantin. I hadn't told Darren about it, with everything that had been going on. I figured the last thing he needed to stress about was Jayden's grades and behavior.

The game got underway twenty minutes after we arrived. Jayden was practicing when we took our seats, trying to concentrate. We didn't bother him before a game, but made as much noise as possible to support him once the first whistle blew.

Jayden wasn't short for his age, but he was nowhere near the height of the tall kids in middle school. Because of that, he was a fantastic point guard, Darren told me. I didn't know enough about basketball to understand precisely what his role involved, but his shorter height combined with his nimble speed allowed him to steal the ball from the bigger kids and move the action in the right direction. He often sank about a quarter of the baskets his team scored during a game.

The game was neck and neck the entire time, and the score was tied with less than a minute to go. Jayden's team was on the defense and could lose at any second. Darren and I were on the edges of our seats. I felt like I was in the game, along with everyone else in the small stadium.

A player on the opposite team drove the ball in to take a shot and Jayden stole it from under him. We all went wild on both sides, cheering and yelling as Jayden charged away from the pack to make a perfect layup without any defense to slow him down.

Darren and I leaped to our feet in celebration as the clock ran out a few seconds later.

Jayden's teammates jumped all over him and hoisted him half into the air as the opposition stewed in defeat. I could hear curses from the other side's family members, while our team congratulated the hell out of Jayden. I guess it's hard for parents not to become emotionally involved.

When Jayden strolled over to us, Darren gave his son a big hug and congratulations. "That was incredible."

"Thanks, Dad," Jayden said, as his father ruffled his hair.

"Come here." I opened my arms wide and cuddled him, whether he wanted it or not. He tried to push me back at first but allowed me this one moment of physical contact. My clothing stuck to his sweaty skin, but I didn't mind. This was the best interaction we'd had all week.

*

After the game, we took Jayden out for an afternoon slice of pizza before he headed back to his friend's house for the night. Darren and Jayden went over the highlights of the game as we ate, while I listened contentedly. Despite Jayden's team not having much chance of getting into the finals, the victory felt like the most significant win of the season.

I sat back and soaked in the wonderful feeling our little family outing had generated within me. The smile on my face soon faded as the realities of the week came flooding back into the forefront of my mind. I tried not to imagine what Karlo would do next.

CHAPTER 32

Four hours later, Darren and I ventured out to a restaurant and to the movies. It felt like forever since I'd done anything fun with my husband. Even though Jayden was old enough to stay home by himself for a few hours or hang out with some friends, we rarely spent any time alone anymore. The business took most of Darren's spare energy, and my job and running the house stopped me from making much effort. We had fallen into a rut of our own creation, which was only growing deeper by the minute.

We enjoyed a lighthearted comedy at the mall and got out of the movie theater at around ten.

"What do you want to do now?" I asked Darren.

He gave me a grin and pulled me in tight like we were a couple of teenagers. "I think we should rush home and go to bed." He raised his eyebrows at me before kissing my neck. I threw my head back and giggled a little, loving every second of the attention. His idea was a perfect one. We both needed to relieve some stress.

We hurried out to Darren's truck, excited to get home. He drove like the world was about to end and got us back to the house in record time.

We pushed our way through the front door and continued where we left off, kissing each other with genuine passion instead of the usual businesslike greeting we gave one another most days. Darren's keys and my handbag landed on the ground where we tossed them, our shoes and clothing forming a trail behind us.

We had all night to make as much mess as we wanted to. Jayden wouldn't be back until late morning.

As we made our way upstairs to our bedroom in nothing but our underwear, we both heard a loud bang come from outside. More specifically, the noise came from our backyard. I instantly thought about the other day, when Bessie had been barking at the fence, and realized that the disruption could have been Karlo.

"What was that?" I asked, breaking off our kiss.

"Probably just the wind or something." Darren moved back to kissing my neck, ignoring whatever it was. I joined him and found myself in our bed a moment later, ready for my husband to make love to me in a way we hadn't done in far too long. As he moved over the top of me on all fours, I felt my skin prickle with anticipation. Darren lowered his face down to my chest and kissed me. I reached around to unhook my bra, but Bessie's bark stopped me.

"Ignore her," Darren said. "She's yapping at what we heard a second ago."

I couldn't ignore it. Bessie sounded distressed. Her barking didn't stop. Instead, it got worse. "Darren," I said, preventing him from going any farther. He looked beyond frustrated.

"What?"

"We need to see what's wrong with the dog. Then we can come straight back up here, I promise. Believe me, I want this more than anything in the world."

"Okay," he said, his head hanging low in defeat. He climbed off and helped me up. We both collected our clothing as we rushed downstairs, throwing it all back on in a hurry.

Bessie kept barking, refusing to stop. She almost sounded like she was trying to warn something away from our house.

"This had better be good," Darren said as we charged for the back door. When we got there, he unlocked the deadbolt and yanked it open.

I peered over his shoulder to see nothing but some light snowfall on our yard and Bessie barking her way back toward the house.

"Bessie!" Darren yelled. "Shut up!"

She whimpered a little at being told off, but pushed through the punishment to continue barking. Whatever had her spooked was too threatening to ignore. The thought sent a shiver down my spine worse than the cold air outside.

"What is she barking at?" Darren asked out loud as he walked down the two steps to the concrete footpath. "There's nothing out here."

That's when I spotted them: two eyes half glimmering in the night, reflecting the moon. A man was staring at us over the tall fence from the corner where Bessie had been barking the other day.

"Darren," I managed to say as I frantically tapped his arm and pointed toward the eyes.

"What the hell?"

"It's a man, watching us. We should call the police."

"Forget that," Darren muttered. He stepped farther into the yard and started yelling. "Hey, you! What do you think you're doing out here? This is private property."

I had to give Darren credit as he stomped with confidence straight up to the man peeking in over the fence. Back when we were first dating, Darren didn't take crap from anyone. If another man gave me a hard time, he wasn't afraid to put himself in harm's way to defend me.

Bessie got more aggressive with her barking at the sound of Darren's angry voice. She knew something or someone was threatening her family.

For some reason, I absorbed their combined confidence and headed out toward the person myself. I thought of all the things I'd say to this asshole for what he had put our family through this week. It wasn't until I heard Darren go quiet that I realized what we had been getting excited about.

Sitting on a branch just beyond the fence was the neighbor's cat.

Darren recognized it at the same time and turned to me with a chuckle. "It's a goddamn cat."

We both laughed at our stupidity as the cat slunk away, unaffected by our meager threats. Bessie stopped her barking and trotted back toward her kennel by the back door.

Neither of us was wearing anything warm enough to be outside for more than a few minutes, so I gestured for Darren to head back inside.

"I'm sorry," Darren said.

"For what?"

We stopped halfway to the door as he faced me and grabbed hold of my arms. "For overreacting. With everything that has been happening, I feel so paranoid."

"It's okay, honey. Let's just get back inside." I smiled at him and rubbed his biceps.

We never made it back inside, though.

The back door to our house slammed shut. The loud noise turned us sideways in an instant.

I spun back to Darren and half choked on my words. "That couldn't have been the wind."

CHAPTER 33

We both ran up to the door and tried the knob.

"It's locked," Darren said with a huff.

"That can't be," I replied. I'd left it unlocked. Our doors had a system that allowed them to automatically lock from the outside if we depressed a button before closing up. I swear I hadn't touched it.

"You must have set it."

"I didn't."

"Then what?"

We both turned to the door and stared. I could tell the same thought had hit our brains simultaneously. Someone was inside our house. I stepped back without thinking.

Darren spoke first. "There's no way someone just crept past us and ran inside."

"They must have," I said as I continued to inch away from the door. "There's barely any wind out here."

"It doesn't make any sense. Why would—"

A slam upstairs startled us both, confirming there was an intruder in our damn house.

Darren remained confident on the outside as he clenched his fists, but I could still see his nerves showing through. He turned to me and said, "I'm going for the spare. Head to the neighbor's house and call the cops."

"But—"

"Don't argue with me. I'm going to let myself in with the other key so I can grab the keys to my truck from inside and—"

"Please don't," I begged him as I took hold of his wrist. "I know you've got a gun in your truck. Don't use it. You could get hurt, or worse."

He stopped for a moment to think but shook his head before turning to me again. "Go next door."

"No," I said. "We do this together. You can't stop me."

Darren closed his eyes for a few seconds while pinching the bridge of his nose. "Fine. You grab your cell while I grab the truck keys. After that, I'm going back in with my gun."

I nodded. I didn't know what to say.

Darren took off slowly as we headed for the gate. It was protected by a thick combination lock to keep anyone from accessing our backyard. Darren entered Jayden's birthday into the dial and unlocked the shackle. He pulled it out of the door with care then quietly opened the gate. We slipped through and shut the door behind us, stopping Bessie from escaping. The last thing we needed was to be chasing her around the streets while some intruder walked freely through our house.

The thought made me wonder if Karlo really was this stupid. Surely he wouldn't sink this low to scare us? Sending threatening messages and taking photos from a distance was one thing, but breaking into our home while we were in the backyard seemed a tad psychotic.

I followed Darren as he headed for the spare key, which we kept under a potted plant by the front door. It wasn't the most original hiding place in the world, but it did the job.

Darren retrieved the key and crept up to the front door. We heard another loud bang upstairs.

"I'm going in," he said to me as he unlocked the front door. I stuck close to him as we moved in. The house looked different with most of the lights off. We'd only switched on what we needed to move from upstairs to the back door, so the kitchen light was off.

There was the sound of something breaking upstairs, followed by a thud.

"What the fuck?" Darren whispered as he picked up his keys, which were lying on the floor where he'd tossed them as we'd charged for the bedroom earlier.

"Let's hurry," I said.

When we reached the kitchen, I spotted my handbag sitting on the floor. I needed my phone so I could call the cops. I took the whole bag, opting for silence over trying to fish around inside it.

"Let's get out of here," Darren said.

We slunk back to the front door while more noise came from upstairs.

We made it back outside and left the front door open. Darren rushed down the steps and headed to his truck. I didn't like the fact that he'd been keeping a gun inside his work vehicle, but at this point I couldn't argue with the decision.

He returned to the front door after silently opening and closing the truck. I used the time to retrieve my cell from my bag.

"I'm going back inside. I want you to call the cops and tell them to get their asses here right now."

I nodded sharply, my hands shaking uncontrollably as I struggled to unlock my phone.

Darren grabbed my wrist and steadied my shaking. "You can do this. Just stay calm, okay?" He turned to leave.

"Don't go in there," I said. "Let the cops handle it."

"No, I can't. I won't let some stalker come into my house and start trashing the place to scare us. I'm going to catch this prick. Now make the call."

I heard myself sobbing as I entered the number. After only a few seconds, I was connected to emergency services.

Darren disappeared into the darkness as I went through the process of getting the police out to our home. The operator told me to stay calm and remain in a safe place until help could arrive.

Her words were just noise as I found myself going back into our house. I couldn't let Darren do this by himself.

I spotted him at the foot of the stairs. He hadn't gone too far yet. He saw me coming in and tried to wave me away. I shook my head and ignored his frustration.

"I told you to stay out there."

"I told you I couldn't do that."

"Fine," he said. "Just stay out of my way. I might have to use this thing." He held up the pistol.

"I hope not." A second later, another thud hit the floor upstairs. We could almost feel it vibrating through the ceiling above.

The noise hastened Darren forward. I followed.

We moved silently upstairs, as if we were intruders in our own home. I knew the police wouldn't be here in time to stop Darren from confronting our unwanted guest, so I tried to formulate a quick plan in my head.

I couldn't sort my thoughts out, though. I felt like I was heading into a trap, that a killer was waiting for me at the top of the steps. I could picture a loaded gun pointed at the back of my head, seconds away from splattering my brains all over the carpet.

Then suddenly, we were at the top. Darren swept his pistol left and right. The last noise we heard sounded like it was coming from our bedroom.

Tilting his head toward the door, Darren told me he was going to enter the room and face the man who had been tormenting us.

We approached the half-open entry. We were both wearing slippers we kept stored by the back door, now ruined by the light snowfall outside. There hadn't been enough time to slap on anything better.

I tried to ignore the mess our slippers were making on the carpet and focused on what might happen inside our bedroom. Instead of some much-needed sex between a stressed-out couple, the room would now be the scene of something sinister. I couldn't imagine any other outcome.

Darren raised the pistol as we reached the threshold to our room. He kept one arm free to push the door the rest of the way open. When he pressed on the wood, it creaked and groaned. The noise disrupted the quiet night air. I cringed at the thought that whoever was inside would hear our approach.

There was no turning back.

Darren entered the dark room, gun first. He stepped farther in and left my sight.

"Darren, wait," I said after him, so quiet I doubted he heard me.

I tried to follow him, but my legs froze. I couldn't seem to take another step.

"What the hell?" I heard Darren say. "Bessie?"

I let out a sigh of relief as I realized who had been making the noise. The dog had managed to find her way into the house. I stepped into our room with some confidence and took a seat on the bed. Darren squatted down beside Bessie and patted her head.

"You gave us a fright, girl. What are you doing in here, huh?" He turned to face me. "It was the damn dog. You'd better cancel the cops."

"Right, of course," I said. "I'll call them now. Hopefully, it won't cause too many problems if I—"

The back door opened and closed with a slam downstairs. Darren bolted past me and gave chase. Bessie rushed out after him, sensing danger. I sprinted downstairs after them both.

I arrived at the door just as Darren flung it open. As we looked out into our backyard, we saw a figure climb and leap over the back fence, disappearing into the night.

Our breathing grew heavy as we tried to process what had just happened.

Darren faced me with a thick, twisted brow. "Forget about canceling the police."

CHAPTER 34

After

"How did you feel knowing someone had violated your home in that way?" Doctor Shaw asks me.

"About as scared as I could be. Some psycho was in my house while we were there. It's hard to think of a house as your home after someone decides to let themselves in and do God knows what."

"So the police had no clue as to why a man would break into your home while you were both there?"

"None. They figured it was a robbery. According to their report, we interrupted a thief who was about to take our things and nothing more."

"Even with the recent threats?"

I nod. "No one took us seriously."

"That must have been frustrating for you."

I sit in silence for a moment. "Yes. It all went perfectly for our intruder. That night was simply a test of our capability to defend ourselves. It was almost a dry run for something else."

"Something else?"

"You know what I mean."

"No," Doctor Shaw says. "Please clarify."

I let out a huff. The doctor understands I don't want to talk or think about that night, but I can tell she is working up to the point I have so far avoided. James might be trying to achieve the same goal, but it's different with him. We're family.

"You really want to know?" I ask.

"Yes, of course. Please continue."

"Okay," I say, closing my eyes for a moment. "In my head, the something else is the night everything changed."

"What happened?" the doctor asks. She knows the answer, but she is attempting to force it out of me.

"How long do we have left?" I ask, trying to change the subject.

"It doesn't matter," Shaw says. "We can continue the session and go beyond the hour if needed. What's important is that you say what's on your mind."

I cross my arms. "And what if I don't ever want to speak about this? What if I can never allow myself to talk about that night?"

Shaw leans in closer to me, placing her notes down carefully. "Then I cannot see you leaving this place any time soon."

※

I exit the doctor's office trying to be positive. It's hard, though, when Shaw is seeking to persuade me into reliving a moment I wish I could laser out of my brain and replace with anything other than the truth.

Of course, my brain has been trying to destroy that memory, one way or another. I never knew it was possible to block out a horrible event in this way. But as much as my mental breakdown has spared me from that night, it has also landed me in here against my will. All I can hope is that I don't end up making things worse than they already are when James takes me out for the weekend.

※

Dinner is fast approaching. I've gotten used to the early meals, which taste mostly like cardboard. The staff brings around trays of food to everyone, along with our prescribed meds. I swallow them whole and instantly think about the other medication I no longer have access to. The image of Tom follows the thought and makes me want to gag.

I find myself wondering if it actually happened. Did Tom try to force me into screwing him in exchange for some tablets that help me keep away the demons at night? Anything is possible in this place, and that scares the hell out of me.

I finish eating my dinner and head to the bathroom we all share on the day ward. Usually I don't use them unless I'm too far away from my room to bother. A foul smell hits my nose the second I walk into the ladies' room. The cleaners around here do a lousy job of keeping the ward clean, and this row of toilets is no exception.

I've only ever used this lavatory once before today. That first time was no different. Urine covers the floor, poorly cleaned feces stains are smeared over most surfaces, and I'm quite certain someone has thrown up in one of the stalls. I decide to use my bathroom instead and turn around to leave.

"How was your dinner, darlin'?" Tom asks, blocking the exit.

My heart leaps out of my chest. "Fine," I say. I try to walk by him, but he moves toward me and fills the gap with his tall frame.

"Whoa, now. Why the rush? There's still another hour left in the day before we send you crazies off to bed."

I can't help but feel like the lowest possible person in the world when someone like Tom holds a higher standing than me. The thought squashes me down as he continues to leer at me.

"Now, what should we do to kill an hour?" Tom leans in closer to me, propping himself up with one arm on the tiled wall of the bathroom. "A few ideas spring to mind," he says with a sneer.

"I need to go to the toilet in my own room. Excuse me." I attempt to push past, but he shoves me back with one arm. He has physical strength that I can't match. A shudder runs down my spine as I try not to let my frustrations show. Karlo enters my mind again.

"Is there something wrong with the facilities here?" he asks with an open palm.

I know he's just messing with me. None of the staff would ever be caught dead using one of these toilets.

"Don't pout at me. These are some of the best crappers in the hospital. Why don't I show you one?" He grabs me by the shoulder and turns me around. He guides me along with one arm around my body. "Let's check out that stall at the end. That's one of my favorites."

I keep my eyes closed as he walks me forward. Every word out of his mouth is like a razor blade over my skin. I want to scream and run away, but I can't have Tom blab to Doctor Shaw about the tablets without losing my weekend leave with James.

Tom pushes the stall open and walks me inside. "I like this one the most because it has that little bit of extra space." He leans in, his mouth close to my ear as he grips both of my shoulders from behind. "Plus, it's nice and private down here. No one can hear you."

I take a deep breath as I try to prepare myself for what's coming. My mind slips back to the event in flashes. I try to squash down the fractured memories.

How have I let things reach this point? How did I let myself get turned so quickly in the wrong direction? It seemed like only a short time ago that most of my life was on track.

"Now, about our arrangement," Tom says. "The way I see it, you owe me, and I think it's time you paid up."

His hands slide down over my chest and keep going down to my crotch. His rough skin feels like torture through the layers of clothing I'm wearing, pushing me to breaking point before anything major happens. I can't do this.

"Take off your clothes." The order falls out of his mouth so arrogantly, like he's given the command a million times before without consequence. Something inside me snaps as I realize where I am and who I'm about to let violate me.

Tensing my elbow, I duck down and strike Tom in his testicles as hard as I can. His grip lets up as he falls back to the ground and loses all air in his lungs. I don't waste time and step past him as he tries to grab me. He fails to get the slightest hold on my leg, as all his strength has been rerouted to deal with the pain keeping him down. I shake my head and walk away.

"You bitch," he cries, almost shouting. "You're done, you hear me? I'm going to tell the doctors everything. You won't ever leave this fucking place."

I stop and turn to face him. With as much confidence as I have left in me, I walk back toward Tom and come to within a few feet. It takes every ounce of strength I can muster to keep my voice steady. "If you say a word to the doctors, I'll tell them you tried to rape me."

He starts to laugh at my words. "What? You think they'd believe you over me?"

"Maybe not, but a single accusation is all it takes for them to start watching you like a hawk. Even Doctor Shaw can recognize how much of a creep you are. I can see it in her eyes every time you drop me off at her office."

Something flickers across Tom's face as he realizes I'm right. "You bitch. I don't care. You'll still be locked up in this hellhole for longer. It'll be worth the hassle to keep you down in the dirt where you belong."

I shake my head at him without thinking. "You can't kick me down any lower than I already am. From where I'm standing, you're the one who has room to fall."

I walk out of the bathroom without looking back. Tom yells more curse words at me, but I continue out of the room and head for my bedroom.

I don't know if Tom will go to the doctors or not. At this point, I don't care. Anything is better than what he could have done to me. I almost want to go to Doctor Shaw myself to get ahead of everything.

As I reach my room, I decide I will tell her about the pills and Tom as soon as I can. I just have to beat that creepy asshole to the punch.

CHAPTER 35

I don't sleep that night. The events of the day won't leave my mind for a single second. I need to push it all away, but I can't. The only solace I can take from my lack of slumber is in knowing I won't fall into that nightmare world that accompanies my dreams.

The main thought dominating my every attempt to rest isn't Tom but James. He was going to whisk me away from the hospital for the weekend and take me to that place, give me a chance to find out the truth and come one step closer to winning Darren and Jayden back. I can't help but feel like I've lost an opportunity that will never present itself again.

"No," I say out loud as I think of the alternative. If I had let Tom do to me what he had intended, I would have come out of that toilet more broken than I already am. I can't let myself become another one of his victims. God knows how many people are out there thinking about the time he claimed them. The image of his mustache rubbing against my neck forces me out of bed and to my feet.

I head to the bathroom and run the tap. I splash water on my face, trying to clean myself. Even though Tom didn't rape me, I still feel dirty. I almost consider jumping in the shower, but an orderly will hear it running and assume I am up to no good. I don't need more of them coming in here, that's for sure.

❋

Morning comes around after a seemingly endless night. I try to work out if I even slept for a minute. I only remember being awake, so I assume the worst.

Tom doesn't come to unlock my door. I'm not sure whether that's a good thing. He might have the day off, or perhaps he has switched patients with someone else to avoid me. Either way, I'm happy not to see him. I can't assume he won't try it again. People like that can't handle being told no. I never actually said the word, but my actions spoke loud enough for him to receive the message.

My new orderly is quiet and less intimidating. I don't bother to learn his name, though I hope to hell he has swapped with Tom permanently.

I'm guided out to the day room and left to wait for breakfast. I need to get as close as possible to where Doctor Shaw can be found before she heads to her office. The doctors all come into the ward via a secured hall that I'm not allowed to access alone, but I can certainly stand by the locked door that opens onto it and try to catch Shaw's attention through the glass when she arrives.

I press myself against the window when no one is looking and see the doctor at the far end of the hallway. She will be passing by soon enough. A smile finds my lips as I begin to practice what I will say to her.

My muttering is interrupted when a voice behind sends a jolt through my body.

"Well, well, well. What do we have here? Waiting for Doctor Shaw, are we?" Tom stands behind me with his arms crossed. "You're not allowed to be near this door, patient."

I ignore him and focus on Doctor Shaw down the corridor. She's still too far away from me. I almost decide to bang on the glass, but it will capture the wrong kind of attention.

"Please step away from the area, Turner."

"No," I say to him—possibly the worst word to use at this moment.

"What did you say to me?" Tom says through gritted teeth. He's practically hissing.

I turn and face him. "Go away."

A smile breaks across his face. "I don't think I heard you correctly, Turner. Did you just tell me to go away?"

I stare into his wild eyes and once again try to ignore thoughts of Karlo as I stand firm.

"Well?" Tom asks, tilting his head. "Did you?"

I back up against the door I'm not allowed to be near. "No, Tom. I told you to fuck off."

Tom's face clouds over as his brow drills into the bridge of his nose. He stomps up to me and lowers his head down. "What did you say?" he shouts. The noise gets the attention of the other patients. In less than a few seconds, they react and start yelling and moaning.

I hold my ground. Doctor Shaw will be here soon. Tom can't harm me in front of all these people, especially now that his shouting is forcing the other orderlies into the area.

"Tell me again," he roars into my face. "What did you say?"

I can't resist. "I said, fuck o—" I don't finish my insult. A punch of energy rushes through my body and sends me to the floor in half a second. Before I can put two and two together, I see him holding a stun gun in his hand. My body shakes and jitters on the ground beneath his feet.

Tom squats down to me and puts the weapon back into its holster. "Didn't quite catch that one, Turner. Now if you'll excuse me for a moment, I need to speak with Doctor Shaw about a troubled patient."

As I twitch and spasm, I stare back at Tom, trying my hardest not to let him win. But I can't change what has happened. He hit me with enough volts to render me speechless.

All around the day room, the other patients have been whipped up into a frenzy. Orderlies are running around in every direction.

Tom steps over my body and unlocks the door. He goes through and leaves me in the chaos. The door magnetically locks behind him.

I try to roll over and reach for the handle, but a voice stops me. Doctor Shaw is speaking to Tom.

I'm too late.

CHAPTER 36

Later in the day, I find myself in Shaw's office, sitting in the chair opposite her desk. I've recovered from the unknown number of volts that was sent through my body at the hands of Tom. The doctor keeps shaking her head at me as she reads through a report handwritten by the piece of crap who shocked me. I feel a dead weight sitting on my stomach that no amount of false reassurance can dislodge.

"What happened?" Shaw asks me as she continues to huff and shake her head.

I don't think she wants me to answer the question yet. I let a silence form between us, hoping it will somehow protect me from what will happen next.

"Well?" she asks again.

I lower my eyes to the table for a moment. "What does he say happened?"

Shaw's brow tightens. "How about you tell me what you think this report says."

A glimmer of hope washes over me. Tom will have exaggerated the truth beyond belief. If I tell her what really happened—all of it—then Shaw will recognize it is my word against his. It could be enough to make her doubt Tom's credibility. It's not much, but it's all I have to go on.

"This all started a few days ago. I've been having trouble sleeping."

Over the next few minutes, I tell Shaw the truth, including Tom's attempts to blackmail me into sex. The only detail I change is who I got the drugs from. I leave Andrea out of the picture for now. I might still need her. I tell Shaw that Tom provided the diazepam to me all along. She writes everything I say down in her notebook. It almost feels good to get this off my chest—and even better to put the blame entirely on Tom.

"That's a big accusation. Are you quite sure this is what happened? Read through my notes twice to double-check. If you are going to do this, you'd better make it stick. A patient putting in a genuine complaint against a member of staff is not something we take lightly."

Doctor Shaw's reaction tells me I'm not the first patient to complain about Tom and his creepy ways. Even in her short time here the doctor has analyzed Tom from a distance and recognized that he is the kind of person who exploits psychologically unstable people. All I can hope is for her to believe me over him.

"Obviously, we will need to reconsider your weekend trip with James. With everything going on, it might not be the best idea for you to be away from our care for two days."

Her words crush me, but I'm not surprised. I knew the truth would cost me. All I can hope now is that James can forgive me for ruining everything.

"Is there any possibility I can still go?"

Shaw stares at me for a moment. I can see her thinking it through. "Give me some time to consider things first."

"Sounds fair." A sigh of relief escapes my lungs. I realize she can still say no at any moment, but the fact she hasn't put me into isolation—or worse—for this whole mess is a good sign.

"Emma?"

I lift my head up, not realizing it had dropped.

"Are you okay?"

I shift in my seat and gaze away. The question seems so foreign to me. How can I possibly answer it in a few words, the way a normal person does? I know I'm not okay. I know Doctor Shaw knows I'm not okay. So why do we do this little dance where I try to pretend everything is fine while the doctor acts like she doesn't notice how dead I am inside?

"Emma?"

"Yeah?"

"You didn't answer my question. Are you okay?"

"Depends."

"On?"

"Define okay. Am I okay physically after being hit by a stun gun? Yes. Am I okay mentally after being assaulted by the asshole hired to look after me? No. No, I'm not. But I don't want to admit that to you and give you another reason to keep me in here."

Shaw purses her lips as she taps her pen lightly against her chin. "Emma, admitting you are not okay with something that should never have happened in the first place is not the kind of information I'm going to use against you. I'm not here to guarantee your stay at the hospital never ends; I'm here to progress you through the system and get you back to your life."

"My life?" I ask. "I don't know what that means exactly."

"More than you seem to realize. You have James, for one. I can tell from your interactions that he will be a positive force if you are ever to move forward."

"And what about Darren and Jayden? Where are they in this life of mine?" I ask.

Shaw's brow tightens as she gives me that face she always does when she's studying me in detail. "You will see them again."

"How can you be sure? They should have come to visit me by now."

"They aren't ready to see you yet."

I tug at my clothing. What did I do? What happened that night that was so horrible my own husband and son are refusing to see me? "This isn't fair. Why can't they just talk to me about everything?"

Shaw holds up her palm to silence me. "Please, keep your voice down."

My mouth hangs open. I want to say more, but what's the point? Shaw is ready to take my weekend leave away from me as it is. This can't be helping things.

"This is why you need to move forward to that night. If we can find that memory again, I truly believe you will learn to forgive yourself for this event—an event over which you had no control. What happened is not your fault and never will be."

I sit down and run my hands through my tangled hair. I resist the temptation to turn my face away. I know there's no place to hide away from Shaw's eyes.

I start rocking in the chair as a different set of eyes gaze at the back of my head. They belong to Karlo.

"Then why do I feel like everything that happened was my fault?"

Shaw doesn't answer. Instead, she stands from behind her desk and guides me out of the chair and over to the couch. She sits me down and does something no other doctor in this place would ever do, something that takes me completely by surprise. She hugs me.

I want to resist at first and push her away. It's how I am now. But I can't stop everything from coming out. I burst into tears and cry more than I have in the entire time I've been here. I moan into Shaw's cardigan, clutching at it for security like a newborn in the arms of its mother.

"It's okay. Let it all out, Emma."

I melt into Doctor Shaw's hug. After a long while, I stop, wipe my eyes, and apologize for crying. She reassures me that I can cry like that whenever I want to and that it is normal.

After a glass of water and a few tissues, I'm ready for our session.

"Let's pick up from our last talk. I want to hear what happened after the police left."

I shut my eyes as I think back to the break-in.

CHAPTER 37

Before

"This is such bullshit," Darren said as he paced up and down our living room. I was sitting on our couch in the half-lit room, watching my husband try not to lose his temper with the world.

Only a few minutes earlier, the police were sitting opposite me, asking questions about the man who had broken into our house with the knowledge that we were home. They didn't believe that this person could be Karlo, despite the recent threats to our family.

"How could it not be?" I asked the officer.

The officer sighed at me like I was the one who had ruined his night. "There has been a string of break-ins in the area over the past month. We believe this was just another break-in and nothing more."

"Why?"

"Well, ma'am, this man ran away the second he realized you were home. Plus, he took one of your computers."

Our laptop in the kitchen was missing. It was the only thing in the entire house unaccounted for. "We didn't witness him take it."

"But it's not here, is it? We believe you interrupted this guy and scared him off before he could steal much else."

"You can't be serious?" I asked, sounding like my son.

Before the officers headed off, I asked them the one question burning in my mind. "Will you at least check out where Karlo was tonight?"

"We'll see what we can find out, ma'am." The officer nodded. I doubted they would do anything more than grab a cup of coffee on their way back to the station.

I came back to the present as Darren groaned with his hands covering his face. "Can't we have one night where nothing crazy happens?"

I didn't have an answer for him. I felt the same. It's like we were prisoners in our own home. "What are we going to do?" I asked.

Darren shrugged and let his hands slip back to his side. "What can we do? This whole thing is a fucking mess. All I can say is thank God Jayden wasn't here."

I nodded as my stomach turned, thinking about Jayden having to witness what had happened. My head dropped down as something clicked in my brain. "We can't tell him about tonight."

"What?" Darren asked. "Are you serious?"

"Yes," I said, lifting my head up. "Think about it. He'll be terrified of his own home. I know I am. Imagine how a fourteen-year-old boy will handle this."

Darren rubbed at the scruff of his chin. "Fine. I guess it makes sense."

"We just need to keep it together in front of him," I said. "Don't let him figure out that anything bad happened."

"Agreed," Darren said. "But tomorrow I'm taking him down to the range. It's time he learned how to defend himself."

I didn't argue. Instead, I stood and asked, "Can I learn too?"

*

Darren and I climbed into bed so late that I didn't bother to check what the time was. We made sure the doors and windows were locked before we set the alarm system for the first time in months. I had almost forgotten about the expensive addition to our home.

As I settled into bed, I felt like we were huddled inside a fallout shelter, waiting for the bombs to drop. Living in a constant state of alert had me on edge.

All I could think about was the man running through our backyard and leaping over the fence. I described him to the police as of average height and build, wearing a black trench coat and a black mask. Karlo fit the man's build based on the information we had gathered from his Facebook profile. All I could hope now was the police followed up with Karlo, but I had little faith they would do the right thing.

Darren scrolled through his phone. From a glimpse, I could see that he was still working on business matters. These days he did little else. His hobbies had taken a back seat to the job. He probably spent fifteen hours a day working if you included times like now.

I snuggled up to him and fell into his chest. He opened his arm and let me into the perfect spot. I could feel his warmth keeping me safe. His arms were the only place in the world that could do that in an instant.

"Why don't you take a break, honey, and put the phone down?" I asked.

"I can't. I've got too much work to prepare for next week."

"I know you do, but you need to take it easy. With the lawsuit and the contract, you're taking on so much stress. I'm worried it's going to give you a heart attack or something."

"Heart attack? How old do you think I am?"

"You know what I mean. You've been burning the candle at both ends for too long now. I understand it's hard, maybe even impossible to push work to the back of your mind right now, but you have to try. I don't want to have to face a future without you."

"That's not going to happen," he said. "We're going to beat this lawsuit and take that contract back. I'm not letting a couple of jerks ruin what I've busted my back to build."

I smiled up at him. "We'll get through this. I promise. One way or another, we will move forward and think about this time as a tough moment in our lives and nothing else."

"That easy, huh?" he said with a smile.

"That easy."

Darren put his phone down and kissed me. Before I knew it, we were back to where we left off before the noise ruined our night.

CHAPTER 38

In the morning, I woke to Darren snoring heavily. I decided to get up without disturbing him. He needed the sleep more than I did.

After a quick shower, I headed downstairs and started tidying up. I'd let the house go to hell in the last week. Housework had been the least of my priorities lately, but now I could no longer ignore the problem.

An hour passed as I took care of the mess around the kitchen. I fell into one of the seats at the counter when I finished, deciding to do the rest of the house later in the day. After a few minutes' rest, I started to make some breakfast, and then a car pulled into our driveway. I quickly checked through the curtains as my heart leaped out of my chest. Jayden was being dropped off after staying the night at Douglas's house. I could see Douglas's mom in the driver's seat of her minivan. I silently prayed she didn't want to come in and chat, but thankfully she began to reverse. I mouthed a thank you to her as I disabled the alarm.

Jayden came in the door, using his key. I greeted him with a firm hug, not bothering to read his body language first to determine whether he wanted one or not.

"Okay, Mom," he said, pushing me off. "Good to see you too."

"I missed you. Did you have fun?"

"Yeah, it was okay." He dumped his bag down on the clean counter.

"That's nice. Have you eaten? Let me fix you something."

"Mom," he said with both palms raised, "calm down. I've already had breakfast."

"Okay, sorry," I said, feeling a dagger of rejection. He used to love my cooking. "Just making sure my boy grows up strong and healthy."

Jayden tried to escape my embarrassing ways, despite no one else being there. "Where's Dad?" he asked, changing the subject. I absorbed the typical favoritism coming from my son. He loved his father more than he would ever love me. They shared a bond we'd never have.

"He's sleeping in. Can you believe it?"

"No way. Dad taking time off—what's next?"

"Well, funny you should ask. Your father has a surprise for you today."

Jayden stared at me as if I was about to ruin his day. It was a fair enough assumption, considering he was supposed to be grounded.

"It's nothing bad. In fact, I think you might be pretty thrilled about it."

"What is it?" he asked with an overly eager smile. He stood straighter than I'd seen him do so in a long time.

"Your father is taking you down to the range."

Jayden's eyes lit up. "You're shitting me."

"Language."

"Sorry, Mom. I can't believe it. Is he really?"

"Yep. As soon as he's up and ready, you'll be heading down there to practice."

"Hell yeah," Jayden said, pulling his smartphone from his pocket, no doubt bursting to tell his friends.

"Jayden, this is not only for a bit of fun. This is a dangerous thing you are about to learn about."

"I know," he said. "I won't screw around. I promise."

I could make Jayden clean his room without a single complaint right now. He'd been bugging Darren since he was twelve to go to the range.

"Good boy," I said. "Now, are you sure you've had enough to eat?"

"Plenty, thanks. Douglas's mom made us pancakes for breakfast."

"Wow. Lucky you. I was just going to slap together some toast and a glass of juice. Remind me to thank his parents next time we see them. I think I owe them a bottle of wine."

Darren came down the stairs as the light on our coffeemaker flicked from red to green. It's like his brain knew when the precious liquid would be ready to consume.

"Hey, Dad," Jayden said too eagerly. "How did you sleep? Did you and Mom enjoy the movie?"

Darren half smiled as he looked at me. "He knows, doesn't he?"

"Sorry, it slipped out. As you can tell, Jayden is quite excited for the range."

"Is that right, son?"

Jayden nodded his head more times than was needed. I hadn't seen him this keen to do something with either one of us in a long time.

"Well, I don't know if I should take you or not," Darren said as he crossed his arms.

"Please, Dad. You've got to."

"Are you going to stop sneaking out of the house late at night?"

"Yes, I promise. Never again."

Darren pursed his lips for a moment. "Then I guess you'd better go get ready."

Jayden gave us a quiet cheer and rushed off with his backpack.

I smiled while I made breakfast.

"What?" Darren asked.

"Nothing. Just that you're a big softy."

Darren scratched at the back of his head with a coy smile. "We've had a tough week—all of us. I think it'll do everyone some good to let their frustrations out."

"So you don't mind me coming along, then?"

"Mind? Hell, I think it would be hot, seeing you firing a gun."

"Shut up," I joked. "But in all seriousness, I want to learn. With the threats and that guy last night, I don't feel safe anymore."

Darren moved closer to me and wrapped his arms around my waist as I fried up some eggs. "We'll push through this, honey. You'll see."

❀

After breakfast, Jayden practically dragged us out the door, and we took Darren's truck down to the range. When we walked inside the building—somewhere I'd never considered visiting before—it was like I'd strolled into a different world. In the shop, I found more rifles, pistols, and shotguns than my eyes could handle. The store was covered in pro-gun messages and posters from manufacturers.

I didn't usually like to be around guns of any kind, but now there was a need for it. Knowing that Darren had one close by at home, with the knowledge on how to use it, made me feel safer. Him teaching me the basics would only add to that feeling.

We made our way through to the range with Darren acting as our supervisor. He was the only licensed one among us. Jayden would no doubt sign up for a future license after today. I even considered getting one myself, but recognized that I'd never go through with it.

Darren ran through some basics with us before we got out to the shooting area of the range. I didn't think this was required of him, but I'm glad he was taking it so seriously.

We took a slot down the far end, away from three shooters who appeared to know what they were doing. Darren obviously didn't want to distract them.

He guided us through a few additional safety drills now that we were out on the range. I had to keep removing my earmuffs in order to hear him. Of course, this allowed the constant sound of bullets being fired in the room to penetrate my ears. My body jerked with each shot. I'd never realized how loud guns truly were.

I watched as Jayden took his first shot. He missed the close target by a mile, but after a few magazines' worth of Darren's input, he started to hit the mark. When his bullet slammed through the sheet marked with a human body, I hoped that Jayden would never have to take another person's life.

"You're up, honey."

I twisted to Darren, semi-confused. "Sorry?"

"Your turn to shoot."

"Right. What do I do?"

Darren gave me the same advice as he had with Jayden. He stood behind me and squared my body up in preparation to fire. "Try not to be too rigid, but also don't go too floppy. You want the gun to feel like an extension of your arm. Now take a deep breath, and once you've let the air out of your lungs, lightly squeeze the trigger."

I took in a lot of oxygen. I could sense my heart beating like a drum in my chest. I didn't understand why I felt nervous, but I was. I exhaled everything I had and closed my eyes for a moment. When I opened them, I squeezed. The gun fired, kicking back in my hands, but I didn't lose my grip on it. I was stunned to see my first shot had managed to hit the outer section of the target.

"I got it," I said with wide eyes.

"Don't sound so surprised. You listened to what I told you. Now, let's see if you can do that again."

We spent the next couple of hours taking turns shooting. Darren gave us a few demonstrations of his own. He could hit the target every time. His shots stayed close together, all scoring the body in the middle of the chest. He could kill anyone in seconds. Karlo had better watch his back.

*

When we arrived back home, Jayden was over the moon about our trip. I'd never imagined going to the range would bring us all together as a family. The idea made me chuckle, but I couldn't argue with it.

Jayden naturally headed for his room, while Darren and I decided to cuddle on the couch and watch a movie. He'd promised me in the truck that he would take the rest of the day off from the business. I almost felt guilty for making him do it, but he needed the break. Our marriage also needed the time. Things hadn't been exactly stable before or during this recent chapter in our lives.

"Do you want some popcorn?" I asked Darren as he loaded up a selection of movies to choose from.

"Why not?" he said while he planted his feet up on the coffee table. "Can you grab me a beer too?"

"Beer and popcorn coming up," I said. I didn't mind that I was the one to make all the food and drinks most of the time. I could argue about the unfair balance of labor that existed in the household, but what would be the point?

I opened the fridge and pulled out two beers. I didn't regularly drink the stuff, but today I felt like making an exception. When I turned toward the pantry, I saw something out of the corner of my eye, sitting there on the kitchen counter. One of the beers fell from my hand and shattered all over the tiles. Glass fragments scattered across the room, and the sharp odor of the beer hit my nostrils.

"You okay?" Darren shouted from the living room.

"Darren," I managed to choke out. I wanted to scream, but my voice failed.

"What is it?" he asked as he rushed in.

My spare hand shook as I pointed to the laptop sitting on the counter—the laptop that Karlo had stolen. There had been nothing on the counter when we left for the range.

He had been back in our house while we were out. I thought about Jayden upstairs all alone and ran for the stairs. Darren was close behind, obviously thinking the same thing.

CHAPTER 39

"Jayden!" I yelled as I reached his door. Darren was right on my heels. We didn't wait for our son to respond. Instead, we barged into his room to find him sitting on his bed, stunned by our sudden arrival.

"What the hell?" he asked as we rushed inside and checked for signs of an intruder.

"Are you okay?" I asked him as I sat down on his bed and stroked his face.

"Yeah, I'm okay," he said, pulling away. "Why are you guys smashing into my room like this?"

I started to tell him but stopped with an open mouth. I didn't want to freak him out. "We thought we heard you yelling out for help. Sorry, honey. We didn't mean to—"

"What the hell is this?" Darren asked, lifting a corner of Jayden's sheets and uncovering what I did not want to ever discover in my son's room.

"I can explain," Jayden said as we stared at what could only be a box of marijuana. I counted over a dozen joints rolled up, sitting inside a small container. There was more weed wrapped in plastic, along with some papers. There was enough there to send Jayden to prison, by my calculations.

"How could you possibly explain this?" Darren roared. "Are you selling this crap to people?"

"No, it's for a friend."

"Bullshit!"

"I swear, Dad. It's not mine. I'm just holding it for a friend."

"And rolling them up, by the looks of things," I said, all too familiar with the drug. In college, my roommate regularly smoked weed. I'd joined in when things got stressful, but after I graduated I never touched the stuff, let alone helped a friend to sell it. The gravity of the situation hit me like a bus.

"We have to get rid of it, now," I said.

"But Douglas will—"

"Douglas?" Darren asked. Jayden realized his mistake a second too late. "You can forget about ever staying at his house again. What is he? A dealer?"

Jayden tried to speak again, but Darren cut him off. "This is unbelievable. Not only do I have to deal with your bullshit, but now I have to tell his parents that their son is a goddamn drug dealer."

I pulled Darren back for a moment. "Is that the right thing to do? Maybe it's not our place."

"The hell it isn't. I don't want this stuff so close to our home. Not to mention someone who's selling it." He turned back to Jayden. "Are you selling this shit for him?"

"No, Dad. I would never. I was holding it for him. Anyway, his parents already know. They've caught him selling it before. They do random checks of his room, so, from time to time, I hold it for him. Nothing else. I don't sell it, and I don't use it. I tried it once, and it wasn't for me, okay?"

"Not okay, son. None of this is okay. If the cops found this much on you, they'd assume you were the one selling it. You'd be in juvenile detention like that." Darren snapped his fingers inches from our son's face.

Jayden's eyes welled up. He'd been holding back tears the entire time. I pulled on Darren's sleeve. "Come on, let's have a quick chat in the hall."

"Fine," he replied to me, before turning back to Jayden. "Don't go anywhere."

We closed Jayden's door behind us and moved a few paces up the hallway.

"What the fuck?" Darren said, both hands on his head. "Where the hell does this come from, huh? We give that kid everything, goddamn everything, and this is how he repays us?"

"Calm down, honey," I said, placing both hands on his chest.

"I won't calm down. Not while our son is storing drugs for a dealer."

"He made a mistake. A stupid one, but still a mistake. I think the next decision we make could be a crucial one in Jayden's life. We have to tread lightly, understand?"

He huffed. His rage was dying to come out. I could almost smell it. "I'm listening."

I locked eyes with Darren. "Jayden will be punished. He won't be allowed to stay at Douglas's again, that's for sure, but we can't ban him from seeing him."

"What? Are you crazy?"

"Think about it. If we ban him from Douglas, that makes the kid a source of rebellion. Next thing you know, Jayden is selling this crap under our noses. Right now, he's just a stupid friend trying to be loyal. Also, he doesn't like smoking the stuff. I believe him when he says that, so we're lucky with that end of things."

"Lucky? It's been nothing but hell for our family lately. How are we lucky? Tell me how this all plays out. All of it."

I ignored Darren's outburst. "We need to talk to him about this like he's an adult. It's the only way he won't lose respect for us."

Darren screwed up his face as he swallowed his instincts and cast his gaze away from me. "You'd better be right about this. So help me God, if I find a single joint in our house after today…"

I grabbed his bicep. "We can do this. I promise it's the right thing to do."

"Okay," he whispered in defeat. "After you."

I didn't like having to do what I'd just done to Darren, but I understood what happened when you treated someone like an inferior after they'd made a mistake. I didn't want my relationship with my son to reflect the one I had with my brother.

We knocked on the door and waited for Jayden to grant us the all-clear. I walked inside first and saw him with his head lowered down in the same position we'd left him. I couldn't even imagine what was going through his brain at that moment.

In all the chaos, I'd almost forgotten about the laptop in the kitchen. I shifted the thought as best I could and decided to deal with that situation later.

Our son needed us.

We spent the next ten minutes or so talking to Jayden about the dangers of drugs and the position he had put himself in by agreeing to help a friend in such a way. We told him he could still be friends with Douglas, but he needed to inform him that we knew everything. There would be no overnight visits and no more drugs to be stored by Jayden ever again. If we found a single piece of evidence to suggest Jayden was involved in that world again, we'd bypass Douglas's parents and go straight to the police.

"I take it I'm grounded?" Jayden asked.

"Until we say otherwise, yes," Darren said. "Now hand over the weed. It's going down the toilet."

"No, you can't. Douglas says it's worth a lot of money. He'll be pissed. He won't ever talk to me again."

Darren snarled at our son. "You think I give a shit about Douglas losing some money?" He snatched up the box and stomped off before I could at least discuss Jayden's side of things with him. I knew without a doubt that he was rushing to the nearest bathroom.

"Darren, wait," I yelled at him. "Let's talk about this first."

"I'm done talking."

I caught up and tried to pull the box out of his hand. Darren shrugged me off without much effort and raced to the toilet. He stuffed the weed into the bowl, including the joints, and started flushing.

By the time I was within reach, the box's entire contents were in the water. "Why did you do that?" I asked. "We should have discussed it first. What did I say about treading lightly?"

"Forget that. He needs some harsh truths. If you store weed for your friend, there's going to be some consequences."

Jayden stood behind us with tears in his eyes. He didn't need to say a word. We both realized we'd ruined his friendship with Douglas forever.

CHAPTER 40

After

Doctor Shaw stares at me, nodding her head.

"What's interesting?" I ask.

"It's nothing," she says as she scribbles away.

"Okay," I reply. She's keeping it all to herself. I know exactly what she is finding interesting. I caught my son holding drugs. I later get busted using drugs. I'm sure the doctor has some wild theories, but I don't want to hear them.

"So, what about the laptop?"

"What about it?"

"How did it find its way there? You all assumed the intruder had stolen it."

"He did steal it. Trust me."

"Maybe you misplaced it. Maybe you're remembering the story wrong."

"How could I misremember that?"

Doctor Shaw leans in closer again. "You don't remember the event. How can you trust any other memory from that time?"

I know that she knows what happened next. Surely this is a test. In my mind, what happened in the lead-up to the event is as clear as day, until...

The doctor continues without an answer from me. "This kind of post-traumatic stress can alter a lot of things: your grip on reality, your memories of key moments, even your personality."

"If that's the case, then why are we bothering with this? Why not lock me away and drug me the hell up, so I don't remember who I am?"

"That's not what we do here."

"No, what you do is let orderlies violate the patients in exchange for their silence."

Shaw raises her voice. "Tom will be investigated and dealt with. You have my word. Now, back to the issue at hand. We bother because the only way for you to move forward is to come to grips with what happened that night. I know the truth, and so do the police. All that is left is for you to face it. Then we can begin the healing process."

I scoff. "Healing, huh? How do I heal when I know I did something so horrific that neither my husband or my son wants to see me again?"

Shaw allows a lungful of air out and lowers her head. She refocuses on me. "You will see them again."

I hear her words, and they sound like a load of crap. "You keep saying that, but I don't believe you. I did something unforgivable; I know it."

"You were forced to do something that night that no one should ever have to face in their life. You are not to blame for what happened."

"If that's true, then why do I feel this way?"

*

I leave the session wanting to die on the spot. Shaw is pushing me along her path whether I like it or not. I don't know if she's the right person for me to go down this road with. I'd rather take it with James, especially if Darren and Jayden are still not ready to see me.

The whole mess has me feeling completely powerless again. Whether it's an orderly trying to have his way with me, or a doctor forcing me to relive a moment in my life I would preferably have cut out of my brain, I hold no control.

What Tom tried to do to me still springs to mind. I can't let that ever occur again. I need to find something to protect myself with.

I think about the doctor's goals for me. She wants me to run through her program and release this memory. She will cripple my mind over and over until I shut down. I'm better off allowing those memories to flow with James. I feel more confident that his presence will hold back such a negative result.

I try to force any dark thoughts out of my head. I don't want to fall victim to this place and become a permanent patient, but I'm losing the fight.

What do I have to fight for anyway? A husband who will never look at me again. A son who will despise me forever. And who could blame them? I did something that destroyed our bond.

I arrive in the day room. With the drug problem on my record, the orderlies are now watching me like a hawk. A new orderly—not Tom—is staring at me wherever I go. I no longer have the limited freedom I once enjoyed. Now, I'm nothing but a dog on a leash, but I need something, anything, to protect myself from these people who can't be trusted. I just have to be willing to find it.

CHAPTER 41

That night, I attempt to sleep. Nightmares or not, I need rest. I get maybe thirty minutes here and twenty minutes there as my brain runs into overdrive. I am so tired at this point I believe I could die. I don't know if that's even possible, but it sure feels like it.

When morning arrives, I head out into the day with a slow shuffle. I'm dead on my feet, and no one cares. I see Andrea outside in her usual spot. She gives me a nod. I take it Tom didn't say anything about her, and neither did I. Her dealing can continue.

I spot the new orderly nearby, doing his job and nothing else. He has been tasked with following and watching me as if I'm about to explode. He looks like he could break me in two with a few fingers if I decided to pull any stunts—not that I would. Not until I have what I need.

I almost feel sorry for the hulking mass of a man, then something twigs. If I present myself as the most boring subject possible, maybe he'll slip up. Maybe he'll decide the directive given to him was overkill.

I sit down in a seat in the day room and start meditating. Without Tom lurking around, I can achieve some level of relaxation. I don't bother to wonder what happened to the bastard, assuming he's on some sort of forced leave during the investigation.

A calm fills me after thirty minutes of controlled breathing. I don't look at the orderly. I want him to think he isn't needed, that I'm a threat to no one.

My session with Shaw is not until later in the day. I have plenty of time to mess with this guy. I open my eyes a slither, checking in my peripheral vision to see if he is still there.

With my eyes closed, I focus on my hearing and wait for his leather shoes to creak. I do a quick visual check and see him heading off to the bathroom. Now is my chance. I dash outside as quickly as I can without raising any alarm bells, and find Andrea alone. After what happened with Tom, I have found a bit of fight that I didn't think still existed within me. I head straight toward her with a tilted head.

"Well, if it isn't Miss—"

Whatever insult Andrea had planned is snuffed out by my hand around her throat. I squeeze tight and pull her aside out of sight of anyone, patient or staff. I shove her against the wall and then let go.

"What the hell?" she coughs out.

"Shut up and listen, bitch," I say while keeping one arm on her shoulder. I give her a stare I wish I could have given to Tom. She sees the glint of crazy in my eye and keeps quiet. "I need you to do me a favor. I figure you owe me one after the whole Tom thing."

"Okay," Andrea mutters.

"I need a pair of scissors. Sharp surgical ones."

"What? Are you insane?"

I half chuckle at her poorly phrased question. "Haven't been officially declared nuts just yet, but there's plenty of time left. And besides, I figured you'd rather do this for me than watch your little drug operation come to a screaming halt."

"You wouldn't."

"Wouldn't what? Tell the doctors about the pharmacy you've been running in this place? I know your primary distributor is out of action, but I'm sure you have more Toms out there keeping things going. Just one word from me will point those in charge in the right direction, particularly now that they know I've been taking smuggled diazepam."

Andrea tries to move away, but I pin her back against the wall.

"You'll die if you do that," she spits, "and it won't be me that kills you, but someone from the outside. I'm just a dealer in here. This shit comes from an operation bigger than you could ever realize."

"You think I care if someone kills me?"

Andrea squirms. "Then they'll go for your brother instead."

"Is that right? But who do you think they'll kill first? I'd say the dealer inside who failed to stop me from spoiling everything."

Her eyes widen. I've got her. Even if she works out I'm bluffing, she has no choice but to comply. The alternative is too risky. I hold her gaze as long as I can without faltering.

"Fine. You win. I'll get you your damn scissors, psycho."

"Good. You have until the end of the day to bring them to me. I don't care what you need to do or who you have to bribe." I release her and walk back to the day room.

"Jesus, you belong in here," she calls to me as I leave.

I pause for a moment and turn back. "Maybe I do."

Andrea screws up her face and mutters something under her breath. I ignore her and head inside. The orderly hasn't returned yet, so I resume meditating in the same spot.

I hear the creak of his shoes a few minutes later and let a smile form on my lips.

CHAPTER 42

My therapy session is the last one booked for the day. My new orderly commands me to follow him. I do as instructed and realize we are heading back to my room. I wonder if Andrea is making a move to take me out.

"Look under your mattress, at the top left-hand corner," he says when we arrive.

I slowly walk over to my bed and do as I'm told. I feel around and grab something wrapped in tissues. It's a sharp pair of scissors.

"Don't lose them," he says bluntly.

"Tell her thanks," I reply. He ignores me and heads for the exit. "Time for your session."

I follow the orderly and wonder if there is anyone in this hospital who isn't corrupt.

*

I sit in Doctor Shaw's office and wait for her to return from the front desk. The orderly—whose name I still don't know—stands in the door like a statue. When Shaw returns, she dismisses him with one of her looks. It's obvious she doesn't trust the staff. Nor should she.

"Sorry about that, but I have something for you." She places an envelope on the desk in front of me. I reach out and pick up the paper, but Shaw stops me from opening it.

"Before you peer inside, I want to go through our session."

"What?" I ask, feeling annoyed by whatever tactic she is employing.

"Today will tell me if you are ready to read this letter."

I let out my breath and toss the envelope on the desk. "Best get to it then."

"Yes, indeed. Unfortunately, we are short on time by about ten minutes."

I plonk myself down on the couch and allow the comfort to take over. I would kill to be able to sit here all day long, instead of hanging out in the day room.

"How are you sleeping?"

"You serious?" I scoff. "I'm not sleeping. Hence the desperate need for the diazepam."

Shaw ignores my response. "How did you used to sleep in the past?"

"Mostly fine, up until that night."

"What about the week before the event?"

I rub my face in thought. "You know, not great. I missed a few nights."

"Did you take anything? Sleeping pills?"

I sigh. "Diazepam."

"Did it help?"

"Yes. It was the only thing that worked. Without it, I would just wake up in terror."

"It can be quite useful when properly administered. Of course, it's not a solution to the problem, merely a temporary fix which will eventually fail."

"What are you saying?"

"I'm trying to understand why you haven't been sleeping in here."

My mouth falls open. "Have you seen the facilities? It's not exactly a welcoming place. It's winter, and I only have a few sheets and blankets. All I can hear are people moaning and screaming all night long. Stress or not, it isn't the ideal place to rest."

Shaw writes something down. It irks me no end when she does this. I wish I could steal an unfiltered printout of her thoughts. At least then I would know what she thinks of me.

"It's obvious to me that your inability to sleep is stemming from something more than your environment."

"What do you mean?"

"That you are having nightmares."

I don't look her in the eye. "I keep having screwed-up dreams about that night."

"What if I prescribed you some diazepam for the short term? Do you think you could work on taking some to aid you in a better sleep cycle?"

I almost lose the ability to speak. "Yes."

"I'll get that sorted for you as soon as possible."

"Thank you," I say, unsure what has just happened.

"That's all it takes, Emma. There's no need to sneak around getting drugs from crooked orderlies. If you have a problem, tell me first. We are here to help."

I think about the surgical scissors in my bed. Maybe I don't need them at the moment, but having the protection from any other Toms out there gives me a sense of control that nothing else in this place could ever provide.

Shaw is studying me, waiting for an answer.

"I'm sorry. I guess I got swindled a little by Tom."

She nods at me. "There are people in here who will try to exploit you. Regrettably, the department is always low on skilled staff, so we have to be a little lax when it comes to new hires. It's not ideal, but until we can land the budget we need, things aren't going to change any time soon."

I don't respond to her slight rant, nodding instead to show how much I agree with her every thought.

"Shall we begin?" Shaw asks.

I close my eyes for a moment. "I'm ready."

CHAPTER 43

Before

Jayden was beyond pissed at us. I asked myself how we could be the ones to feel guilty when he was the fourteen-year-old boy caught with drugs. He locked himself away in his room and refused to come out. Darren tried to barge in, but I stopped him, saying we needed to give Jayden some space.

We took the conversation downstairs, checked every door and window for signs of another break-in, and swept up the broken glass. After ten minutes of double-checking the doors and windows, we headed back to the kitchen. Darren and I stared at one another, the returned laptop between us. I decided not to press him about the choice he'd made to flush the drugs down the toilet. It might have been the right call. What was bugging me more than anything else now was the laptop that had been placed back in our home through locked doors.

"What are we going to do about this?" I asked.

Darren shrugged as he opened the fridge and grabbed a fresh beer to replace the one he hadn't got to drink. He popped the lid and took a swig without asking if I wanted anything. "There's nothing we can do," he said once he caught his breath.

"What about the cops?"

"What about them? They won't believe us. There's no sign of forced entry. Whoever did this has a key and put that right there where we would find it."

"So, what? Are they screwing with us? What is the point?"

Darren held his arms out, beer in hand. "Same damn reason it's been all along: they want me to pay out for Victor's accident."

"Maybe we should," I said as I toyed with the laptop.

"What?"

"Think about it. Our lives have been getting worse by the day. These people seem to know what they're doing. I'm starting to suspect that Victor's family are either criminals or psychopaths. What else are they planning?"

Darren took a massive gulp of beer. "Not they. He."

"Karlo?" I asked. "You think this is all just him?"

"Has to be. He's the only one with a record. The rest are squeaky clean. I had someone look into them for me. Didn't find a single thing out of the ordinary."

"Doesn't mean they aren't into some illegal things, though. How can you be sure that Victor didn't ask Karlo to do all of this?"

"I guess I can't, but he fits the profile—he's been to jail for aggravated assault, breaking and entering, fraud, of all things, and a whole bunch of other misdemeanors. I think he's the black sheep of the family, going behind Victor's back. Of course, the others are pissed at me, but I don't think they're capable of this kind of thing."

I realized in all the excitement with Jayden that we hadn't checked if it was working or not. I opened the lid and found a note on the keyboard:

"TURN ME ON."

"Jesus," I said, holding up the paper to Darren.

"What now?" Darren said as he slammed his beer down on the counter and rushed around to my side of the island to see the screen. "Turn it on. I want to see what this prick has for us."

I pressed the power button with a shaky hand. I took a moment to center myself as the system loaded up from hibernation. Darren was standing beside me with crossed arms. I didn't want to look at the display, but I forced myself to.

I tapped in our basic password and cursed myself for using something so damn easy: "jayden." I knew it was weak, but it was simple for me to remember.

The login screen faded away to the desktop. Our background had been changed, and all of the icons except one had been removed. The wallpaper had a message written on it that said, "Play," with an arrow pointing to a video file.

"Oh God," I moaned. "I can't look."

"Screw that; we're watching this. And then we're going to the cops again." Darren took over and opened the video file. It started playing after a short delay.

A lone man sat at a table in a room devoid of detail. It had concrete walls and a single light source flickering above. It could have been anywhere. Worse still, the man was wearing a black hoodie and a black balaclava with a white skull painted over the material. His eyes held no color and appeared black in the video. He was either using contacts or he'd been sent straight from hell.

My hand found my open mouth as I staggered back from the image. The man sat calmly at the table with his gloved hands folded together. "Hello, Turner family," he said. His voice had been modulated beyond recognition.

"Turn it off," I said.

"No," Darren replied. "We're watching this."

The man continued, "As I am sure you are aware, things have not been business as usual in the Turner home. If I were your neighbors, I'd be wondering why the police keep coming to your house. They must think you are criminals."

Darren planted both hands firmly on the counter and leaned in closer. Either he wasn't intimidated or he was trying to convince himself this man wasn't serious.

"Turners, you have only one choice. One way to stop what is happening to your family." The man moved in closer to the camera. "Have you worked out what it is? Yes, money. As you know, compensation is in order, and only a payment made in cash will stop the madness. And I'm not talking about some out-of-court settlement."

"Asshole," Darren muttered to himself.

"Two hundred thousand dollars cash is owed for what you did. You have forty-eight hours to get it together by whatever means you have at your disposal. You will soon be told where to bring the money. Once this is done, your debt will be wiped clean. Simple as that. But if you do anything stupid, like calling the police, then no sum of money will be able to recover that debt. A different course of action will be required to make things right. And trust me, you don't want that."

The man fell silent for a moment as he stared at us with his lifeless eyes. His hand dropped down out of sight and came flying back up with a hunter's knife in his grip. He then slammed the blade into the wooden table.

"Don't think any of this is for show, Turners," the man said as the knife glimmered in the light. "I will kill all three of you if needed."

The video cut out.

I stumbled backward and found myself unable to utter a single sound. I turned back to the screen to see Darren frozen in the same position over the laptop. He pressed play and watched the video again.

CHAPTER 44

"What the hell are we going to do?" I repeated for the third time.

Darren kept watching the video, over and over. It's as if he thought there was some cryptic message I wasn't seeing.

"Darren?"

He silenced me with a finger while keeping his eyes glued to the screen. I had no choice but to wait for the video to finish again.

"Please, Darren. Talk to me."

He stood straight and shut the lid on the laptop. He turned to me and saw how shaken I was. I couldn't hide behind a wall of bravado. My eyes were full of tears, my hands trembling. "What are we going to do?" I asked again.

"I won't pay Karlo," he said, shaking his head. "Not a cent."

"But—"

"I'm not paying him, you hear me?" Darren shouted. "He thinks he can intimidate us."

"Yes, he can," I yelled. "You saw what I saw. This isn't a joke. We're talking about a psychopath who was involved in organized crime."

Darren stomped away from me. "That's all bullshit. He's no mobster; he's just trying to scare us. Why should we lose everything for that?"

I followed him as he climbed the stairs. I didn't know where he was going. All I hoped was that Jayden hadn't heard a thing.

"I'm not going to pay them," Darren said. He rushed into our room and stormed into the walk-in closet. I caught up as he shifted a few items around on the top shelf to reveal a gun safe. I'd never seen it before and had no idea if he'd had it installed after he'd bought the gun I saw in his truck, or if it had been there all along. Now wasn't the time to find out.

"What are you doing?" I asked.

"Getting prepared. These people think they can threaten my family. Well, I think it's time I visited Victor."

"Are you insane? Karlo will kill you. At best, Victor's lawyer will get you on record intimidating a man who is suing you."

"No, they'll back off. They'll stop doing this shit to our family. I know it."

I moved in close to Darren and placed a hand on his tense shoulder. He flinched. I realized he was just trying to find the courage to protect his family.

"Honey, it's okay. You don't have to do this. We can pull this money together and pay them off."

"I can't—"

I cut him off with a hug from behind. He stopped opening the safe and grabbed hold of my arms around him.

"It's okay," I said. "We'll push through this."

"What if we can't?" he asked.

I could hear the tears in his voice. The facade he had been putting up started to crumble. The real Darren was coming out.

"We'll send him the money and be done with this hell forever."

"What about the business? I'm going to have to rip it to pieces to do this."

"We'll worry about that later. What's important is that we do what he asks. Otherwise…" I trailed off as I thought about Jayden. If anything happened to him because of all this madness, I would never forgive myself.

"Okay," Darren said. "We have forty-eight hours to get the two hundred thousand together."

"We better get started," I said. "What's the best way to do this?"

Darren and I spent the afternoon in the kitchen, gutting the business. Our personal savings could only cover about ten grand if we left ourselves with enough to stay off the streets. The business would be completely ruined after we'd dissolved the accounts, and my salary alone couldn't handle our current expenses.

"You won't like this," Darren said, "but I've got wages for the month coming up. I can drain the account. It means the guys won't be paid, but we can worry about that later. Hell, they can form a queue and jump in line with Victor for all I care."

I chuckled at the terrible joke. What else could I do? Our life was falling apart around us. We were going to have to cook the books to make it seem like Darren had made a huge mistake and sent the business bankrupt to cover everything up.

We spent the next two hours going through every possible account we could shift around and drain. Every liability we owed would be used to make up the difference. I felt sick taking cash that wasn't strictly ours, whether it belonged to the IRS or our own employees, but Karlo had given us little choice.

My mind drifted around as I wondered if Karlo really was working alone, or if he had gotten as many people in the family involved as possible. It seemed to me that everything that'd happened so far was too much for one man to handle. It made me sick to my stomach to think that Victor could be in on something like this, but I guess becoming a cripple overnight could do things to a person's way of thinking.

"That should do it," Darren said. "We just need to convert this all to cash."

"How?" I asked, somewhat ignorant.

Darren scratched at the back of his head and gave me a grin that only came out when something not quite right was on the cards.

"I know a guy. He'll give me the equivalent in cash and transfer it to an offshore account. He'll then cook the books for us so we can declare the business bankrupt. Beats me how he does it, but we lose ten percent for the service. I've accounted for that, though."

I shook my head and looked away. It dawned on me that I should have been asking him how he knew such a person, but we were well beyond that point in the process. I figured Darren had wanted to have the option of liquidating the business illegally, for reasons I could never know. But how could he not tell me about the contingency? Was he afraid of my reaction? Or just ashamed?

More doubt circled in my head as I wondered what Darren had put his team through in the past. Victor had been there since day one. Were there any projects he'd worked on without being paid what he was owed while Darren pretended everything was fine? I didn't want to have such doubts about my husband running through my head, but Darren was giving me little choice in the matter.

I had thought I knew my family. I had thought Darren would never be involved with a criminal. I had thought Jayden would never be involved in the selling of drugs. But there I was, clueless about the world.

"I'll give the guy a call and get the ball rolling," he said as he headed for the front door.

"Where are you going?" I asked as I squinted at a piece of paper covered in figures.

Darren was already playing with his cell, tapping away to drown me out.

"Honey?"

His eyes leveled with mine, both brows raised. "Ah, sorry. This guy doesn't like to be screwed around. I need to be ready to meet him with the figures ASAP. I don't know when I'll be back."

"But what about Jayden and me? We'll be here by ourselves while those psychos stalk the house."

Darren's head dropped down as he realized what I was saying. "Shit," he muttered.

I wanted to tear strips off him for thinking of us last in the entire ordeal, but there was no point. He had too many problems on his plate.

"Maybe you guys can come with me. It won't be exactly safe—"

"But we will be together," I said, finishing the sentence he should have been saying.

"Right. Exactly. Get Jayden ready. I'll contact this guy."

"What do I tell him?"

Darren looked at me with narrow eyes. "Who?"

"Jayden!" I shouted.

"Right. Nothing. Just tell him we have an important business meeting, and he is not to be trusted on his own. Make it part of the punishment, I guess."

"Okay," I said as I moved for the stairs. I tried not to let the lies I was about to force upon my son nauseate me.

CHAPTER 45

Jayden came along with Darren and me without argument. Typically, such a request would be met with complaints before, during, and after, but now, well, Jayden had nothing left to do but silently hate us for ruining his friendship with a drug-dealing teenager.

Darren drove us across town to a small diner we hadn't visited in a long time. He asked us to stay in the truck while he met with his contact inside. He didn't want Jayden to overhear what was happening. I agreed to stay in the truck, though I would have preferred to wait inside the diner, closer to Darren. I didn't feel safe out in the parking lot.

I distracted myself by trying to work out which of the few customers in the diner was Darren's guy. There were three men to choose from: a stocky, balding man wearing a cheap suit and reading the paper; a thirty-something laborer ordering some food; and a big hulk in the corner with a shaved head and tattoos on his neck. If watching movies had taught me anything, it's that the guy with the tattoos was too damn obvious. My eyes swept back to the quiet businessman, and sure enough, Darren sat down with the criminal hiding in plain sight.

"Knew it," I muttered to myself.

"Knew what?" Jayden asked from the back seat.

"Nothing," I replied, looking away from Darren.

"Why is Dad meeting with some guy inside a diner?"

"He's a potential client," I said. "He might be able to help your father out with a new contract."

"Okay," Jayden said, sounding somewhat convinced. "So why meet here? And why did we have to come along?"

I swiveled in my seat and crossed my arms. I gave Jayden the mom stare to push him off the scent of the meeting. "Was that a complaint?"

"No, Mom, I—"

"It better not be, because I can tell you now, your father and I are not happy with what we found in your room. I wouldn't be surprised if a discussion about military school came up over dinner tonight, you get me?"

"I'm sorry, Mom. Happy to be here. Dad's got my full support."

I gave my son a forced smile laced with sarcasm. "Well, thank you, Jayden. It means the world to us both that you are always so eager to please."

He let out a fake chuckle. "You know me, Mom. Just part of the team."

I shook my head as I turned away from his nonsense. I didn't know where I'd pulled that BS from, but it worked.

Jayden went back to playing with his cell. We'd taken away his Internet, but the device could still run some of the apps he'd installed. I'd rather he did that than question why his father was meeting with some dodgy businessman at a diner of all places.

I stared back at Darren and wondered how he'd found this guy. How many shady contacts were hidden away in his cell? I tried to focus on getting through the day unscathed, but every second I watched Darren interact with this criminal only made me lose more faith in my husband.

*

Fifteen minutes later, Darren rushed back to the truck with a small bag he hadn't walked into the diner with. Jayden's mouth opened to ask what was in the bag, but I shot him a glare that silenced him before he got the chance.

Darren said hello to both of us and started up the car.

"How did your meeting go, Dad? Do you think he will give us a new contract?"

"Contract?" Darren asked.

"Yes, honey," I said. "A new building contract to replace the one we lost."

"Oh, right. Yeah, it sounded promising, Jayden. Things will be okay soon enough." Darren stared off into the distance as he gripped the steering wheel.

"Dad?"

Darren didn't respond. I gave him a subtle nudge to bring him back to reality.

"Sorry. What is it, buddy?"

"Can we have burgers for dinner? I know I'm grounded and all that, but I think we've all had a long day and could use a treat. I'll even pay."

Darren and I shared a look. We both smirked with surprise at Jayden's offer.

"Sounds good to me," Darren said, "but we'll pay. Keep your pocket money for another day."

"Thank you for the kind offer, Jayden," I said. "I think it's an excellent idea."

Suddenly, I felt like we were a family again. Even though Jayden was grounded and shouldn't be given the luxury of fast food, I was happy to take a moment to celebrate securing the money needed to pull ourselves closer to the light at the end of the tunnel. Plus, we hadn't exactly been a functional family lately. The dinner would help to bring us together for a change.

                                      *

We grabbed some burgers and fries on the way home and arrived back at the house a few minutes later. Darren's cell chirped away, and he answered it. "Darren Turner."

Jayden and I were already getting out of the truck. I had the bag of food in my hands, enjoying the warmth. I turned to Darren and saw him shake his head at me before glancing toward Jayden. I received the message.

"Take this and wait by the front door," I said to Jayden. He agreed without complaint and grabbed the food. I climbed back into the truck to see Darren still on the phone. His face dropped as he lowered the cell from his ear.

"What is it?" I asked.

"Our contact. He knows we have the money."

"Okay," I said, nodding away as I took a deep breath. "He's been watching us. But at least he realizes we have the money now. What's the next step?"

"He wants to meet… tonight. He wants to collect at midnight."

I closed my eyes and tried not to freak out. Everything about the past few days had felt unreal until that moment, as if I were just watching someone else's life unravel on TV.

I opened my eyes and stared at Darren.

"Okay. We can do this."

CHAPTER 46

After

"Were you confident things would work out?" Doctor Shaw asks as my brain snaps back to the present.

"Not really. But Darren needed that projection of confidence. We all did."

Shaw stares at me as she taps the tip of her pen on her chin over and over. The habit is starting to irritate me.

"Tell me what went through your mind when Darren said he knew of a criminal who could liquidate your business illegally for cash."

I sigh as I lean back on the couch and cover my face with both hands. I am reaching that point in the session where I can no longer stand the doctor pulling apart the relationships in my life. "How do you think I felt?"

"I'm asking you. That's what this is all about."

I fight the urge to curse out loud as I remember Shaw hasn't told me if I'm going on the weekend trip with James or not. "Okay," I say.

"Take your time. We still have another ten minutes."

I glance at the clock on the wall. Its incessant ticking drives me insane on a good day. It's a constant reminder that Doctor Shaw is not my friend but a worker on the clock. She's like every other doctor in here, waiting for five to come around so she can get the hell out of this hole and drive home to a fancy apartment or whatever it is a highly paid doctor lives in.

My eyes fall to Shaw. I give her my session smile and continue. "At the time, I didn't have the ability or luxury to fully analyze why my husband would have such a man on standby, ready to turn his business into a sack of illegal cash. Sure, it made me lose some faith in him, but we had a job to do."

"And now?"

"Now, I think that this shady contact couldn't have been the only one Darren used from his list. It makes me question if Darren was cutting corners with the business before that night."

Doctor Shaw leans forward. I continue.

"Like I said, I couldn't figure this out at the time, but something is clear to me now: Victor's case against us had to have been legitimate. His injuries were most likely the result of Darren's neglect. Victor knew what his boss was like and expected him not to pay up."

Shaw scribbles away, writing down what she apparently didn't know about Darren. I guess the file she has for my family and me isn't quite complete after all.

"So to answer your question, my mind was focused on getting these people off our backs and nothing else. Darren's questionable behavior could wait until another day."

"Okay, Emma. I think we'll leave it there for the moment. I have something I would like to discuss with you before our time runs out."

Doctor Shaw stands from her seat and places her notes down. She takes off her glasses and puts them in her pocket. Something serious is about to come out of her mouth, and I don't know if I should prepare for the worst.

"What is it?" I almost whisper.

"You are ready for that letter."

I had forgotten about her mysterious letter. I take a slow moment to open it up.

"It's about your weekend leave with James."

My heart skips a beat. I think about what will happen if I can't go. James will be devastated. This trip seems more important to him than it does to me. As much as I don't want to face the moment that destroyed my relationship with my family, I know in my soul that it must be done.

I glance up to Shaw's eyes like a puppy waiting for punishment and hold my breath.

"I'm giving you two days with James away from this place. You just need to sign it."

"Thank you, doctor," I say as I bounce a little on the couch.

"On one condition," Shaw says over the top of my excitement.

"Anything. You name it."

"You are to check in with the hospital. I want to have a five-minute conversation with you each morning and again before I leave for the day so I can get a reading on your state of mind. Do you agree to those terms?"

I don't. The thought makes me feel like a child, one who needs Mommy's permission to tie her shoes. But I can't say what I'm thinking. I try, instead, to focus on my lies.

"I agree," I say, holding my hand to my heart for emphasis. The doctor gives me a scan with her therapist's eyes, probing for deception. I do my best to persuade her.

"Very well. I will contact James and let him know that the weekend away is on. I think some time alone together will be helpful for you. A supportive network of family and friends is an important part of your recovery."

"Thank you, Doctor Shaw," I say without thinking. "It means a lot to me." I go to hug her, but I stop halfway over. I still feel uncomfortable touching another person during my time in the hospital. Doctor Shaw seems to be the only one I can handle embracing.

"It's okay, Emma," Shaw says with open arms.

I accept the offer and wrap my hands around her. I sink into her chest and feel secure in an instant. The hug is only brief, but I could let it go on forever.

*

I head back to the dining area for a meal. After I finish eating, I am given my usual meds, along with some diazepam, as promised by the doctor. The stuff goes down a treat. Within fifteen minutes, the world starts to fuzz over. Suddenly things aren't that bad. My problems are problems, but they don't feel like their usual nagging selves. I decide to head back to my room in preparation for sleep, for once feeling almost at ease in this place.

When my head hits the pillow, the darkness swallows me whole, even though the light in my room is still on. Nothing can keep me awake now.

I fall asleep not worrying about tomorrow. No nightmares can haunt me for now.

CHAPTER 47

I wake up in the morning without having had a single disturbance in the night. If I had a lifetime supply of those beautiful diazepam pills, I swear I could leave this place in a heartbeat and never have to face the truth. I could disappear from the world and live out my days away from the lives I ruined. I'm almost at peace with the idea until I remember those lives: Darren and Jayden's. No amount of calming peace can ever replace them.

In a flash, I realize that James will be picking me up today to drive me back to where it all happened. My mind wanders to Darren and Jayden. Will I run into them when we are out of the hospital? I'm tempted to ask James if he'll take me home for a few hours to see them despite everything.

My fantasy is blown away like sand in the breeze. I don't want to face that night, but I have to. To face this event that I can't remember, the one that had pulled me to pieces, one string at a time. Fear consumes me as I imagine what I will do when I find out the truth. Only the thought of having James by my side keeps me sane.

My door clicks open a few minutes later. Tom is still nowhere to be seen. I doubt he'll ever be back. I figure Doctor Shaw suspected as much as I did and asked the powers up the top to do a full investigation into the allegations. There must be enough people in this place who know something about Tom to make him go away. At the very least, we could keep him from working at this hospital. I can only hope he is fired and possibly arrested for the numerous sexual assaults he has no doubt committed over the years.

I head to breakfast past an arguing bunch of patients. There's always a debate going on in this place. It's enough to drive a healthy person crazy. I chuckle. I should never think of myself as one of these people, but time does that to every individual locked in the facility. You come in assuming the world is wrong about you, that you couldn't be the one with the problem. Unfortunately, it doesn't take long to realize that it isn't normal to have a full-blown mental breakdown and repress an entire night of your life.

After I finish my breakfast and swallow my pills, I spot James out of the corner of my eyes. Doctor Shaw is accompanying him. They are both smiling, and I can't help but grin back.

"Hey, Emma," James says, with a cheeky grin I haven't seen in far too long. "Doctor Shaw was just going over everything with me. We have to have you back here by six on Sunday night."

It's Saturday morning. We'll have more than enough time to skip over to where it all happened. I only hope I can handle it, so James doesn't have to deal with an all-out mental breakdown.

The doctor hands me a number to call so I can contact her this evening at five. I also need to do the same on Sunday morning.

"No problem," I say. I hand the card to James. "Can you hold on to this for me?"

"Of course. You'll be needing my cell to make the calls." James places the card inside his wallet.

"So, shall we get going?" he asks both the doctor and me.

"Leave when you're ready," Shaw says to James. She glances at me. "I've prepared this kit for you with some clothing more suited to the outside. You can change before you leave. And if at any time you don't feel right, please head back. The real world can be overwhelming and scary after any time spent inside a hospital like this. Take it easy, avoid anything stressful, and enjoy your brother's company."

Shaw leans over and gives me a quick hug. I could lift her up off the ground for making this happen. It's not just about confronting the events of that night; it's also about seeing that there is life after this place. Even a brief glimpse of the world outside is enough to motivate me to keep moving forward.

"After you," James says as he gestures for me to leave. Doctor Shaw escorts us through the checkpoints in the hospital, taking us past all the locations I haven't been in since my admission. Shaw waves us off at the exit and returns to the ward without looking back.

I stop off in the reception toilets to change into something less crazy. I throw on some jeans, a black button-up top, and a light gray cardigan. There's also a thick coat I slide on in preparation for the cold weather waiting outdoors.

I stare into the mirror, which is made of actual glass. I look like hell and need a lot of makeup, but I don't care. I'm not trying to impress the public or convince anyone out there of my sanity. I just want to taste the normal world while they let me and do what's right for my recovery.

I leave the bathroom and smile at James.

"It's good to see you out of those hospital clothes."

"Thank you," I say as we move toward the exit. James opens the double doors that lead to freedom. I follow through. When my eyes catch the light outside, I swear I'm stuck in a dream. Despite it still being the end of winter, the daylight engulfs me, pulling me from the hospital lurking behind. For once, I don't feel the beast on my back following my every move.

"Right this way," James says. He leans into the cold with both hands in his jacket pockets. We find his car a minute later: a recent-model BMW. I'm still getting used to the idea that James has money now. When I climb inside, I find leather wrapped around every surface. He keeps the car immaculate. Not a single scuff mark or bit of dirt can be seen. I feel unworthy.

"How can you afford this?" I ask.

He sighs. "A few years after we lost contact, I decided to get my act together and make something of my life. I started a landscaping business. It took off after six months, to the point where I managed to get a few teams up and running to do all of the work for me."

I'd forgotten James used to work in landscaping. I smile at him and rub his arm. "That's amazing."

He turns away. "It's nothing major."

"It sounds like a big deal to me. You should be proud."

He waves me off. "Best we get a move on."

I see the shyness James has always had when it comes to his achievements. He was never one to boast. I keep the thought of his successful business in my head and decide to ask more about it another day.

He taps away at the GPS built into his car.

"How far away from the place am I?" I ask, as I realize I have no idea where we are in terms of distance.

"About three hours. Might be able to cut off a few minutes here and there if I drive fast enough." He winks at me.

I return his attempt at humor with a quick smile. "James, are you sure you want to do this? That's a lot of driving to do."

"Are you kidding me? I'd drive you across the country if it meant I could help your recovery. I'd do anything for my family."

"Family?" I ask, narrowing my eyes.

"Yes, family. Look, I'm sorry I haven't been there for you guys over the last eight years. Part of me wonders if this whole mess could have been avoided if I had stopped being an asshole and just made contact sooner. But I'm here now—for the long haul."

I try to stop the tears, but it's damn near impossible. "I'm sorry too. This is all my fault."

"No," he says as he grabs me and pulls me in for a hug. "This is not your fault. You didn't cause any of this shit, okay? You got caught in the middle. Sometimes it happens. But I can tell you now, we're going to find out what really happened that night."

I nod and turn away, thinking about what I can remember. It's a mess at best. I glance back to James. "How much do you know?"

"About that night? A lot, from the police reports. You and Darren had informed the police that you were being harassed by one of Darren's former employees and his relatives. The report said you had taken it upon yourselves to pay the employee off so he would tell his family to stop bothering you."

"What happened next?"

James takes in a deep breath. "The rest you need to remember for yourself."

I nod. "I don't remember the night in full, but I know we were trying to pay Victor's cousin Karlo off. Victor was Darren's best employee until he fell off a house and broke his spine. I seem to be able to remember everything up until the meeting. After that, it all gets a bit hazy. Only glimpses come to mind, and then my brain goes blank. The next thing I remember is waking up in the hospital."

"We'll uncover it all. I promise you," James says as he presses the start button on the BMW. He pulls out and away from the hospital, leaving the overbearing building in our wake.

After getting out of the town, we hit the I-55. I close my eyes and try to imagine what I'll do when we reach the spot where it all went down.

CHAPTER 48

I doze off in the car. It's hard not to when you're cruising down the highway on a three-hour trip. Without enough diazepam in my system, I inevitably have a nightmare of two black eyes staring at me through the window of my real home as I stare out from my bedroom. I surprise myself when I snap awake and find a pool of drool on my jacket. I thought driving to the spot where my life changed forever might keep me wired and awake, but I guess I am still quite exhausted from everything that has occurred over the last few days.

"So you still snore your butt off," James says with a grin from the driver's seat when he notices I'm awake. He has one hand on the wheel while the other keeps his head propped up.

"Sorry about that. I didn't mean to fall asleep."

"Forget about it. You obviously needed to rest. Plus, this is a long trip. Why did these doctors feel the need to drag your ass all the way out here?"

"Probably to keep me away from home. Away from Darren and Jayden."

"I'm sorry, Emma. I was only joking," James says.

"It's fine," I say as I stare out the window. Nothing but flat, green farmland meets my eyes in all directions. The occasional overpass comes and goes.

For the next hour, we pass by town after town along the I-55 and fall back into our old rhythm of conversation. We talk about the past like the last eight years never happened. We even share a few memories of Mom and Dad without getting into an argument. The wall that was between us is coming down, brick by brick.

"You hungry?" James asks. "We can pull in at the next gas station and grab a bite. Won't be the best meal in the world, but it's food in our bellies."

I sit up a little. "After eating the hospital's food for the last month, that sounds amazing."

James gives me a smile and taps on the GPS in his car to locate a rest stop. He finds one a few miles away.

"Bingo."

*

We spend the next twenty minutes eating and stretching our legs. The stop is slowing down our progress, but there's no point driving so far in one go. James has to fill up his tank regardless, so it's not a complete waste of time.

I head to the bathroom on the outside of the gas station and push my way into the shared facilities. A smell worse than I could find at the hospital greets me. "What the hell?" I mutter as I force myself to go inside. I get the task over with as soon as possible and rush back out.

I spot James at the car, talking on his cell. He seems a bit agitated and keeps looking around as if someone is following him. Has the hospital worked out where we're heading?

I want to charge over and ask what's wrong, but the conversation finishes before I reach the car. James shoves his smartphone back into his pocket. I slow down and act like I never saw anything out of the ordinary.

"There you are," he says when he sees me. "We gotta go. That was my one of my guys on the phone. I've got some emergencies with my business that I need to deal with."

"What does that mean?"

He sighs. "It means I'll have to cut our two days short by a day, sorry."

I walk up to the car with my mouth half open. "So what does that mean for the plan?"

"We keep going and get you to that spot. After we've spent some time there, I'll need to take you back to the hospital tonight and leave town to deal with some problems at home."

I feel my face drop. "What if nothing comes back to me in time?" I ask with one hand on the handle.

James flashes his smile again. "It'll come back. And if it doesn't, we'll do this again and again until it does. I'm so sorry, Emma. I hate to do this to you." He stands straight. "Come on." He taps the roof of the BMW. "Time to move."

I nod before climbing in. I feel so defeated. I wanted to spend time with James and build up to going to the spot. Now I need to face it in a hurry. Maybe this wasn't such a good idea after all.

We make it back on the road and keep going the way we started. James fills me in briefly on his business and the emergency situations that will be waiting for him. One of his suppliers had delivered a huge order to the wrong site and set back a major job by several days.

"Why don't you take me back to the hospital now?"

"Nonsense," he says. "We can still go there for a few hours. My problems can wait until tomorrow."

"Are you sure? I don't want to be a pain."

"Positive. I'm sorry we can't do this right."

"No, it's okay. Getting me out of the hospital, even for a minute, is more than anyone's done for me recently. I dread going back more than anything."

A moment of silence forms between us.

"Who says you have to go back?" James says eventually.

"What?" My heart beats too fast in my chest.

"Think about it. You're out. Why go back? I can help you start over. I have enough money to support you."

"But what about Darren and Jayden?" Though I still don't know if either of them will ever want to see me again.

"They'll understand that you need to get your head right before seeing them. Maybe with enough time, you could go visit."

I cover my face with my hands. James has hit me with too many things at once. The BMW starts to close in around me as the seat belt cuts off my circulation.

"Stop the car," I whisper.

"Sorry?" James asks. It's unclear whether he can't hear me or if the demand concerns him.

"Stop the fucking car. I can't breathe."

James slams on the brakes and pulls over to the emergency lane. He undoes my seat belt for me, and I pile out of the car and fall into the grass. I struggle to catch my breath, but the open space gives me enough grounding to refocus and prevent my fears from escalating into a full-blown panic attack.

"Are you okay?" James asks as he kneels beside me.

I stare at him for a moment. He has no idea what I've been through. He is trying to patch up an eight-year hole with a quick fix. Why did I agree to this?

"No, James. I'm not okay. I'm as far from okay as someone can be."

I hear a sigh come from my brother that borders on frustration. It reminds me that I am nothing but a burden to every person I have left in my life, and there aren't many.

"I'm sorry," I say without looking his way.

"Don't be. This is all my fault. I shouldn't have brought you out here to start with. Maybe we should head back now while we still can."

"No," I say as I climb to my feet. "I won't let this control me. I have to keep going and face what happened. Otherwise, I'll never be free from this existence."

James smiles out of the corner of his mouth and offers me his hand. I take it and follow him back to the passenger seat of the car. I climb in and face the road ahead. When he gets into the driver's seat and buckles up, I lean forward, eager to get going.

"Let's do this."

We drive for another hour, until I see a sign up ahead I haven't seen in a long time. It welcomes me to the town of Clearwater Hills, Illinois. In a few minutes, we'll arrive at the one place in the world I despise more than the hospital.

I can feel my chest start to tighten as my breathing increases in speed. I tug at the seat belt again, convinced it might kill me. I feel hot and cold at the same time and try to quiet down the thoughts running through my head. What if I can't handle this? What if going back to where it all happened makes things worse for me?

I close my eyes. *I can do this. I have to do this.* I need to know what I did to destroy the relationship I have with Darren and Jayden. It's the only way forward, the only way to rebuild what I lost.

With my eyes closed, I feel the car come to a stop. James shuts off the engine and turns to face me. "We're here."

I open my eyes. "Okay."

I watch as he slowly climbs out of the car and comes around to my side to help me out, as if my legs don't work. We're at a park not far from where I live. I've been here before with Darren and Jayden to run Bessie around. It is just a simple patch of grass lined with trees, near a school. How can such an area make me feel sick to my stomach?

"We'll take it slow," James says as he guides me away from the car. We walk beyond the parking lot and out onto the grass, which has only just begun to recover from the extended winter season. Patches of snow still remain.

"I can do this," I mutter to myself. "I can do this."

With every step, I feel a stab in my gut. We're getting closer to where it happened. I can feel the beast behind, mocking me with its dead eyes. We are about to reach the location of the meeting.

I drop to my knees as a flood of memories hit me all at once. I clutch at my temples and squeeze my eyes shut. I know what happened that night.

It's all there. I can't avoid the truth any longer.

CHAPTER 49

Before

"Why midnight? And why there?" Darren asked out loud for the tenth time that evening.

It was only 7 p.m. We had received the location an hour previously, accompanied by a threat not to go to the police. And of all the places in the world for Karlo to pick, we were going to meet at a small patch of grass near the elementary school called Vista Park.

"I don't know. It's as good a place as any, I suppose. And the time will guarantee no one is around."

Darren looked at me with a twisted brow and squinted. "Whose side are you on?"

"What?" I asked. "Do you think I understand the first thing about what is going on? This is all insane. We're about to unload all of our money to keep some lunatic away from our family. I'm just trying to make sense of it all."

"We have no choice!" Darren yelled. "You convinced me of that. Don't try to change my damn mind now."

"I'm not," I said, quieter than before. I didn't want Jayden to figure out what was going on. "I'm only saying that you need to take a seat and calm the hell down. If we go in all wired up and agitated, they'll think we've gone to the cops. They already know we've been talking to them."

"Not since that video came our way. Karlo is probably watching us right now. All for two hundred grand. It's hardly worth the effort."

I'd thought about that myself. We weren't exactly the best targets to farm for a payday. I grabbed Darren by the arm as he moved by me. "What if this is about more than financial compensation? What if he wants the money, and to see us dead too?"

Darren shrugged me off and continued stomping around. "He doesn't. He just wants money and to know my business will be in ruins. If we go through with the drop-off, everything will be square."

"Then what? He magically leaves us alone?"

Darren stopped pacing and squeezed his head tight. He rubbed at his temples with closed eyes. Finally, something snapped.

"What do you want from me?" he yelled in my direction. "I'm trying my best. All you're doing is making me question my every instinct. One minute you're telling me to pay up, the next you're acting like we have other options."

I slumped. "I guess we don't, do we?"

He shrugged. "Maybe we do."

I shook my head at him. "No police. He said so in the video."

"Not that," Darren said. "Maybe I could bring my gun along."

"And what?"

"Scare them. Make them think twice about messing with us. Shoot them if I have to."

"Shoot them? And go to jail?"

"No. It would be self-defense, right?"

"Not out in a park by a school in the middle of the damn night. That's also forgetting the fact that you are one man against a complete psycho. You think he won't bring a gun himself?"

I dropped my head into my hands and tugged at my hair. How could Darren be so stupid? What ignorance was coming out of his mouth? But he was desperate. We both were. We wanted a solution, a way out of screwing ourselves over and exposing our lives to a revenge-hungry criminal.

I heard crying and realized it was me. I sniffed away the tears and wiped my eyes with my sleeve. How could this situation get any worse?

Darren moved in by my side and placed an arm on my back. "I'm sorry for yelling. I didn't mean any of it. I'm just as scared and confused about this as you are. I'll leave my gun behind."

I grabbed him and stood. I fell into his chest and tried to find an answer in the security it provided. Usually, I felt safe in that position, but not tonight. I could sense Darren's anxiety overriding everything. He was a ball of stress, close to exploding. How were we going to make the drop-off without seeming guilty, as if we'd gone to the police?

*

The time came for us to leave. We made Jayden stay at a friend's house so he wouldn't have to know about anything. It was late notice, but one of the moms on the basketball team believed my BS story about a family emergency. Jayden questioned why he was allowed to stay at a friend's house despite being grounded. We told him that we needed a night to ourselves and to go along with it or he'd be grounded for even longer. He didn't argue.

Saying goodbye to my son was difficult, as I knew there was a possibility it could be the last time I ever saw him, but I had no other option. If the drop-off went horribly wrong, at least he wouldn't be in any danger. Karlo wasn't the type of criminal who would go after a teenager. Or was he? I had no idea.

We sat inside Darren's truck, staring at the clock. The park was only a few minutes away. We headed out and arrived early, in the exact spot we had been told to wait in. No one was around. A deafening calm hung over the area. Every tree was stiff in the wind-free night. I'd never seen the weather like this before. I prayed for a breeze to show me that I wasn't losing my mind.

"Take this," Darren said as he pulled an object from his pocket. He placed a stun gun in my hands. "I meant to give this to you sooner." He showed me how to disengage the safety so I could utilize the weapon. "From there, you just point and squeeze the trigger."

"I don't know if I can handle that," I said with a shaky voice.

"Hopefully you won't need it, but I'd rather you had this on you in case things go pear-shaped."

"It's all going to go smoothly, right?" I asked.

Darren didn't answer me. He focused on the park ahead.

"There's a car," he said, gripping the steering wheel tight. He closed his eyes and let out a staggered lungful of air.

"Are you sure you don't want me to come?" I asked.

"No, forget that. If this all goes to hell, start the car and get out of here as fast as you can. Get Jayden and then go straight to the cops."

"Okay, but what about you?"

"I'll be fine, honey," he said with a smile to cover a quivering lip. "Just a young punk trying to squeeze some dollars from an old man. Nothing else." Darren opened the door.

I threw my hand after him and grabbed hold. "I love you."

He glanced down at me and smiled. "Love you too, honey." His smile faded in an instant as he shut the door and threw the bag of money over his shoulder.

The car drove straight onto the field of the park, keeping its distance from our truck. I recognized the old sedan that had been sitting outside our house, this time with two figures inside.

Karlo wasn't working alone.

Darren slowly walked straight toward the blinding headlights. I wanted to scream out a warning to him, but I knew it would only cause a panic.

The old car came to a rough stop. The first figure climbed out and walked around to the passenger door, casually taking his time. I couldn't make out his face, but it had to be the body of a man. I could tell by the shoulders alone.

He opened the door for the second person as if they were royalty. I imagined all kinds of crazy in the form of mob bosses. Was Karlo connected?

My rambling thoughts no longer mattered when I realized who the second person was.

There was no mistaking it. Jayden was now standing by the man, with both of his arms bound in front of him.

CHAPTER 50

"Jayden!" I yelled as I jumped out of the car and ran toward him. Darren turned back to me with wide eyes as he realized why I was screaming our son's name.

"That's far enough," a modulated voice called out from behind a mask. It was the man standing by Jayden—the same one from the video. He had a pistol pointed straight at me. I froze on the spot beside Darren and stared at my son. He had no idea what was going on or why.

Darren stepped forward. "He isn't part of this. Let him go."

"Shut the fuck up. Did I say you could talk?" The robotic voice boomed out at us and chilled me to the bone. Darren remained stationary. We both did, not wanting to give the man a reason to kill Jayden.

"Listen, Karlo," Darren said, "I have the money right here. Just take it."

The gun lowered for a moment before the man kicked Jayden down to his knees. "Don't move." He brushed past our son and headed straight for Darren, who held the bag out. The man snatched it free from Darren's hands and tossed the pack aside.

"Get the fuck over there by him."

"Karlo, wait—"

"Don't say my name," he yelled, striking Darren across the face with the metal gun. Darren dropped down to one knee. Karlo grabbed him by the collar of his jacket and dragged him over to Jayden's side and pushed him onto both knees.

I couldn't move a muscle. My legs felt like they weighed a thousand pounds each as I stared at the psycho in the mask. He slowly circled Jayden and Darren, his gun pointed at their heads. He pulled back the hammer on the pistol.

"Please don't," I said, my voice an insignificant squeak.

"Shut up. Do not speak unless spoken to, or I will kill them both right now."

I nodded, not sure if I could reply with words. Karlo wasn't messing around. This had always been a dangerous situation. Why had that only dawned on me now? We should have gone to the police. What did we have to lose?

"Two hundred grand isn't going to cut it. I want more. I know you have it."

"We don't," I said. "That's all of it. The business is gone now. All we have left is our house."

"That's right. That fucking expensive big house in the nice part of town. You're going to hand it over, understand?"

I agreed as fast as I could. "It's yours. Take it." I reached into my jacket pocket to fetch the keys. I felt the stun gun beside them. Karlo aimed his weapon at me.

"I'm just grabbing the keys." I held them up with a shaky hand to show him I was serious. What good was a large house if your family was dead?

"Don't move," Karlo said as he opened the car door. His engine idled as he pulled out a document and slapped it on the hood.

"You and Darren own that house outright. I want the deed transferred to me. Both of you sign this right now."

"Okay," I said. I cast my eyes to Darren and realized he wasn't scared; he was angry. Blood leaked from the cut on his skull. I shook my head at Darren as subtly as I could. He ignored me—with good reason. The pistol he'd promised to leave behind poked out of the side of his jeans.

Darren jumped up and drove his elbow into Karlo's gut. The blow emptied the masked man's lungs and gave Darren an opportunity to reach for his own gun. Karlo saw Darren's move and rushed straight at him. They both fell to the ground. I ran into the fight, heading for Jayden, but Karlo regained the upper hand before I had a chance to reach my son. He shoved Darren off and held both pistols to his chin.

"What the hell did I say? You think I'm messing around?" Karlo got back to his feet and kicked Darren in the face. I watched as my husband toppled over and crawled away. Karlo holstered one of the pistols and stormed after him. He lifted Darren up and around, tossing him back to his spot beside Jayden. I moved away as Karlo shifted his aim toward me.

"You Turners don't seem to learn, do you? Well, I might have to teach you all a lesson."

"Please, he didn't know what he was doing," I begged.

"Bullshit."

"I'm sorry," Darren got out. I could hear him struggling with the multiple injuries he had suffered.

"You shut the hell up," Karlo said to Darren. "Sign this. Now!" He spun back to me. "You're next."

I turned to Darren and pleaded with him. "Do it, Darren, please." I stared into his eyes and tried to dissolve the hatred flowing through him.

"Okay," he muttered.

"Okay? You think you have a choice?" Karlo shouted. He lifted Darren up to the hood of the car and pinned him down, putting a pen in his hand. "Sign it." Karlo drew out a penlight and guided Darren through the process of transferring the title to our house. He shoved Darren back onto his knees, and then I was dragged over. I obediently signed everywhere he ordered me to. All Karlo had to do now was fill out his details and take the document to a crooked notary. I began to understand how he had planned this whole thing out. All except one detail.

"Now was that so hard, Turners? See what happens when you work as a team?"

He shoved me back.

I already knew what would happen next. All I could do was beg for Karlo to be reasonable, but I realized this had been his plan from the start.

To properly secure our house, we needed to be dead.

CHAPTER 51

"You don't need to do this, Karlo. We can leave town right now. We won't stop you taking it. The house is yours." I tried every line on the angered criminal, but Karlo just stared at me. I could see the same black eyes from the video staring at me through the mask. Were they contacts? No one had eyes that color.

The hue wasn't the only thing upsetting me. When I stared into Karlo's eyes, I realized that I was nothing to him but an obstacle to be overcome and discarded. How did a person reach that point?

"You Turners had your chance to play nice. Now it's time to play a little game."

"No, please, we don't have to play any games," I said.

He squared the gun at my head again and wrapped his gloved finger around the trigger. I cowered down and looked away, waiting for the bullet to hit my skull and scatter my brains across the thin layer of snow on the grass. I couldn't help but picture the red spray slicing across the air to stain the ground.

I peeked and realized the gun was no longer pointed at me. "Too easy," Karlo said. "I've got a better idea." He placed a hand on Jayden's shoulder.

"Don't touch him, please. Can't we just let Jayden go? He has no part in this. You can take the house without involving him. Darren and I are the ones you want."

Karlo's mouth was covered by the modulator, but I saw his smile in his eyes. This entire ordeal was making him happy.

"Jayden can't go," he said. "If I let him live, he inherits the house. You see the problem I have."

"No, you could claim the house before that happens. Inheritances take time. He's not even eighteen yet."

"Sounds logical, but I'd rather you were all dead instead. It'd be easier." He aimed the gun down at Jayden. I lost control of my body. I pulled out the stun gun and charged at Karlo. Before I could shoot him, he drove the side of the pistol across my face and slammed me in the temple. A bright flash of white sent me to the ground, freeing the weapon from my hand. I couldn't tell which way was up for a moment until I saw him standing over me.

"Next time one of you attacks me, I shoot. Got it?"

I nodded my understanding as blood flowed over my eyes. I cleaned the wound with a wipe of my sleeve.

Karlo paced around us with total control. "You Turners need to relax a little. The plan never involved killing any of you. I am taking your shit either way. Once those documents are processed, that house is mine."

I closed my eyes and let out a quiet word of thanks.

"However," Karlo said. The word hung in the air and dropped down on me hard. I almost stopped breathing.

"You have all shown me nothing but disrespect tonight. I think it's time one of you paid the price." Karlo stepped up to Jayden and Darren and stared me in the face with those beady black eyes. "Emma."

I shuddered as I met his gaze. "Yes?"

"Choose."

My mind went blank. I couldn't speak. All I could manage was to repeat his command. "Choose?"

"You heard me. One of them must die to make things right. Jayden or Darren: who's it going to be?"

"What?" I whispered. "You can't make me do this."

"Either one of them dies, or they both die. Simple as that."

My eyes darted between them. Darren was steaming with rage, ready to burst, while Jayden pleaded with his eyes, conveying a single message: "Don't let me die."

"Come on, Emma. Choose. Your husband or your son. One lives. One dies."

"No," I said. "Fuck you. I choose me. You can kill me and let them go." I was standing when I said this. Karlo shoved past and seized me by the arm. He dragged me across the snowy ground and placed me behind them.

"It doesn't work like that. You make the selection. You decide their fate."

I heard myself crying. "No, I won't."

"Then they both die, Emma. Right now, in front of you. Is that what you want?"

I tried to look away as Karlo aimed the pistol between Jayden and Darren. "I don't want any of this."

"Of course you don't. No one wants bad things to happen to them, do they? But bad things happen to good people, Emma."

I gulped air in and spewed it back out, desperate to breathe. I felt like the open field didn't hold enough oxygen to keep me conscious. I tried to focus my energy on finding Karlo's dead eyes. Why were they black? Why were they so damaged? I locked on to them and begged. "You don't have to do this."

"I know, Emma. But sometimes you just have to bite the bullet, so to speak."

I slumped. I was defeated. There was nothing more I could do or say.

"The clock is ticking, Emma. Time to choose." He turned my head back to my husband and son and wrapped his powerful arms around me. The next thing I knew the pistol was in my hands. Karlo kept control over me by gripping my wrists like they were in a vice.

"What are you doing?" I asked. I thought back to Darren showing me how to shoot. His lesson was still fresh in my mind. And a gun was now in my hands.

"Giving you a choice." He forced my finger into the trigger guard and positioned the gun between them both.

"No, I won't do it. I won't pull the trigger."

Karlo slid his left hand back and unsheathed a knife, which he then placed by my throat. He pressed it against my skin, drawing blood.

"You will."

I shook my head again. My brain flicked between the two: Darren. Jayden. My husband. My son. I shook my head, trying not to vomit. I couldn't believe I was contemplating what Karlo wanted.

I didn't get to consider an alternative scenario before Darren jumped up and said, "Kill me, asshole. I'm the one."

Karlo knocked him down with a solid kick in the back. "No. You don't get a say." Karlo pulled me tighter; his arms locked in. "Time to choose."

I stared at my family as my heart skipped a beat.

"You don't have to do this," Darren said to Karlo as I aimed the pistol between him and Jayden. My finger wrapped around the trigger as a decision entered my brain.

I'd run out of time and options. I'd run out of excuses. There was no other choice, and my refusal would have a far worse outcome. Karlo had gone to great lengths to bring us all to this moment. How had I not seen this coming?

The signs had all been there. The warnings had been clear. His past threats floated into the forefront of my mind on a loop, preventing me from thinking of an alternative.

"I have to," I whispered, eyes closed. My words were weak and crippled, but they could all hear me.

"Please," Darren said. "There has to be another way. There's still time to undo this."

"I have to," I whispered. Too many thoughts ran through my head at once.

"Time to choose," Karlo said again, ignoring Darren.

"Clock is ticking, Emma. You've got five seconds. Who's it going to be? Five…"

I drowned out Karlo's countdown as the pistol hovered between Darren and Jayden. If I let him kill me instead, would he spare them?

"Two. One." Karlo dug the knife farther into my throat.

I felt the blood seeping out. I couldn't die. Not like this. "Stop," I said in a whisper. I moved the pistol to the person I'd chosen. It was all Karlo needed from me— then he would do what he had planned all along.

Time slowed down.

My heart didn't beat.

I left my body.

I squeezed the trigger.

The sound of the gun firing ripped through my core as the pulse of the bullet jolted my body backward. I fell to the ground in a heap the second Karlo released me. He laughed to himself as he stepped away and scooped up his documents from the hood of the car and the bag of money from the ground. He strolled back around to the driver's seat of his idling car.

"Was that so hard, Emma?" he asked me.

I stared up into his soulless, black eyes, the light glinting off their pure evil shine.

He climbed into his sedan and drove off, leaving me sitting over the body of the one I'd murdered while the survivor crawled away from me.

The dark night swallowed me whole, pulling me down into the void. I passed out.

CHAPTER 52

After

It all comes back to me the second we reach that spot in Vista Park. Karlo, Darren, Jayden, the gun, the choice I'd made. This is the place where my life changed forever. It's too much for me. I hear the sound of blood rushing in my ears, and collapse.

I wake up in a pool of sweat inside James's car. We are sitting in the parking lot, facing out onto the patchy grass. James stares at me from the driver's seat.

"Are you okay?" he asks me, concern dotting his eyes.

I can't remember how to speak; my eyes dart around in all directions, looking for Karlo.

"Emma?"

"No, I'm not okay. I'll never be okay."

"What happened? Why did you faint?"

I turn to him in my seat. "I remember now. All of it."

"Jesus."

I stare at him. Silence fills the air as our eyes lock.

James clears his throat. "Do you mind if I ask you something?"

"What?"

"Do you remember yet who..." He pauses. "Do you remember who died?"

I twist away. I see the look in the eyes of Darren and Jayden. They both knew one of them was about to die. They stared at me with a sting of betrayal, but one of them had known their fate was sealed the minute Karlo made me choose.

I had no other option.

It had to be Darren.

Jayden was still so young.

Jayden was our son.

I let out a scream as I pummel my fists against the dash of James's car. I pound and punch every surface until my knuckles bleed. I yell so loud my throat starts to burn.

James takes in every painful moment. He reaches out a hand and places it on my shoulder. "It's okay, Emma. You're free now."

"Free? I'll never be free. I killed Darren. I murdered him."

James doesn't say a word. Does he know that I don't want to hear a bunch of therapy lines, how this was all the fault of a psycho in a mask and not mine? Does he finally understand how broken and fucked up I truly am?

"Take me back to the hospital," I say, looking away from him.

"Are you sure?" he asks.

"Yes. I'm done here."

*

We drive in silence for at least an hour. James is the one to break the quiet.

"I'm sorry I took you there. I—"

"It's okay," I say. "I was too scared to face this on my own. I should be thanking you, not yelling like a maniac."

"Emma, no. I shouldn't have gotten involved like this. I screwed everything up again."

"No, you didn't. I know the truth now. I can move forward with Jayden and start over. I can—" The reality of a life without Darren hits my brain. It doesn't take long for the tears to flow. We had our problems, as so many married couples do, but he didn't deserve to die like that because I was too scared to sacrifice myself. "Darren," I whisper. "Why?"

"It's okay, Emma. He would have saved Jayden too."

I feel it boil up inside me again. I snap at James. "Did you know?"

"Know what?"

"That Darren is dead?"

James lets out a huff of warm air. "Yes. Everyone knows. The doctors told me never to mention it, that you needed to arrive at this moment on your own."

I shake my head. "How could I have done it? I killed my husband."

"It's not your fault, Emma. You didn't cause this."

"I did. I failed to stop Karlo. And now I'm left with a son who will never speak to me again." I can see the shock in Jayden's eyes. I killed his father. He will never forget that. How could he? "He'll never forgive me."

"Maybe with enough time he will."

"Have you seen him?"

"No, I didn't want to disrupt him. I've been told he's back in school and coping somewhat okay. He's a tough kid. Maybe right now he blames you, but soon he'll realize it wasn't your doing."

I sniff as I try to stop crying. I hate my vulnerabilities being out in the open like this, especially with James. We haven't seen each other in years, and this is how we end up reconnecting. Life is one screwed-up train wreck.

We fall back into silence, and another hour passes. I stare out the window as the daylight begins to fade. I will see Doctor Shaw soon. I don't know how I'm going to face her without breaking down. She will recognize that something happened during my leave. One glance at my bloody knuckles will tell her everything she needs to know.

"So," James says, breaking the silence, "have you given any thought to my idea?"

"What idea?" I say with a grunt.

"About not going back to the hospital. I can take care of you. You won't need to worry about money. I have a place for you to stay so you can start over."

I think about his idea for a minute. Would it be right to wipe the slate clean and reinvent myself? I could do all the cliché things people do to start over. Change my name, cut my hair, become a new person. The only thing stopping me is my son. He hates me enough as it is. If I abandon him now, his hatred will be cemented forever. I owe it to Jayden to complete my treatment at the hospital and be fit enough to take care of him again.

"I'm going back," I say to James.

"Are you sure? I can help you more than those morons at the hospital."

"They aren't all bad," I say, thinking of Shaw. The rest can go to hell as far as I'm concerned.

"Well, the offer still stands if you change your mind."

"I won't. At least not any time soon."

James doesn't give me his reassuring smile. He can't hide his disappointment.

"We'll be back before five," he says. "What are you going to tell the doctor?"

"What do you mean?"

"Well, we're coming back a day early. She might get suspicious."

I hadn't thought of that. I had too many dark images running through my head instead. "I'll say I felt overwhelmed and needed to come back. She'll understand." It wasn't much of a lie.

James nods, giving me the skeptical look he used on me when we were teenagers.

CHAPTER 53

We arrive at the hospital with a few hours to spare before five. I think about what I can do with my memories of Darren's murder. I have no proof Karlo killed him, but I know he was the one who forced me to pull the trigger. All along I sensed he was at the heart of the event, but I couldn't see it clearly in my mind until now.

I want to shout his name from the rooftop of the building, but I doubt it would get him arrested. According to James, the police have no leads, despite Jayden telling them about Victor. After I killed Darren, I shut down and provided no assistance whatsoever to the investigation. The next thing I knew, I was waking up here.

Karlo has gotten away with murder, and there is nothing I can do about it. And all for a family member. How can loyalty like that drive a person to such a horrific crime?

James takes me inside and walks me to the doctor. We find Shaw in the day room with the help of an orderly. James has a visitors' badge on and does what he can to avoid the stares and shrieks of the other patients.

"Emma. I wasn't expecting you to be back until tomorrow. Is everything okay?" Doctor Shaw asks.

"Yes. I wanted to come back tonight and sleep here. I need the familiarity."

"That's perfectly fine. You can still spend the day with your brother tomorrow, if you like."

I turn to James. "I think he's had enough of me." I remember he has to head back to his home to sort out his business.

"No," James says. "I'd be more than happy to visit you again at the end of the day for a few hours."

"Very well. We'll see you later tomorrow," Shaw says.

"Sounds good, doc. I'd better head off, then, hadn't I?"

"You can stay for a little while longer."

James smiles at Shaw. "Thank you. I think I will."

We take a seat in the day room and try to talk. It's hard after what I went through today. An awkward silence fills the air, reminding me of the first time he visited. I don't know what else to say. He knows that I killed Darren. I know I killed Darren. What happens now?

Do I go to the police and tell them about Karlo? It will be my word against his. They're not exactly going to believe a crazy woman, are they?

"Maybe I should go," James says.

"You don't have to. I enjoy sitting here with you. Sometimes it's all I need." I'm still shaking a little as every memory floods my brain on repeat. The flash of the gun glinting in the moonlight, the cold night air freezing me to my core, the dead black eyes of Karlo. I feel a migraine coming on.

"No, I should make sure everything is okay with my business. Sorry to leave you like this."

"It's fine. Do what you need to do. I've already wasted too much of your time with all of this."

"You haven't wasted it at all. Seeing you again has been worth every second." He smiles at me.

I try to do the same in return. It was hard for me to smile before I knew the truth. It's only going to be harder after today.

"So how much longer do you think you'll be in here for?"

I shrug. It's the last thing I've thought about. "As long as it takes for me to be able to face everything and be a functional mother again for Jayden."

He frowns. "What if you never reach that point?"

"I have to. He needs me."

"My offer still stands. You can still leave right now with me. It's got to be better than staying here."

I can't meet his gaze. "No. I have to stay here. After today I'm more of a mess than I was before. Jayden deserves a mother who can look after him, instead of the other way around."

James breathes out loud and shakes his head. "I guess running away isn't for everyone, is it? Maybe therapy is the only way to move on."

"It is." I look out of the window to the empty courtyard. The snow is starting to melt. Patches of grass are showing through. I turn back to James and place my hand on his. "It won't be easy, but it's the best option for me."

James's eyes are glued to the table. I'm not sure if he's even listening. I can't blame him. I wouldn't want to be caught dead in the same room as me. After a long moment, his eyes flick to mine.

"Are you going to tell Doctor Shaw everything you remember?"

The sound of the gun firing in the night forces my eyes closed for a second as I remember the event in full. It echoes in my mind. I will have to go over this again and again with Doctor Shaw.

"Emma?" James asks.

My watery eyes jump to his. "I don't want to have to relive that moment. I can't face what happened."

"Maybe you'll have to, though. Sometimes you just have to bite the bullet, so to speak."

I pull my hand away. I feel as if I'm going to fall out of my chair. "What did you say?" His words rattle around in my brain. *Bite the bullet.*

James looks at me, puzzled for a moment, but then his eyes focus in on me like a laser. "Nothing. Just a stupid phrase."

I attempt to concentrate for a second. Maybe he accidentally used the same expression Karlo had just before he made me kill

Darren. It's a common enough thing to say, right? I need time to think straight.

"I'm exhausted. I might head to bed early," I say.

"What about your dinner?"

"Not hungry," I blurt as I stand. "Lost my appetite after today."

"Fair enough. Why don't I escort you to your room so I can give you a proper goodbye? I don't like doing it in front of these people." James looks at one of the patients with a sneer.

"Okay," I stutter. What else am I supposed to say? I have no idea if what I suspect is true. How could it be? Why would James be helping me as he has? I must be wrong. I have to be.

My mind runs into overdrive while we walk back. My brother stays close. I try to piece it all together, but there are so many questions that need answering.

Why did he show up now after eight years?

Why was he so keen to take me back to where it all happened?

Why does he want me to leave this place?

Those black eyes swirl around in my head again, staring at me in the video, staring at me at the park moments before I pulled the trigger and killed my husband while a knife dug into my throat.

James can't be involved in any of this. We're twins. It's always been us against the world. The only person to have ever have gotten between us was Dad. Could our falling out have driven James to such lengths? It doesn't seem possible, but his words echo in my brain on a loop.

He strolls casually beside me and smiles. "What would you like to do tomorrow, sis?" he asks. His voice sounds different. A hint of sarcasm has replaced the care and understanding. He's never called me sis in my entire life.

"I thought you had to go back and take care of things with your business?"

"No, I've decided it can wait. You're more important."

I nod. Does James even have a business? Was that another lie? I start to think about how he suddenly has all of this success. He was never like that. James was always happy to put in his time and go home at the end of the day. He doesn't have the strength it takes to run a small business while your personal life takes hit after hit.

We pass an orderly, and I try to give him a look that I hope will grab his attention. The man ignores me, like they all do. It isn't too unusual for the staff to witness all kinds of weird faces.

The orderly turns away and heads in the opposite direction from us. We are utterly alone in the last stretch of corridor to my room. What I wouldn't give to see Tom poke his ugly head around the corner and hit on me.

"Here we are," I say, doing my best to hide my concern. Do I really think James is the one? I thought it was Karlo harassing our family, but the man I saw that night at the park was a cold-blooded killer. Now that I think about it, the police never found any evidence to suggest Karlo had been stalking us. Had our assumptions led us astray?

"Well, bye," I say.

"Hold up a minute," James says. "Let me see your room. I want to make sure these people are taking proper care of my sister."

I close my eyes for a moment. His request sounds plausible, but the voice in the back of my head is screaming at me to run. My legs fail to act, and the next thing I realize, I am walking into my room. James follows and shuts the door behind him.

"That's supposed to stay open."

"It'll only be closed for a minute. Give us some privacy."

"Okay. So, this is my room. Not much to it," I say as I sit on the bed.

"No, there isn't. I gotta say, Emma, this place is a real shithole."

I suddenly get the urge to defend the hospital. "It's not the best place in the world, but it's my home for now."

"Yeah, right," he says with a chuckle. "You really should come with me. It's not too late to change your mind. I can take care of you now. I have the funds we need to leave this place forever. And I'm not going to waste them."

James is talking about more than the present moment; he must be. I think about the last bit of defiance my father aimed toward James when he died. He left me all of his money. Not a single cent went to James. I would have given him half if he had only returned my calls. Hell, I would have given it all to him if that's what it took to reconnect. Is that why he made us sign over the house? To reclaim what he felt he was owed? The next words out of my mouth could be my last. I either play along or accept my fate.

"Okay. I should go with you. You can take care of me."

"That's right. I'm the older brother. It's time you acted like a younger sister and accepted your place."

I fight the urge to tell him that we are twins and that he is only older by a few minutes, but I can see in his eyes he is about to say something far worse.

"I didn't want things to reach this point, Emma, but what choice did I have? He forced my hand. He made me do these things to you."

He? Is James talking about our father? I realize it doesn't matter. James's words are like daggers through my heart as everything comes together. James was the man in the mask. He took our money and our house. He stalked our family. He killed Darren. The black eyes were a false memory. I finally see James's green eyes staring at me.

Tears fall down my cheeks as I cringe away from him. I can't play along with his twisted fantasy anymore.

"Emma, Emma, Emma," he says. "It had to be done."

"Why?" I let out. "He was your brother-in-law."

"And he was a decent man to you. Maybe not to the rest of the world, but to you, he was everything."

"Yes, and you killed him."

"I didn't kill him, Emma. *You* did. You made this all happen when you accepted Dad's money. You thought you could take it all for yourself and not give me what I deserved, didn't you?"

"No, I—"

"Don't lie to me!" he yells. He comes close to my bed and stands over me. "One more word of deceit and I'll gut you." He produces a knife from his pocket and grabs my chin. I've been in the company of this blade before.

"I'm sorry," I mutter.

He lets go and steps one pace back.

"James, please."

"What? Are you going to beg me not to do this? Should I hand myself in? Not likely. Once I offload that house, I'll have half a million dollars sitting in offshore accounts, thanks to you and your idiot husband. The way I see it, you still owe me. Dad's money should have been all mine from the start. Instead, it went to you and your simpleton husband."

"How could you do this to me?" I ask.

He smiles that smile again. "Well, sis, if you must know, I never intended for things to get this out of hand. At first, I was only trying to ruin Darren's business. That's why I sabotaged his contract."

"You caused Victor's fall?"

"Guilty," he says. "It's funny, I thought that would be enough to satisfy me, but it wasn't. The next thing I knew, I was stalking you idiots and making it look like the work of a disgruntled former employee."

His words are like poison to my ears, but I have to know more. "It was never Karlo, was it?"

"Please. Do you honestly think that family could have pulled off what I achieved? They would have stomped right up to your front door and kicked it in. I had better plans."

"Like killing Darren?" I shout. Will anyone hear my cries, I wonder?

"Keep your voice down. Don't give me a reason to finish what I started." He holds the blade up to the light scar on my throat, forcing me to shy away.

"I never intended to kill him. I simply wanted to see you all in ruin and make you feel the way I have for the last eight fucking years. The money was the best way to do that."

"Well, it's yours now. Just let me go. I'll never bother you again."

"I wish it were that simple. But you know too much." He leans in closer to me and raises my chin with his knife.

I shake my head. "Just do it, already. Don't draw this out any longer than you have to. I've suffered enough." I close my eyes, ready for the end, ready to give up and let him win. My mind falls back to that night, when James pushed Jayden to his knees and held a gun to his head.

My eyes fly open and I stare James down. I won't let him off this easy. A thought hits my brain. "Why did you take me back there? To the park?"

He steps back a touch and lowers the knife. A sinister smile stretches across his face.

"You wanted to see me go through it all again, didn't you? You wanted to relive that moment, you sick freak."

He slices his hand through the air and slaps my face. I fall back on the bed, but I don't let my eyes wander from his.

"Just kill me, James. You've taken everything else. End my life."

"No, Emma. You need me. Your life is not over until I say it is. You will be dependent on me from here on out."

I want to defy him, but I've thought of a better idea. I lower my head with defeat. He closes in, leaning over me with the knife still out. I stare up into his eyes and submit. It's the only move I have left.

"You're right. I need you, James. Now and forever."

He leans down and kisses me slowly on the forehead.

A tear rolls down my cheek and catches his attention. He comes nearer to my face and dominates me with his steely gaze. "You are mine, understand? I own you." He grabs my wrist with his spare hand and begins to pull me off the bed. "It's time for us to leave."

I hold his stare long enough to distract him from what I'm doing. My hand drops down, searching. He doesn't understand what I'm about to do. How could he?

I shove the scissors I'm clutching in my fingers into the side of his throat with every piece of energy I can muster. In his arrogance, he didn't notice me fishing them out. It never occurred to him that I would have a way to defend myself. I twist the metal into his jugular and push him back from the bed. The knife in his hand falls as he tries to claw at his neck, but I refuse to stop pressing down as visions of Darren hit my mind. I ram the blade harder into James's throat as he continues to grip my wrist in shock until the floor runs thick with his blood.

"You don't own me. No one does. No one ever will."

He gurgles the last lungful of air he'll ever breathe as he stares at me with a sickening grin. His eyes glaze over and give up their fight. His face is frozen in time.

I finally let go.

CHAPTER 54

Over the next day, I help the police understand why I killed my brother with a pair of scissors that were hidden inside my room. The officers are skeptical at first, but after a week the investigators understand everything that happened, including the sudden and illegal transfer of my house into an offshore business James owned. The transfer had already been under investigation, but the police were having trouble tracking down who had stolen our house until I pointed them toward James.

With me locked away in the hospital and Jayden staying with Darren's sister, James planned on eventually selling the house anonymously and wiring the money to some offshore bank accounts he had set up. The police also found what was left of the two hundred thousand dollars in cash at an apartment he was renting nearby. He had spent most of it already to give himself the appearance of success. He'd even purchased a landscaping business with some of the money. I would have been none the wiser that the large payday he was about to come into had been stolen from my family.

A day later, the lead detectives tell me I have been cleared of any wrongdoing, ruling that I acted in self-defense. It's a hollow feeling, and it changes nothing, but I'm glad no one thinks I killed my brother for no reason.

*

A few months go by at the hospital. I make excellent progress after a few dark weeks, according to Doctor Shaw, and I'm finally at the point when I am ready to receive a visitor again. There is only one person I want to see, and I am terrified of how he will respond.

Jayden doesn't seem himself when he walks into the room. He appears older, as if that night has aged him. He steps up to my table, Doctor Shaw at his side. He is clutching at his elbows with both hands as he tries to avoid looking at the other patients.

A wave of shame washes over me. How could I let them bring him here? A shudder sinks me down into my seat, and I close my eyes for a few seconds. I shove the thought aside and try to focus on the positives, the way Doctor Shaw taught me.

Jayden sits down and avoids my gaze for what feels like an eternity. I don't know if I should speak first. What are you supposed to say in a situation like this? No combination of words can bring his father back.

I take a deep breath and find some courage. "Jayden, you don't have to see me. You can leave right now, and I will never hold it against you—ever. I understand that you hate me more than anyone else, and I want you to know it's okay. I'm just happy knowing you are safe."

Jayden continues to stare at the table. I go to speak again, but he cuts me off with a shake of his head.

He stands from the chair and walks around to my side. Before I can work out if he is going to leave, he wraps his arms around me, kneeling down to squeeze tight.

"I'm sorry about Dad," Jayden says. "I'm sorry Uncle James made you do that. I'm sorry about everything."

I cry. It all comes out in a nonstop mess. Darren and James fill my thoughts, pulling me down into a dark spiral until Jayden's hug takes over and heals me more than months of therapy ever could.

"Mom?" he asks.

I pull back and stare him in the eyes with the best smile I can summon. I can't speak.

"Everything is going to be okay. You're going to get out of here, and we're going to start over."

I draw Jayden back in for another hug and whisper into his ear, "Thank you."

"I'm here for you, Mom."

"I'm here for you too."

We comfort each other while Doctor Shaw smiles down at us with that face she gave me the day we met.

For the first time since I arrived at the Hopevale Psychiatric Hospital, I can see a future beyond its gray walls. A future where I exist.

A LETTER FROM ALEX

I wanted to say a huge thank you for taking the time to read *The Last Thing I Saw*. If you enjoyed reading the book and want to keep up to date with all my latest releases, then just sign up using the link below. Your email address will never be shared, and you can unsubscribe at any time.

www.bookouture.com/alex-sinclair

I hope you got a lot out of this book. I loved every minute I spent writing it. If you enjoyed *The Last Thing I Saw*, I would be very grateful if you could write a review. I'd love to hear your thoughts, and your review would make a huge difference in helping other readers discover my book.

I also love hearing from my readers—you can get in touch with me on my Facebook page, through Twitter, Goodreads or my website.

Thanks,
Alex Sinclair

ASinclairAuthor

ASinclairAuthor

alexsinclairwrites.com

ACKNOWLEDGEMENTS

Firstly, I have to thank the entire hard-working team at Bookouture for making this happen, and in particular commissioning editor Abigail Fenton, for giving my submission the time of day and helping to make it the best story it could be.

A big thank you to my wife for her years of support and for listening to me drone on and on about writing. Another big thank you to my little girl for inspiring me to work harder and get up each day at five in the morning to write before work.

Thank you to my first editor, Melissa Gray, who fit me into her busy schedule to work on the original manuscript.

Thank you to all of the authors at Bookouture who have welcomed me into the family with open arms.

And finally, thank you to anyone who has given my work a chance and spent their valuable time reading this book. Without you, none of this would be possible.

Gibbon Public Library
PO Box 138 1050 Adams Avenue
Gibbon, MN 55335